WILD CARD

WILD AT HEART SERIES, BOOK THREE

BY CHRISTINE HARTMANN

WILD CARD

Limitless Publishing, LLC
Kailua, HI 96734
www.limitlesspublishing.com

Formatting: Limitless Publishing

ISBN-13: 978-1-64034-181-4
ISBN-10: 1-64034-181-1

DEDICATION

To Ron, still my Mr. Romantic.

CHAPTER 1

Did anyone notice?

The question excited Bree as she tugged the opulent carved handle of the ladies' restroom. The hotel's dark walnut door swung on well-oiled hinges, releasing a cacophony of chatter on a warm, sweet-smelling breeze. The sounds hung briefly in the overly air-conditioned hallway. Keeping her eyes fixed firmly on the carpet, she squeezed her straining dress past sleek girls in short satin and chiffon numbers that exposed teenage thighs tapering like delicate exclamation points to spiky heels. She reflexively smoothed the material over her plump tummy.

Around her, conversations faded as though someone had pulled the plug on a radio. Bree pretended to study the silver bangles on her wrist and slipped past shimmering, sweaty adolescent shoulders that parted to reveal a spot at a wall-length, gold-framed mirror. She leaned in, grateful the decorator had positioned it low enough for her to see without standing on tiptoe. Her stubby little finger traced the outline of her lower eyelid, wiping away mascara streaks, while her eyes darted to catch glimpses of nearby faces. Her teeth clamped her lower lip to repress a smile that tickled her cheeks. *Yes*, she thought, *they noticed.*

She felt rather than saw the angry gestures, assumed rather than heard the whispers, and wanted to savor and not escape from the attention. But her hands trembled as she reached for a paper towel, the noise of its crinkling bouncing gently off the brocade padded chairs in the uneasy stillness of the faux Louis XIV surroundings. She twisted her lips into a frown. But it curved up at the corners, hinting at glee about to burst like a balloon too close to a flame. After flinging the towel into an overflowing stainless steel bin, she fled, a grin bisecting the dimples on her cheeks.

"Slow down, *amiga*." Outside the restroom, the familiar voice halted her scamper across the floral carpet.

Bree took in the tall, slim figure of her best friend, who looked, she thought, even more than usual like a runway model in the strapless orange and black dress that clung to her outlines as though sprayed on. "You should have seen them, Stephanie." Bree laughed, holding her hand to her chest. "They're still picking their eyeballs off the floor."

"Blame them?" Stephanie tugged at her bodice, lowering it an inch. "Sophomores at senior prom. We stand out."

Bree's eyes sparkled. "It makes up for a lot."

Stephanie led Bree away from the door toward a

row of white linen-covered tables laden with porcelain towers that dripped with thick sandwiches, colorful vegetables, and gooey desserts. She dropped a few celery sticks on a plate. "They're jealous, *chiquita*."

Bree's hands adjusted the material around her middle. "Right. They're all dying to wear a size sixteen."

"Dying to dance with your hot date." Stephanie sucked seductively on a light green sliver.

Bree punched her arm. A flock of heavily perfumed girls flitted past them, trailing a wake of flowery scent and evil looks the way a cigarette trails wisps of smoke. Bree coughed and crossed her fingers behind her back. "The date with him's a fluke. Like a hundred-year storm." She scanned the thronged ballroom's dance floor.

Stephanie's eyebrows lifted. "More like a missile homing in on its target." She pointed. "He's over there. By the stage."

Bree glanced in the direction Stephanie indicated then shrugged her shoulders and turned to the buffet, choosing with exaggerated nonchalance a brownie from among the sugary selections. She held it in a napkin, smiling as she chewed, enjoying the consternation evident in Stephanie's features and glad Stephanie couldn't see how quickly her heart was pounding. "No rush." She mumbled between bites. "He's not the only thing I can enjoy."

"The only thing *worth* enjoying." Stephanie yanked the last morsels of brownie from Bree's fingers and gave her a shove toward the crowd on the floor. "Remember to do everything I would do.

And more, if you get the chance."

Bree grinned as she excused her way through the pulsing dancers. The closer she got to the stage, the more out of breath she felt, as though her heart raced ahead without her. Her tight crepe dress conspired to hold her back, so she hitched it up to mid-thigh and pushed ahead, her hips bumping gently against rail-thin frames. She ignored the affronted looks that flashed from under heavy makeup, keeping her eyes focused on the corner to which Stephanie had pointed.

She reached the stage panting. On it gyrated a band that tried to make up for its conspicuous middle agedness through judicious tears in clothing, gobs of sweat-proof rouge, and speakers the size of hot tubs. She leaned against the stage's smooth birch planks. Her knuckles knocked the wood. She tried to ignore the thought that slithered forward and coiled cold tendrils around her stomach. Had he left?

The thumping beat from the speaker obliterated all hope of concentrating. Under the glittering glass wall sconces that threw a nonstop shower of confetti-like sparkles into the crowd, she edged against the cream-colored walls, suddenly welcoming their support. He was nowhere in sight. Her throat constricted. She watched the room spin without her, like a complete, lithe, contented entity that cast her off. Her eyes searched for the nearest exit.

A hand gripped her elbow. "Couldn't stand the noise."

Upon meeting his calm, blue eyes, a sudden

warmth rose from Bree's chest, melting the chill the way summer sun pushes through clouds. She disengaged from the wall and posed deliberately, one foot at right angles to the other. Behind her back, her fingers uncrossed.

The boy stuffed a napkin into the vest pocket of his dark suit so it stuck out like a folded handkerchief. He gripped her hand. Dancers parted for them as he led her to the center of the room. He didn't seem to notice boys and girls who tried to catch his eye.

Breathless, not with fear but with exhilaration, Bree floated behind him, remembering the time she went tubing on the lake near Stephanie's family's summer house, the wind whipping her long hair across her face, the giddy excitement of being pulled behind a speeding motorboat that skimmed across the water, trailing a frothy silver wake. He was exactly like that motorboat. Rushing her into situations before she could ask why or consider the consequences, such as how she would feel tomorrow when she saw him pin a willing girl's hands against a locker and grind into her with a kiss that slammed the breath out of Bree.

She focused her eyes on his and danced, centering her awareness on the next step, the next brush of his arm, the next inhalation that drew in his half men's deodorant, half teenage sweat, all-delicious scent. He smiled down at her, moving in sync with her rhythm but with few gestures, as though fun for him came from the inside.

"Don't you like dancing?" Bree ran her fingers through her hair and let the music's rapid thrum stream through her limbs.

He twinkled a smile. "Too much like sports." He spun her under his arm, twirling her into the crowd of strangers then scooping her back into the space only they inhabited.

Eyes wide, she raised her voice to be heard above the music. "But you're great at sports."

He thrust his hands in his pants pockets, wiggling his shoulders in time to the beat and looking, for an instant, younger than his eighteen years. "Just trying not to disappoint people."

Bree waved her arms over her head. "For me, dancing takes away pressure."

"Because you're good at it." He spun her again into the surrounding melee. "Wish I had your guts."

Bree squinted. "You're dancing with the math league secretary. I think you get the award for guts."

He seemed not to have heard and she closed her eyes, allowing the rhythm to take over, like a drug. She moved her feet and arms as though they belonged to a different self. Then the music paused, the lights dimmed, and a slow song floated on the thick air. She stood bewildered, legs splayed, as couples partnered or traipsed from the floor. Her mind still vibrated with the previous song's lyrics. Her extremities tingled with exertion that had no outlet in the quiet swaying.

He stretched his arms and beckoned her to him with a quick tilt of his chin, a fisherman hooking and reeling in his catch. She stepped forward, her nose level with his armpit. Not knowing where to lay her head, she hovered it an inch from his chest, twisting like an anxious carp on a line. A moment earlier, she thought, everything seemed easy. Now dread inched up her body like wet cement. What was she doing in his arms? Her feet dragged, stumbling across each other.

"Relax." He pulled her closer, resting one hand on her hips and one on her neck.

Her hand slid up his back. She tried to shut out the thought of the contrast between her own spongy contours and the hard, rippled surface that strained beneath the wool and polyester mix. A gentle pressure eased her head onto his chest. She thought discerned his breathing, even and deep. Her own came in shallow, rushing snatches. Slow dancing, she thought, left too much space for doubts.

Her platform shoes ground into his toes with a crunch. He pulled away and squinted at her, one eye closed in mock agony. She turned away, face reddening. "I should let you dance with someone else."

His warm hand curled around hers. "Let's get out of here." He again tugged her in his wake through the staring crowd, this time toward the exit. Outside the ballroom, the music barely audible behind padded doors, he strode toward the hotel's deserted shopping arcade. Its window displays provided the only light in a wide hallway that curved away from the ballroom. Periodic benches ran down its middle like paint on a highway. As she trailed slightly behind him, flashes of empty jewelry cases, women's silk scarves, and men's swimwear impressed themselves fleetingly on her mind, billboard images on an empty pedestrian highway.

She slowed her pace. The last bubbles of intoxication from the dancing drifted into the shaded recesses of the pressed lead ceiling. She imagined walking hand-in-hand with him down a hallway in their high school, the image so incongruous that she jerked her hand from his, slowing her stride to a crawl. The icy feeling of uncertainty once more crept along her limbs.

"Shouldn't we get back?" She studied the floor's black and white marble tiles.

He swung one leg over a bench and patted the space in front of him. Bree peered into the dim light and noticed for the first time the silence. She perched far from him, at the end of the bench, like a sprinter ready to leap at the first crack of a gun. He laughed and scooted forward. She jumped up.

He stood a few feet away, hands in his pockets. His eyes roamed the empty hallway. "Reminds me of the beach." His voice sounded small, as though he too were cowed by the quiet.

The unexpectedness of the comment made her sit again. She gazed at the ostentatious displays. "It makes me think I don't belong here." She sucked in her stomach, trying to minimize the rolls and curves around her middle.

He sat and inched closer until she could feel the warmth of his body. "Sometimes I drive to the beach in the winter. When no one's there. And stand on the cliffs."

Bree shivered. "Sounds dangerous."

"Always seems like a good idea before I go. But when I get there, I feel lonely."

She shot him an incredulous glance. "Half the

school would go with you anywhere."

He rested a hand at the nape of her neck. "More isn't always better."

At his touch, a spark coursed through her. Goosebumps rose on her arms. She chewed her lower lip, avoiding his gaze. Her fingers crossed and uncrossed. Any moment, she thought, he would run as fast as he could in the other direction. *So I'd better beat him to it.*

She sprung from the bench. "I'm going home with Stephanie." Her heels clicked on the hard flooring as she stepped backward. The cool air felt suddenly close.

He rose but hesitated, his hand hovering above but not touching her shoulder.

She brushed it aside, furious with the part of herself that wanted to remain. "You've done enough, Ryder." She blinked and cursed the drop of warm liquid that slid down her cheek.

He wiped the tear away with the awe of a child touching his first feather, rubbing his finger with his thumb, as though unable to understand why it was damp. His features softened and she momentarily pictured him at age six, lying face up in a field of soft grass, gazing at the clouds with wonder. *At six*, she thought, *we could have been friends*.

He removed the napkin from his blazer. It hung before her in the still air like a flag of surrender. Her mind swirled with conflicting commands. She closed her eyes.

Something warm brushed her lips. Her eyes snapped open. Ryder's face was an inch from hers. A wisp of golden hair hung down from his forehead and tickled her nose. She rubbed her upper lip to keep from sneezing, her hand lingering in front of her mouth like a shield.

He cupped her face, nudging her fingers out of the way. His breath smelled minty and reminiscent of something warm and earthy.

"I want you with me on the beach." He lifted her chin. His lips fluttered against hers.

Bree swallowed, blood rushing in her ears, a hot flood of longing tingling her insides. Her gaze bored into his, seeming to read in his eyes everything she had dreamt of seeing there since the first day she glimpsed him in the cafeteria and he singled her out for a smile.

He likes me.

She lunged forward, her lips colliding with his, her inexpert fingers roaming through his wavy hair as though lost. She pressed against him, thoughts whirling.

A piercing whistle shot from down the hall. "Check it out."

Ryder's lips stiffened. He pushed her away and stared down the hall at an approaching cluster of suit-clad boys.

"Coming with?" The closest boy, a thick necked stubby youth who spoke loudly, as though afraid of being overlooked, strode forward, snatched the napkin from Ryder's hand, and wiped his face with it.

Bree's fingers searched for Ryder's. But he held them out of reach like the limp end of a question mark. His mouth hardened into a thin, dark line. His eyes flicked from the group to Bree and back.

The stubby youth spoke again. "If you'd rather hang out with underage…" He scanned Bree without meeting her gaze. "You said you'd be done your pity date by eleven." He looked at his watch. "Twelve-thirty, dude."

Pity date. The air caught in Bree's throat, which felt stung by a thousand hornets. Her face burst, an agony of red flames. She bounded from the bench. Her voice, when she spoke, was raspy. "Stephanie's waiting for me." Her feet pounded on the marble, click, clack, like the retort of a machine gun. By the time she had run a few feet beyond the boys who circled Ryder like a pack of hyenas around a tiger, the tears began to drip in black mascara-laden drops onto her white dress, boring holes through her heart and into the cold, hard ground.

CHAPTER 2

The bright sapphire on its platinum band sparkled in the elevator spotlights, snatching Bree's attention and momentarily giving space to a thought she tried to repress: *Is this a mistake?* Her manicured finger hovered over the thirteenth-floor button, whose broken plastic face grimaced like an unwanted stepchild next to full-blood siblings. She drew small circles around the knob's cracked periphery, then touched it quickly with a decisive thrust, as though testing a hot stove. The elevator groaned and creaked its reluctant assent. Her eyes lit with the satisfaction of someone who has recognized danger and averted it.

"It'll work out." Her words melted quietly into the empty space. Behind her back, she crossed her fingers.

Overflowing reusable shopping bags leaned against wood veneer paneling, rattling in tune with the elevator's rumblings. Her eyes absentmindedly scanned the dusty floor. When she caught sight of a dull penny in a corner, a smile spread over her face like a slow sunrise. She plucked it from the linoleum and polished it against her skirt, its surface leaving gray streaks across the tight black silk fabric. Holding the penny between thumb and forefinger of her left hand, she let the sapphire on her ring finger dance ephemeral reflections across the walls. *It's going to be okay.*

When the elevator doors rasped open, the stale air beyond vibrated with the pulse of a distant song that grew in intensity as Bree negotiated the narrow hallway with its burned-out overhead lights. Her heavy bags bumped against her thighs, making her feel like a cow trudging down a cattle chute. Straps dug into her hands. Her leather pumps pinched her toes. All signs pointed to a long night. But her fingers still clutched the penny and the smile lingered on her lips.

No one heard the knock of bag-laden knuckles against peeling varnish. Her knee edged open the door, releasing scents of alcohol, greasy snack foods, and perfume. Beyond the short entrance crowded women aged twenty to sixty. Clothing ranged from svelte navy business suits to jeans and T-shirts so distressed that only threads kept their wearers out of jail for indecent exposure. Bree stumbled across the threshold, throwing the bags onto the wood floor. She raised her voice above the music's beat. "Stephanie, you owe me."

Stephanie appeared from the throng and kicked the door shut with a stiletto boot-encased leg. She embraced Bree with one arm, holding a martini glass aloft with the other. "Nice you made an appearance at your own engagement party."

Bree laughed, backing slightly away and fanning her hand in front of her nose. "Your fumes could trigger warning levels on a breathalyzer test." She surveyed the room. "What did you do, invite the whole class?"

Stephanie shrugged. "Word got out. *Gracias* for the blender and ice." She picked up the bags and drew Bree toward a makeshift bar set up on a cluttered kitchen island. Over a dozen bottles jostled with an assortment of bulbous, slender, and shapely glasses, creating a disorderly and colorful skyline. A blender whirred in the background. "Drink." The word was not a question but a command.

Bree twisted labels toward her and whistled. "It's not me they come to see. It's your liquor."

Stephanie sloshed coconut milk and ice into the blender, tossed in pineapple slices, and followed them with a liberal splash of rum. She winked at Bree. "Remember when we…" A roar from the machine obscured the story.

Piña colada in hand, Bree followed Stephanie to the only vacant chair in the room, a worn brown leather recliner bedecked with white satin ribbons. "For me?"

Stephanie tucked her hair behind her ears and nodded conspiratorially. "Been hell keeping the cats away." She waved a ribbon in the air. "All yours, *amiga*."

Bree sat carefully, perching on the edge of the cushion as though worried her weight would tip it backward. She straightened her blouse over her tummy. "Please don't make me give a speech."

Stephanie shrugged. "Should have thought of

that before you got engaged."

Bree's eyes avoided her friend's. She attempted in vain to tug her down to her level. "Let's keep it low key. We had a fight and I haven't heard from…"

Stephanie ignored her and nudged guests from a nearby sofa. She clambered up, hands outstretched. "Ladies." In the chatter, her voice didn't carry beyond a few feet. Stephanie cleared her throat. "*Yo, borrachos*." Her second attempt ricocheted off the walls like a fog horn.

From the back, someone shouted. "Speech." Another person clapped. Color rose in Bree's cheeks.

Stephanie bowed, almost toppling from the sofa. "Case you hadn't noticed, our guest of honor finally arrived." She pointed at Bree, whose attention was absorbed in wrapping streamers around her wrists like handcuffs. Stephanie grinned. "No one's surprised Bree's getting married. What we're wondering is…what took her so long?" Laughter interrupted, and she swatted it away like an annoying insect. "Starting in high school, I kept thinking she'd found the man for her. But Malcolm Patel beat them all." She closed one eye and focused with effort on Bree. Bree kicked the retro shag rug at her feet. Outside, a siren trailed its lonely cry through the city. "A man who's allergic to dogs but has a dog wash business. A man of mystery." She dodged a balled up streamer Bree threw at her. "*Mi hermana*, he's lucky as hell. Better treat you right." She pumped a threatening fist, almost knocking herself from her roost.

"Marines are in our blood. We sisters know how to fight."

Stephanie reached in the pocket of her jeans, removed a spool, and tossed crepe streamers at Bree. Tape fluttered in a pink cascade. Suddenly, streamers, confetti, and balloons bounced off heads, showered from the ceiling, and dipped into drinks. Stephanie bounded from the sofa, yanked Bree from her chair, and propelled her onto the couch, where the pillows sagged.

Bree teetered, hands outstretched like tightrope walker. She regarded Stephanie with a quizzical expression. "Who's that woman?" She ducked the balloon Stephanie batted at her. "Seriously. Most of you know my life would have been…a mess without Stephanie's family adopting me." Her fingers twisted the sapphire band on her ring finger, as though trying to unwind it. "She said Mal was the lucky one. I think she got that backwards. I've got all of you." She bent and knocked on the sofa's wooden armrest. "And if luck stays with me, I'll have Mal and his family too." She blew a kiss to Stephanie. "Thanks for the party."

Hands helped her from the sofa. Stephanie punched her arm playfully. "Thought you'd give us hot details about Mal."

Color rose to Bree's cheeks. "Hardly likely." Her elbow pointed to a woman with zebra striped glasses downing a martini. "That's my boss over there." Bree lowered the level of her drink by an inch. "Anyway, not much to talk about these days."

Stephanie rolled her eyes. "Crazy in-laws getting you down?"

"In-laws to be." Bree marched to the kitchen, empty glass held in front of her like a band majorette's baton. "They don't know I'm here." She hooked her fingers into quotation marks. "They don't value 'ostentatious displays of frivolity.'"

"Or alcohol." Stephanie tipped contents from a gin bottle into a fresh glass with enthusiastic disregard. "Big surprise they're not invited." She handed Bree the drink. "Relax, my *chiquita*. It's *your* party."

Two hours later, Bree lay grinning in the recliner, feet pointed at the ceiling, streamers draped over her stomach, the detritus of unwrapped presents strewn around her. Lacy intimate apparel decorated the chair's arm rests. In its crevices lay suggestive books and a collection of gift cards. The guests had thinned. Only a small group clustered around the open yearbook on Bree's lap.

"What about him?" Stephanie touched the stem of her martini glass to a photo of a lank teenager with curly hair, raised eyebrows, and a moustache reminiscent of a 1920s silent movie swashbuckler. Bree's fingers quickly covered the name in the caption.

Women shouted in unison. "Sergio Fernandez."

Bree flipped through the pages. "Too easy." She chose another photo and hid the name. "What about him?"

"Douglas Park?"

"Nope."

"Scott Scully?"

Bree shook her head. "Give up?" Heads nodded. "Rickie Wolfteich."

17

Stephanie slapped her forehead. "Of course. How could I forget Wolfie the Wolf? Cornered me in physics class and asked if I wanted to see how his…you know…could defy gravity. Ugh." She reached for the book. "My turn."

She skimmed the pictures and laid the album back on Bree's lap, open to a full-page close-up of a football player wearing a helmet. "Your turn, Bree. That guy."

Bree averted her gaze and lifted her glass from the floor. She mumbled into her drink. "Ryder Fitzgerald."

Sighs echoed at her words. Stephanie turned pages and pointed to another photograph. "Looks better without the helmet. He's in here more than anybody else."

A petite, fair skinned woman with bemused hazel eyes and striking red hair spoke. "I was yearbook director. And I couldn't get enough of him."

Somebody fanned herself. "You and half the school."

The redhead gazed at the ceiling. "I wonder what he's doing now?"

Stephanie nudged Bree. "Think Bree knows."

Bree shifted in her chair. She shoved her hands under her thighs. "Involved in startups. Something with a venture capitalist firm."

The redhead peered at her. "You're in touch? So envious. Is he still gorgeous?"

Another woman spoke before Bree could answer. "I'm friends with him on Facebook. And no, he isn't."

The redhead's face fell.

"He's better." The woman laughed. "He has, like, five thousand friends. Mostly women."

Stephanie tapped Bree's shoulder. "Ryder took Bree to his senior prom."

Bree rubbed her temples and shot Stephanie an annoyed look. "A pity date. It was the year after…"

The redhead reached out to touch Bree's knee. "I remember. That was so sad." She took the book. "Here. My turn."

Afterward, at the door to the apartment, Bree clutched a new shopping bag stuffed with gifts. The room behind her looked as though a party store had exploded.

Bree suppressed a yawn. "Sure you don't want me to stay and help clean up?"

Stephanie shook her head. "Uber's waiting downstairs. You're driving to Vegas tomorrow."

Bree nodded sleepily. She leaned in to hug her friend goodbye.

"Crap." Stephanie backed away. "Supposed to give you something. Wait right there."

Bree rested against the doorframe and closed her eyes, letting pictures from the previous hours cascade over one another in a collage. It reminded her of the yearbook and of Ryder. Her eyes snapped open. She felt her cheeks flush. *Serves you right, Bree*, she thought, *for not telling even Stephanie the whole story*.

"Why's your face red?" Stephanie waved an envelope and box in front of her.

Bree deposited the brimming shopping bag on the floor. "What's this?"

"Slipped my mind earlier. Box is from me."

Bree tucked the card under her arm and tore open the box's wrapping. Inside lay a set of six thin silver bangles, each engraved with the name of one of Stephanie's family members.

She glided the bracelets onto her arm. "They're perfect."

Stephanie smiled. "You're always going on about family. Since we won't be in Vegas, I wanted us to be there in spirit."

Bree stuffed the box into the shopping bag and held up the card. "I'll read this in the car."

"It's from Mal. He stopped by earlier." Stephanie helped settle the bag in Bree's arms. "Probably a love letter so, yeah, read it later."

The silver ringlets jingled as Bree clutched the letter to her chest, negotiated the trek to the lobby, and hopped into the waiting car. On the dark San Francisco streets, lit row houses slid past her window at oblique angles to the steep roads. She nestled into the upholstery with a happy sigh and kissed the envelope.

She spoke to herself as her fingernail prized open a corner and ran carefully along the sealed edge, breaking it in a neat line. "Thanks for remembering, Mal. You're not perfect." She pulled out a stiff white card. "But that's why we're a good pair. Neither am I." Her head leaned toward the window to read the note in the intermittent light from the streetlamps.

Mom says you never reimbursed her

for the hotel's advance payment. Send her a check before you leave tomorrow. It's embarrassing to have her remind me.

Drops of sudden rain splashed against the car's window. Bree shivered and stuffed the card into the bag. She wrapped her arms around herself like pieces of a torn blanket and stared out into the night, the reflections cast by her bracelets absorbed by the gray city, the sapphire on her finger dark and morose.

***

It took Bree three trips the next morning to load her luggage into the waiting Uber. The female driver helped lift the final load into the backseat and dropped sunglasses onto her broad nose. "Wedding?"

Bree grinned ruefully. "Engagement party."

The driver nodded, slipped behind the wheel, and tuned the radio station to classical music. "Helps people relax. If your in-laws are anything like mine, you'll need it, girl."

When the car rolled to a silent halt in front of a one-story yellow building twenty minutes later, the driver twisted to face Bree, her dreadlock ponytail bumping against the headrest. "You sure you want to rent from this place? The airport's just a few exits up."

Bree looked out the window at the building's

peeling wooden sign and metal-barred windows. She raised her eyebrows. "How bad can it be?"

"Well…"

Bree smiled, slung her purse over her shoulder, and yanked her carry-on from the backseat. After a minute, the pile of luggage obscured everything below her navel. She crossed her fingers. "Wish me luck."

The driver rolled down the passenger window as Bree struggled past coaxing a hulking roller suitcase, a garment bag draped over one arm. "I can stick around, girl, and drive you to Vegas myself."

Bree's eyes twinkled. "I'm good. *Me time* starts now." The garment bag flapped as Bree waved goodbye and bounced her load confidently across the spider web of cracks in the sidewalk like a BMX rider on a dirt trail near the finish line.

An off-key bell tinkled when she opened the rental agency's door. Inside, aggressively scented air freshener masked the odor of stale tobacco and sweat. Behind a gray Formica counter, a grimy CD player pulsed Mexican pop music. Two attendants in stained yellow Miser Rent-A-Car t-shirts operated enormous gray computer terminals. Poles with retractable belts marked a customer line that snaked back upon itself. Bree stifled a sigh as she edged into the last place and counted the number of people ahead of her. Sixteen. She clamped her suitcase against one leg, hung the garment bag across it, and took out her phone in its pink case.

Twenty-eight new emails glared up at her. Data analysis for a company-sponsored drug study was behind schedule. Marketing had problems choosing a name for a new antifungal medication. Her most recent hire announced she'd broken her arm skiing over the weekend and needed voice recognition software to function. Bree's fingers began to dance across the screen, the oscillating fan in the corner blowing away all thoughts of "me time." Forty-five minutes and two corners of the line later, Bree raised her head and took a deep breath of over-chilled air.

Directly in front of her, an older woman with a stylish bob pounced. "I hesitated to interrupt you. I am familiar with burdensome workloads. But have you rented here before?" She swept her arm in the direction of the door. "I've been here nearly an hour." Her eyes rolled as though they were following the track of an erratic fly.

Bree lowered her phone and massaged her shoulders with a grin. "Interruptions stop me from working twenty-four seven."

"My husband booked this rental for me." The woman put a hand on her hip. "Revenge will be swift and uncompromising."

"Maybe the line will start moving faster." Bree searched for a scrap of wood on which to knock and, finding none, tapped her knuckles on her head.

Her companion glanced at the agency staff and raised her voice. "Does anyone have the Yelp app? Should we consider giving a group review?"

The line suddenly lurched forward, curtailing further conversation as everyone monitored the actions that moved them closer to a rental car. Bree lifted her phone and, over a pause in the music's throb, heard the main door tinkle its welcome and someone roll a suitcase through the slalom of poles behind her. She opened her email and was instantly swallowed again by the myriad concerns she'd left behind in San Francisco.

"Bree?" A man's voice spoke from behind her, tinged with hesitation. "Brianna Acosta?"

Bree pulled her shirt's puckers flat over her tummy bulges with an instinctive motion born of years of practice. Behind her stood a blond man of impressive build wearing aviator sunglasses, an open Hawaiian shirt, and fashionably day-old stubble. His wide smile created deep dimples on either cheek. His hands held a stack of Miser Rent-A-Car note pads that he stuffed into the back pocket of his jeans when he noticed her staring at them.

Her mind tried to fit the face into her professional list of contacts. Nothing. She glanced at his elegantly thin garment bag and sleek black metal roller without a company tag. Her memory raced through images from pharmacy school and college but also came up blank.

She gave up and held out her hand, flashing teeth and sucking in her stomach. "Nice to see you again."

"It *is* Bree." The man gyrated her hand in an excited volley, as though pumping in a desert for water. Before she knew what was happening, he tugged her into his arms. A wave of musky cologne enveloped her as he hugged and released her before she could push him away.

Her eyes narrowed. She crossed her arms tightly across her chest, which this stranger had squeezed with more intimacy than it had known in weeks. Yet something about him made her restrain the volley of righteous indignation poised on her tongue. Something about him was…familiar. Her memory expanded, like a dry sponge soaking up drops of water. Her eyes explored the smooth features of his face.

The impatient woman leaned in across her shoulder. "Are you acquainted with this gentleman?"

He gave the older woman a bow. The matriarch beamed and let out a squeal when an attendant motioned her toward the counter.

Bree dropped her arms. "Could you take off those sunglasses?"

The man grinned and slid them down his nose.

Bree stumbled against her suitcase, knocking her garment bag to the floor. "Ryder?"

He retrieved it. "Freaky, right?"

Bree felt blood rise to her face. "I was at Stephanie's last night. She brought out the yearbook."

Ryder shook his head and lowered his eyes. "That's painful." He eased his glasses from his face. "High school wasn't my brightest moment."

She bit her lips in an unsuccessful attempt to reduce the flush on her cheeks. "For you and me both."

She turned to the counter and sucked in a breath. What kind of idiot was he? Did he think his day-after-the-prom apology made up for everything? That ten years later he could walk up to her and pretend they were friends? In an instant, she second-guessed every decision she made that morning about what to wear, how to style her hair, and where to apply makeup. Her hands tugged again at her shirt, pulling the hem straight down until the fabric ran in a crisp, straight line across the front of her body like a sheet of metal.

Ryder kicked the tile flooring. "Bree, I'm so glad…"

"Next." The sole remaining attendant interrupted, his teeth ground together, head cocked.

She exhaled. "I've been in this line for almost an hour." Her knee nudged her bulky suitcase forward. She prayed for a miraculously quick check-in.

"No have full-size cars." The attendant chewed gum with the absorption of a cow chewing cud as he waited, hands on hips, for her reaction.

She struck the pose she used in photographs, one foot out in front, at right angles to the other, hoping it would work its slimming effects equally well for people looking at her from behind. "I'm transporting a lot of guests. I can't take an economy car."

The man seemed ready for an argument. She held her ground. No, she said, she couldn't take a downgrade. That would be like taking an economy, wouldn't it? Coming back later wasn't an option. That's why she'd made a morning reservation. She ran her fingers through her hair, noticing the sweat on her forehead. "I need to get to Las Vegas tonight. It's my engagement party."

The attendant bent over his antiquated machine. Bree fidgeted, the thought of Ryder standing behind her feeling like the heat from a massive campfire that threatened to sear her clothing. She looked down and noticed the front seam of her skirt was six inches askew. Her fingers itched to readjust it. She put her hands on the dull yellow Formica counter, her fingers bouncing in an invisible speed-typing contest. After years of avoiding even the mention of him, why did Ryder have to show up twice in two days?

A new customer burst through the main door in a flurry of expensive wool and silk that he wore like a suit of armor. He circumvented the poles and belts, stalked to the counter, and flung down a key. "Where is everyone?"

Bree's attendant scuttled sideways with an obsequious smile. "Sorry, Mr. Smith. Everything okay?"

Bree dropped her phone on the counter and opened the app of a national car rental chain. "Don't mind me."

The new customer marched back and forth in the narrow space like a hungry panther. At the keyboard, the young man's hands, marked with a chain tattoo across the second knuckles, flew in a robotic frenzy. In under a minute, he handed the man a receipt. "All set."

The man stomped out, leaving behind him, Bree thought, a whiff of something feral. The attendant's energy vaporized as quickly as it had ignited. He trudged back to the monitor in front of Bree.

"You take upgrade?" He jerked his head in the direction of the exit. "Mr. Smith had SUV. We give you same price. Good deal."

Bree's feet hurt from an hour of immobility in pumps. Her head ached from the stale air and tobacco. Most of all, she wanted out of the building. "Only if you give it to me now."

"No cleaning. No wait. Only ten-dollar-a-day mark up."

Bree's eyes flashed. "Five-dollar *discount*."

The man stared at her, nodded, and handed her the keys.

She didn't look at Ryder on her way to the door.

CHAPTER 3

Once she got through San Jose on Highway 101 South and traffic thinned, Bree loosened her grip on the steering wheel and rolled down the window. *Too much high school.* She let the wind cool her face and wipe clinging cobwebs from her mind.

She called Mal and got his voicemail. "Miser rental was a dump. Let's talk when I get there about being less frugal." A truck hurtled past and she edged the car closer to the shoulder. "Good news is I have an SUV. Not the newest." She sniffed the air. "Smells kinda funny. But roomy."

She relaxed and surfed satellite radio stations until she found a pop music channel. The wild breeze blew the last remnants of product from her hair and long strands whipped periodically across her face, making her feel as though she were driving through patchy fog. "It's good to be young, free, and on the road," her melodious alto hailed the steady trickle of passing cars.

A few miles out of San Jose, she eased her vehicle down the exit ramp for Morgan Hill. Her smile widened when she saw the donut shop's sign. She congratulated herself for having studied the route to Las Vegas ahead of time. The drive to Vegas was, after all, not a punishment but an adventure. Not a failure to come to grips with her fear of flying but a sensible alternative to arriving for the long weekend's festivities drugged, disheveled, and dismayed after a terrifying airplane flight. Instead she would arrive calm, clear-headed, and—with the help of a final stop in a rest area short of the city—cute. Just the kind of fiancée Mal wanted to introduce to his relatives. So what if she gained a pound or two on the journey? The prior weeks of dieting gave her ample wiggle room.

She pulled into a small strip mall, found a parking space, and killed the engine. The aroma of freshly fried donuts wafted on a light breeze. She inhaled deeply, leaned out, and took a photo of the storefront.

Bree: Me. Here. Now.

She added a blissed-out face emoji and sent Stephanie the text.

Her eyes were glued to the enticing photos of glazed, filled, and chocolate delights. She grabbed her purse, rolled up the windows, and slammed the door behind her. Then a car pulling into the space next to her made her jog for the sidewalk.

Out of harm's way, she shaded her eyes, finding it difficult to glare effectively while squinting into the strong sun. The silver Camry's door opened and a familiar voice reached her ears.

"My bad, Bree."

"Ryder?" Her mouth hung open.

He stepped onto the sidewalk, grinning. "Almost faked me out by getting off the highway."

She felt a tightening in her throat, as though someone were closing a noose. "You're stalking me?" She looked at the shop behind her, wishing she'd parked somewhere else.

"Totally." He laughed and sat on the hood of his car. "You left so fast, I never got the chance to tell you."

Bree held up her hand. "Don't say it."

"Vegas. Got a business meeting."

She leaned against the building wall, the warmth of the cement soaking into her like a hot water bottle on a summer night, not soothing but irritating. The frown that had sprouted on the edge of her lips grew. "Nobody drives from San Francisco to Vegas."

"You do."

She cocked her head, placed a foot on the wall behind her, and stared as he gazed back through the aviator sunglasses. His blond, wavy hair fell to chin length. The folds of his untucked shirt fluttered around his waist in the light breeze. Tanned ankles poked out from under skinny jeans. He wore canvas sneakers without socks. His thin but muscular build, she thought, didn't seem to have changed since the last time she glimpsed it in high school.

Figures.

She planted both feet on the ground and turned to give him a more flattering view. He may not have changed. But she had.

31

"Why?" The question popped from her mouth like a shot.

"Why drive?" He shrugged and tossed his keys from hand to hand. "Never crossed the California state line in a car before."

"In a car from a dump like Miser? What did you want to do, try slumming it like the rest of us?" Her hands balled into fists behind her back.

He spun the keys on his finger like toy helicopter blades. "Have a new assistant. She did the booking."

Bree shook her head. "Bet she won't have that job for long."

"Been a long time since we saw each other." He pocketed his keys.

Bree didn't answer, afraid that if she opened her mouth, unknown sentences would tumble out, words she had no control over. The air between them felt thick, as though the universe created a temporary bubble that left her in limbo between high school memories and adult reality. She felt sucked back to the night of the prom, to the airless hotel hallway where she'd last seen him up close, the humiliation and misery as raw as if the past ten years had never happened. She fixed her gaze on the ground, her eyes narrowing, sending daggers of fury toward a crack in the sidewalk.

Ryder pushed himself from the hood and pointed his thumb toward the store. "Going in?"

Bree reddened. "No." She looked around the mostly empty parking lot and pointed at a small grocery store in the far corner opposite them. "I'm going there for a drink and...carrots."

Ryder peered at the tiny, almost illegible sign. "Kind of far. Want a ride?"

Bree took a deep breath. "It's good exercise."

"Was hoping you were going for the donuts." Ryder sighed.

Minutes later, she watched from the store window as he returned to his car with a rectangular box and perched on the edge of the sidewalk by their cars, legs tucked between the curb and the cement parking space marker. She waited inside with the bag of carrots and bottle of water, hoping he would leave. After fifteen minutes, she trudged over to the cars. Beside Ryder lay an open box of mixed donuts and two brownies.

She leaned on her hood, tucking her skirt between her legs. The sun warmed her skin. She tilted her head and let her hair cascade down her back, thankful she'd taken time in the grocery's bathroom to fix it.

"I got brownies." He pushed the box toward her.

Bree shoved the box away with her foot. Her eyelids fluttered as she blinked back a sudden stinging. "I associate brownies with a bad experience. Can't stand them." She took out her car keys and punched a hole in the bag of mini carrots.

Ryder bit into a donut and gulped a frozen mocha latte. "You'll live longer than me."

Bree stared at the rapidly disappearing doughy ring in his hand. "But you'll have more fun. That's what happens when you don't care about what you do."

***

Later in the car, with the black highway stretching before her and a caramel fudge iced coffee in the holder next to her seat, she wondered why everything felt different. Her SUV wound slowly up Route 152 toward the San Luis Reservoir and Highway 5. Only intermittent trees and roads marked the passing miles amid monotonous parched grass, dried bushes, and brown hills. The ride she had been looking forward to now stretched in front of her like a bad dream. Talking with Ryder catapulted her back in time. It felt like trying on a cheap pair of sneakers a size too small, the kind that pinch your feet, cause blisters, and take the spring out of every step.

The pink phone on the seat next to her rang. She picked up her headset without thinking.

"You've got to tell." Ryder's voice sounded tinny. She watched him wave at her through the back window of the car in front of her and cursed herself for giving him her number.

"Tell what?" She kept her gaze on the road.

"About your engagement."

Bree involuntarily stepped on the brakes. Cars honked. She jumped and hit the pedal harder, causing a slight skid. She clutched the steering wheel with white knuckles until the blare faded into the distance.

"You okay?"

Bree swallowed before speaking. "Never been better."

"Want to get off the highway?"

"I need to get to Vegas."

"Right. Your fiancé would never forgive me if I

didn't get you there in one piece."

Her fingers throttled the steering wheel. She straightened the car and pushed the odometer back to above the speed limit. "You overheard at the rental agency. About my engagement."

"Who is he?"

She rolled her eyes and her fingers hovered over the end call button. "His name's Malcolm. Mal for short. And you are *not* responsible for getting me to him."

"Want to meet this guy who stole your heart."

She mouthed the phrase, *Over my dead body.*

"How'd you meet?"

"In a bar." She spat out the words, hoping he would pick up on the acerbity and end the conversation.

Ryder's laughter burst through the headset so loudly she turned down the volume.

"A bar's about the last place I would have looked for you."

"*You* weren't looking."

Ryder's car slowed and Bree took her foot off the accelerator as she waited for him to respond. When he didn't, she continued. "I wasn't desperate. It didn't start out in a bar."

"Love a mystery."

She began the story the way a prosecution lawyer would pester a belligerent witness, hoping the facts would grind him to a stop. "I was on vacation in Cancun with some girlfriends. There was this good-looking guy hanging out in the lobby."

"And that was Mal."

"That was Chad." Bree took one hand off the steering wheel and felt around the passenger seat. She found the box of donuts he had given her, brought a jelly filled one to her mouth, and continued between chews. "We all went up to this guy, Chad, together. I asked him to come with us, but he refused."

"Jerk." Ryder gave a thumbs down through his car's rear window.

Bree choked on powdered sugar. She pulled the last donut out of the box and bit in. "Said he just broke up with someone named Brianna. Couldn't face a girl with the same name."

"How does this get to Mal?"

"I went into the bar for a drink. After a while, Mal sat down next to me. He was recovering from an allergy attack." She licked her fingers and concentrated on the road. "He's allergic to dogs and sat next to a service dog on the flight down." She pulled into the left lane and passed Ryder's car. The Camry revved, passed her, and sidled again into the space in front.

"Rough."

"Mal's sensitive."

Ryder paused. "My girlfriend broke up with me recently."

"Sure you're good at finding new ones."

"It's not that easy."

The air in the car felt stale. She turned up the air conditioning. "Come on, you're a walking magazine cover."

"Says who?"

"All the girls from high school."

Ryder coughed. "What do they say about you?"

"None of your business." Bree pulled at a fingernail with her teeth.

"Maybe they're jealous."

"Of fat me?" Her words discharged like the report of a rifle.

Ryder's tone dropped an octave. "I've known you since you were, like, fourteen. So I can say something, right?"

"No." The donuts churned in her stomach. Her eyes followed the white line marking the shoulder of the road. She raised her hand, ready to take the headset from her ear.

Ryder cleared his throat. "Yeah, Bree, you're heavy."

Bree flung the headset onto the seat beside her. "Thanks." She pushed her purse over the mic and blinked back tears that sprung into her eyes. *Looks like in high school you were just gearing up to become a nasty adult.*

CHAPTER 4

With the word "heavy" ringing in her ear, Bree tried to control her fury by concentrating on the mechanics of driving. Her foot leaned heavily on the gas and she sped by Ryder's car, resisting the urge to bump it from the road. The numbers on the digital speedometer rose past eighty. The car vibrated. Bree's lower jaw felt like it had been forged to the upper with a steel plate. Her eyes were narrow, cold pins piercing the windshield. Her fingernails tore at the vinyl covering of the steering wheel, which she noticed seem to be pulling to the right. She scanned the road for potholes.

A few seconds later, the wheel lurched. Thudding followed. The wheel's tug became more insistent. She wrestled it for control, stepping hard on the brake and veering onto the shoulder amid flying dust and gravel. Her fingers ground into the plastic and she muttered curses, as the car gradually skidded off the asphalt, across dirt, and came, slightly tilted, to a halt.

Bree cut the engine and slapped her hand on the

now docile wheel. Her breath came in heaves. Her heart pounded in her throat. She tried to repress a familiar wave of rising panic.

It's fine. I'm okay. It's fine. I'm okay... The two phrases rose and fell with the rhythm of her breath. She jumped at a tap on the driver's side window and raised her head to see Ryder's anxious face. He pulled at the locked door handle. She unclenched a hand from the steering wheel and opened the door, moving in slow motion as though through mud.

"What happened? Are you okay?" He leaned toward her.

Bree stared at him, unblinking, as a semi roared past them up the incline.

Ryder walked around the car and back to the driver's door. "You've got a flat. Is there a spare?"

Bree didn't answer. She pushed her hair from her face and noticed her hands were shaking. She stuck them under her legs and blinked. *I'm fine. It's okay.*

Ryder scanned the jumble of Bree's purse contents and the donut box in the passenger seat foot well. "Go sit in my car." He handed her the remains of the iced coffee. "Drink this. Be done in no time."

Bree took the drink and shuffled to his car like a reprimanded school child. She felt foolish and angry but incapable of making decisions for herself. If Ryder wanted to catch her in a weak moment, this was it. Accidents opened up a fault line of anxiety within her like an unexpected earthquake.

In the back of Bree's SUV, Ryder untangled a garment bag intertwined with a heap of electronics that spilled from an open pocket of her suitcase. He stuffed charging wires, a laptop brick, and a silver cell phone into the open compartments and transferred all the luggage to the back seat. Twenty minutes later, his greasy hands closed the SUVs enormous hatchback. He kicked the new tire on his way back to his car.

"Full-size spare." He flopped into the driver's seat next to Bree and rubbed his fingers with a donut shop napkin. "You're good to go."

Bree put her hand on the passenger door handle. "Accidents freak me out."

Ryder twisted the napkin into a tight roll. "With good reason." He tossed the crumpled paper into the foot well. "Let's get going." He walked to the passenger side and pulled her out of the car. Palms on her shoulder blades, he guided her back to the SUV.

Her fingers brushed the scorching hood of her car. Gravel crunched defiantly under her feet. The shadow of a stray cloud darkened the road ahead and disappeared. She settled herself again behind the wheel and faced Ryder. "Thanks." The word caught temporarily in her throat as it passed.

He stuck his hands in his pockets. "Haven't changed a tire since driver's ed."

Bree searched through the mess in the passenger seat foot well for her keys. "I hope the thing stays on."

Ryder bent and threw items into her open purse.

She grabbed the bag from him. "I keep my stuff organized."

Ryder peered over her shoulder as the large leather weekender swallowed her arms to the elbow.

"Could've fooled me."

"It's my personal system." She held up the keys.

Ryder rolled his eyes. "Be careful next time. You drive like my grandmother, all gas and no class." Bree bit back a smile. He closed the door. She turned on the car and gunned the engine, feeling better. Ryder strolled to his car, waving a thumbs up.

The smooth pavement welcomed her back as though nothing had happened. She pulled into the fast lane. Moments later, the phone rang. She turned on the headset. "Leave this grandmother alone."

"Bree?"

Her foot slipped from the accelerator as she registered the quizzical tenor. "Mal?"

"Expecting someone else?"

Her foot reclaimed the gas. "Thought Stephanie was calling back."

"Nope. Just me."

"How are your parents liking Vegas?"

"Dad spent so much time looking at the ground that a couple of strangers asked him if he'd lost something."

Bree watched her speedometer, keeping the numbers hovering around seventy-five. "What about your mom?"

"Think the slot machines pushed her over the edge." There was a cough, then the sound of a hand over the phone microphone. "My parents just dropped by." A raised woman's voice filtered through the connection, followed by a man's grumbling, and the woman's rising tone.

Bree absently felt the seat beside her for the

donut box. Her eyes shifted between the empty road ahead and the rearview mirror. "At this rate, I probably won't get there before nine. Maybe later."

"We're all looking forward to seeing you." The voice sounded hollow above the increasingly audible argument in the background.

"I can hear your parents." She reflexively smoothed the front of her blouse and straightened her spine.

"Got to go."

"You need me there to play interference." She stepped on the accelerator, ticking the speedometer above eighty.

"No rush. This end's all set. See you when you get here." He hung up.

The road ahead stretched straight as a ruler. She watched the broken yellow line flash by as her thoughts drifted back to the first time she met Mal's parents.

***

He introduced his childhood into their conversations carefully, bit by bit, as though he feared people could only stomach small doses. So she hoarded scraps of information and, over time, pieced together a tattered picture of what she thought his life growing up entailed. Since he always spoke of austerity, she guessed the family lived in suburban California's version of a monastery. Because his parents' strict religious sect frowned on ostentation, she imagined the house as dull, utilitarian, and uninviting. She envisioned

Spartan rooms without carpets, unappealing meals, and bare walls. No photographs. No piano. Certainly no Internet. Everything in black and white.

So she stared flaccid-jawed as Mal pulled up to the neatly manicured, two-story standalone house with skylights, a welcoming front porch, and pastel blue picket fence.

"I thought your parents…" She trailed off, not sure how to express the image in her mind.

He maneuvered the car to within six inches of the curb, cut the engine, and turned to her. "Are frugal? Despise consumerism? Disavow the commercialization of our culture?"

"Isn't that…" Her gaze rested on an old BMW in the driveway.

"Bought it when we first moved. Before they converted." He swept his arm, taking in both the house and the neighborhood. "First generation born in the U.S. Kind of competitive." He fingered a small mole on his chin.

Bree put her hand on his arm. "Now I'm nervous."

Mal kissed her on the nose. "Don't be. I love you."

Bree pulled back. "You've never said that before."

He caressed her mouth with his finger. "You've never met my parents before."

She laughed. "I can't be the only girlfriend you've brought home."

Mal looked out the window. "The only one who has a chance of coming out alive."

"Appreciate your confidence." She tickled his chin.

Mal's mouth twitched down at the corners. "Watch out for Patel landmines."

Bree giggled and opened her door. "What should I look for?"

Mal traipsed up the walk behind her. "When you step on one, you'll know."

Inside, on a bright floral sofa, with a cup of chamomile tea balanced on her knee, Bree felt oddly at home. The room and people, she thought, were like the Indian version of a 1960s family TV show. What wasn't familiar in the décor seemed like it belonged. But she regretted the hour she'd spent in the bathroom that morning with a department store display's worth of makeup in front of her. Mal's four sisters clustered along one wall, two on a piano bench, one in an armchair, and one on a footstool, with not a hint of product on their faces or in their hair. At least Mal's mother had succumbed to dabbing on muted lipstick and, potentially, a smudge of rouge. But her only piece of jewelry was an enormous gold cross dangling from a thick gold chain around her neck.

"Mal's told us so much about you." His mother perched on a straight-backed chair in the middle of the arch that separated living from dining room, completing a blockade around the living room's empty coffee table.

"And me about you, Mrs. Patel."

Mrs. Patel shook her head. "Call me Faye. My parents named me Fahya. I never comprehended why would they do that in this country. It makes me sound South American." Her eyes darted to Bree. "Not that Hispanic is bad. But you know how it is. A child wants to fit in." She straightened her spine. "I look more like a Faye."

Bree tucked her hands together in her lap. "Guess my parents got it right, since I look like a Bree Acosta."

Mal's youngest sister giggled. Faye flashed her a stern look. "Mal says you're a pharmacist." Faye swept back black hair tinged at the temples with gray. "I was pre-med in high school."

Bree blinked. "I didn't know they offered pre-med classes in high school."

Faye's brow wrinkled. "What I mean, of course, is that I *would have* been pre-med if my parents allowed girls to go to college." She crossed her arms and leaned back in her chair.

Bree's eyes sparkled. "My mother wanted to be a doctor too."

"I had everything I needed to excel."

Bree nodded. "Except a supportive family." She took a sip of tea and looked up to find seven pairs of eyes staring at her as though her blouse had popped open. She ran her fingers down her front buttons and pinched her neck line closed. She turned to Mal. His focus swiveled to the coffee table.

Faye cleared her throat. "I was the youngest of seven girls. My parents didn't have time for luxury."

"Of course not."

"Neither did *his* parents." Faye glanced at her husband. The air in the room suddenly crackled, as though a spark had been lit and threatened to burst

45

into flame.

Bree put her tea on the table and leaned back with a neutral expression. Mal glanced at her. She winked and the corner of her mouth rose, as if to say, "I'm watching this one from the sidelines."

Faye launched into a monologue about the inequities of arranged marriages, Indian parents-in-law, and misogynistic cultures. The rest of the family stared at the coffee table as though it were a screen showing an absorbing drama only they could see. Mal sat erect and periodically squeezed Bree's hand when his mother's attention was elsewhere.

Bree used the interlude to study Mal's father, who sat motionless in an arm chair across from his daughters. Where Mal was youthful, his upper body firm from long sessions at the weight lifting machine in his small apartment, his father's thin shoulders stooped. Where Mal was reluctant to hold people's gaze, his father looked past people, as though preoccupied with something distant and unattainable. But Bree also detected a more distilled image of what had attracted her to Mal: a calm tenor voice that reminded her of her own father's; brown eyes that sparkled when thin lips parted in a smile that bisected and softened chiseled features; deliberate gestures that conveyed an inner steeliness at odds with an outer presentation of accommodating—perhaps even long-suffering—obedience.

Mal's sisters bumped each other's knees when they thought their mother wasn't looking. The youngest, Bree knew, was sixteen but looked, in a plain white blouse and navy skirt, barely out of middle school. The twins had just turned twenty-one but still lived at home during this, their final year of college. The oldest sister, closest in age to Mal and most distant in demeanor, was Val, who sat nearest her mother and nodded emphatically at key points in the stories.

"Val wants to be a man," Mal said when he ran through his siblings one more time in the car on the way over.

"She's transgender?" Bree turned in her seat. "I thought your parents were super conservative."

Mal thought, absentmindedly fingering the mole on his chin. "She's trans-something. Like transferring all her aggression onto me. Used to beat the heck out of me."

Bree squeezed his bicep. "No fear of that these days."

Mal continued like he hadn't heard. "She would take my place if she could get me on a twenty-year expedition to Antarctica."

"The way you hog the covers?" Bree laughed. "You'd never make it past Mexico."

Mal shrugged. "All the worse for Val."

In the family living room, Bree inspected Val. *She looks lonely.* Bree's gaze softened and at a pause in Faye's monologue, she leaned forward. "Faye, your family's so impressive." She opened her arms to include the sisters in her sweeping compliment. "You've accomplished a lot."

"God guides us." Val responded for her mother, rubbing her hands together. "He blesses those who listen to His calling."

"I didn't have a big family."

Faye's glance flitted between Bree and Mal. "Mal told us. It was God's will."

Mal coughed. "Mom…" He reached for Bree's hand.

Bree patted his palm and shook her head, smiling. "Maybe that's why I'm here in a big family today." She stood and moved toward the piano, on which rested a collection of framed photos. "Who are these beautiful women?"

Faye beamed and rose. "That's my aunt…"

Over the next hour, the discussion pitched and heaved its passage through chit-chat, iced tea on the back porch, and appetizers in the kitchen. Bree maintained a steady, consistent hand on the conversational rudder, maneuvering the talk away from Faye's tumult and into calmer waters. At dinner, after a ten-minute standing grace around a white table cloth smothered by large dishes of meatloaf, Brussel sprouts, and mashed potatoes, Bree nudged the tiller between grateful mouthfuls. Any woman who cooked the way Faye cooked had a direct line to Bree's heart. The more Bree voiced enthusiasm about the food, the more Faye's cold demeanor melted, until, by the dessert, she was a pliant mass in Bree's hands.

On the porch when they said goodbye, Bree beamed as the younger Patel sisters hugged her, Val shook her hand, and Mr. Patel embraced her in an unexpected bear hug. Faye pecked her on the cheek as Mal pulled the car into the driveway. Bree squeezed her hand. "I've never had a more delicious dinner."

Faye blushed. "You are welcome back anytime."

After they drove out of view of the house, Mal braked at a stop sign and yanked Bree into his arms, covering her mouth in a deep, voracious kiss. She caught her breath and snuggled into the soft leather of his ancient Jaguar. She tugged her blouse over her full belly. "That meatloaf was to die for."

Mal repetitively stroked the steering wheel. "I've never seen anyone handle Mom the way you did."

Bree sighed. "And I could eat ten more slices of that strawberry rhubarb pie."

"How did you know what to do?"

Bree stretched her legs, sliding lower onto the seat. "I didn't expect your parents' house to be so pretty."

"Keeping things looking neat is a virtue in my parents' religion." Mal pulled onto the freeway and gunned the accelerator.

"And you get along with your sisters."

Mal merged into the HOV lane. "Because misery loves company."

"You have things in common."

"Because we're united by a common…"

Bree laughed. "Your mother's not so bad."

Mal sped down the freeway at eighty-five miles an hour. "I was going to say family history."

"At least you have a history." Bree touched his leg. "There's no rush."

Mal relaxed his foot. "Isn't there?"

Bree scrutinized his face. "I know that look."

Mal took one hand from the wheel and ran it across her thigh, up her blouse, and over her breasts. "I've got champagne in the fridge and fresh sheets on the bed."

Bree kissed his fingers. "A lie down is just what I need. I couldn't eat another thing."

***

A semi roared past Bree's SUV with a gust that made the car quiver and snapped her out of her reverie. The phone rang. She glanced at the screen. *Ryder*. She declined the call. A minute later, the phone rang again. She reluctantly put on her headset.

"How's it going?"

Bree ground her teeth. "Just reminiscing."

"About high school?"

"About the first time I met Mal's family." Why, she thought, did they always end up talking about her?

"Let me guess. His parents are still married. He's got at least two sisters. And they all get together for a family dinner once a month."

Bree's foot eased off the pedal. "W-T-F."

Ryder chuckled. "You're not going to marry a loner. You've always wanted family around."

Bree squinted at his silhouette in the rearview mirror. "I don't think I'm that predictable."

"I don't think being predictable makes you boring."

She wiped a thin film of dust from the radio console on the dash. "I've changed a lot since high school."

"We all have."

"Anyway, family treats you better than friends."

"That," Ryder sucked in his breath, "depends on

the friend."

Bree snorted. "You should know."

A red sports car overtook both their vehicles in an angry roar. Bree took her foot off the gas and watched Ryder's car gain on her, then back off again as she slowed.

"I want to focus on getting to Vegas in one piece." She hung up and dropped the headset into her lap. She opened the window and let her hair blow through the crack. *With some friends*, she thought as the air whipped strands across her face, *you don't need enemies*.

CHAPTER 5

In the CEO's office at the toy company's headquarters, a fluffy lamb spun through air, head over pink tail, like a cotton candy missile. It thumped against the room's wooden door and slid to the floor in a tangle of spindly legs.

"Get that thing back to design." The CEO's deep voice shook with impatience.

A navy-suited young woman bent at the waist with a swiftness and precision evidencing long practice and lifted the sheep by its ear.

"I want a wolf, a grizzly, something boys won't be embarrassed snuggling."

The woman nodded, her mouth in a straight, unperturbed line. One hand rested on the doorknob. The other held the disgraced animal at arm's length.

"Tell them I want a prototype by Monday or I'm making cuts."

"Yes, Mr. Greenwood." The woman closed the door softly behind her.

In a large leather chair behind a massive glass desk, a man with a gray crew cut and closely clipped beard slammed the flat of his hand onto the clear surface as though squashing an ant at a picnic. "Now where's my fucking phone?" He yanked open onyx drawers, sifting through papers and muttering. Next, he overturned a large silver trashcan and accompanied each crumpled paper projectile that he shot back into it with a curse. After hearing a knock on the office door, he stuffed the remaining detritus behind his chair with his foot and, when the door opened, was striding toward the exit.

The young woman wore a plastic children's doll smile. Her iPad rested on her arm. "You wanted to talk about Friday morning's TV show?"

"Fuck that." The man breezed by her.

She scampered to keep up as he marched through a bright, orchid filled atrium toward a golden bank of tall elevators. "Want me to come back later?" Her words kept time with her steps. "They sent questions. Marketing has ideas about policy responses."

The man spun. She avoided hitting him by stumbling to the side. She righted herself as he hissed at her. "*I* set policy."

She lowered her gaze but maintained the smile. "Marketing took transcripts from your recent interviews and ran key points by consumers."

"Why didn't you fucking say so?" The man turned on his heel and punched the elevator button with his elbow. "Got a call from my wife. Family emergency." The doors slid open and he stalked inside. "I'll be back this afternoon."

She stuck a knee inside the door at just the height of the sensor. The door reopened. "You've got two meetings this morning, Mr. Greenwood. What do you want me to tell them?"

"Tell them if they want to talk with the CEO, they'll have to come back when he's around."

As the door closed behind him, the woman's smile dropped from her face like a room darkening when the last light is extinguished. She shrugged and walked back through the atrium, typing on her iPad with one finger.

Inside the elevator, Greenwood slumped against a mirrored wall. "Fuck."

Ten minutes later, stuck in San Francisco gridlock, he tore off his jacket, feeling the side and chest pockets for the tenth time. Next, one hand steered while the other groped around the center island, his fingers straining as he pushed between firm plastic and resilient leather. At red lights, he slammed the gear shift into park and bent double, reaching his arm underneath the seats.

"Fuck."

At the Miser Rent-A-Car facility near the airport, curses showered the attendant who rushed from the side of a family of six to open the door of Greenwood's Mercedes. He stuck out his hand. "Welcome back, Mr. Smith. Do something for you? Need more SUV?"

Greenwood sprung from the driver's seat and slapped the hand aside. "Where's the car I had this morning?"

The attendant shook his head and shrugged. "Don't know. Check with guys in office?" He pointed. Greenwood pounded toward the back door.

Inside sat two youths with high-top sneakered

feet on a white plastic patio table. Joints dangled from their fingers. When Greenwood entered, they pushed back their chairs and stood.

"Mr. Smith." The taller of the two stepped forward, flicking his joint into an overfilled ashtray.

"I need to see the car I rented." Greenwood kicked an empty soda can into a corner, where it clattered against a pile of car child seats. "Left something inside."

The young men looked at each other. The taller thrust his chin out and pointed at his colleague. "What you do with his car?"

"Dude, you rented it. A couple hours ago."

The taller man turned to Greenwood and lifted his hands in a helpless gesture. "Mr. Smith, so sorry. Dumbass rented it."

"*You* rented—" The subordinate received a kick on the shin and stopped complaining. The two men looked at Greenwood, whose face froze. They took a simultaneous step back.

Greenwood edged forward like a roller intent on flattening everything in its path. "Where's the stuff you found when you cleaned it?" He spoke in a whisper.

The two again exchanged glances. The tall one turned away first. He reached the room's other door one stride ahead of his friend. "You tell him." He threw the words over his shoulder as he stepped into the main lobby. "I deal with customers." He slammed the rickety plywood door, making the walls rattle. The thin youth in a dirty yellow shirt swiveled slowly back to face Greenwood.

"Where'd you put the stuff?" Greenwood

advanced to the far side of the table, his question dangling in the air like a tarantula hanging from a thread.

"We didn't find anything."

Greenwood shoved the table aside. The ashtray skidded to the floor. "Don't lie."

The youth held out shaking hands. "Whoa, dude."

Greenwood clenched fists at his side. "Give me…my cell phone."

The man's features shifted from fear to relief. "We don't have your cell phone. Never cleaned your car. We flipped it. I swear."

Greenwood paused. "Flipped it?"

"No cleaning. We give a discount and save the hassle."

"So you're telling me," Greenwood ground the ashtray contents into the cement floor with the heel of a shiny black leather loafer, "somebody's driving my car with my phone still inside?"

"That's it." The young man pulled a chair in front of him and offered Greenwood a seat. "I'm sure they'll find it and call. Or it'll be inside when they bring it back. I can find out when the rental's up." He disappeared through the door to the main area.

Greenwood followed and stepped into the narrow space behind the bank of ancient computers. The two men had their backs turned on a long line of grumbling customers and were grouped around the only modern computer, a laptop perched on a desk partially hidden behind a low cubicle wall. The tall one manipulated the mouse while the short one pointed. Neither glanced at Greenwood, who hovered over them, hands still clenched. After a few tense minutes, the taller one spoke.

"Found your car." He gave Greenwood a sickly smile. "Due back Sunday."

"Sunday's not fucking good enough." Greenwood peered over his shoulder. "Don't you track them?"

Both men shook their heads vigorously.

Greenwood laid a hand on the sitting man's shoulder. "Don't fuck with me."

Large eyes looked into Greenwood's. "We track. But only if car not back. Or in Mexico."

"I don't give a fuck about your business practices. Track my car."

The standing man sucked air through his teeth. "You know how to do that, dude?"

The man at the computer nodded. His hands quivered slightly as he typed and clicked. "Boss don't like us doing this."

Greenwood's large forefinger and thumb flapped a hundred-dollar bill between the man's face and the screen. "Give me the location and keep me updated. I'll give you five more when I get back."

The standing man made a grab but his friend at the computer wrenched it out of Greenwood's hand. The standing man punched his colleague in the shoulder. "Dude, it's my risk too."

"Split later." He rose and strode to the printer at the agency desk. A chorus of complaints erupted. "System down," he said before disappearing again behind the cubicle wall.

He handed Greenwood the paper. "License

number, make, and model."

Greenwood folded it neatly in half and then put it in his breast pocket. "Where is it now?"

The man pointed at the computer screen. "I-5. Going south."

Greenwood slapped another hundred on the counter. This time the shorter youth dove across the chair and pocketed the money with a grin. Greenwood smirked. "Give me a number where I can get you. I don't care if you have to sleep here. I want to know where the car is. In real time." He took out a cell phone.

"Hey." The standing youth tapped Greenwood playfully on the arm and laughed. "You didn't lose your phone. You've got it right—"

Greenwood's glower stopped his monologue. "My *work* phone's in the car."

"Got it, dude."

Out in the lot, Greenwood closed the Mercedes door with an expensive *thunk*. He turned the key and sped the bulky car past the somber youths with the speed and intent of a missile.

"Fuck you," he mouthed out the window. They waved back as though they'd read his parting words as *thank you*.

On Highway 101 south, he gunned the engine, weaving through traffic like someone obsessed.

CHAPTER 6

Driving through the desert approaching Las Vegas, Bree had difficulty keeping her eyes on the road. They felt like pieces of iron, drawn inexorably upward to the magnets of the stars. Earlier, Ryder requested they pull off the highway at a dark and deserted exit. She reluctantly complied but stayed in her car. When he suggested they take a short walk across the sandy dirt, she resisted, questioning his sanity and reminding him of her need to get to Vegas in one piece. He assured her scorpions were active only in the daytime and rattlesnakes curled up to sleep when the stars came out. Only because her legs were cramped from hours of sitting did she comply.

Standing in the frigid night air with Ryder's sweatshirt wrapped around her shoulders, she shielded her eyes from the occasional car's headlights with hands held like horse blinders and stared into the heavens. What she saw wiped every other thought from her mind. Above her, the sky was puckered with dense clusters of stars. The

Milky Way flowed a thick path of light encircling the earth. The only constellations she knew, the Big Dipper and Orion, glowed down at her with many smaller points of light in their midst. Ryder pointed out fuzzy stars he insisted weren't stars at all but rather nebulae, interstellar clouds of dust. Now and then a meteor blazed across the magnificent display.

Bree held her breath. "I used to think I could count every star in the sky." She put down her hands and massaged her aching neck.

Ryder kept his gaze focused upward. "Strange goal."

"Probably thought it was romantic." She looked back at their cars. "How many stars do you think we'll see in Vegas?"

"Vegas shows have lots of stars."

Bree smirked. "Seriously."

Ryder dropped his hands. "If you want to wish on a star, I don't think Vegas is the place to do it."

Bree turned. "Just like you to have no faith." She closed her eyes, listening to the sounds of the desert. A light breeze stirred dried tufts of plant life. A four-legged creature scuttled across the sand. An owl screeched. But mostly she listened to the silence, the long still intervals where the only sound was Ryder's breathing and hers.

She turned and walked slowly back toward the cars, peering at the faint glow of the big city in the distance. When she got to her SUV, she paused. "Do you really think Vegas isn't for romance?"

Ryder stepped toward his car, throwing his answer over his shoulder like a football toss. "They wouldn't have all those wedding chapels if it weren't."

Outside the city limits, Mal called to say he was going to bed. She recognized the shattered tone in his voice, the one that made her heart cry out to help. He sounded like a small child who had crawled into the corner of his bed and curled up in a ball. She told him when he next woke up, she'd be there beside him.

The glow from Vegas on the horizon grew rapidly, from a faint hazy orange bubble to a pulsing dome. The stars faded, the night's deep black replaced by a gray sheen that substituted for darkness. Traffic thickened, intermittent blips from approaching cars transforming into a steady stream of headlights and taillights that accompanied her on the final leg of the journey. She lost track of Ryder's vehicle as impatient drivers cut between them. Her grip on the steering wheel tightened and her heart rate increased as her senses acclimated to the urban environment, from dark to light, from peace to frenzy. Twenty minutes from their destination, with the towers of Vegas clearly outlined before them, Ryder phoned.

"Loving the traffic?"

Bree slammed on the brakes as a car pulled in front of her with only inches to spare. "I thought San Francisco drivers were bad."

"Not usually drunk, though."

Bree shuddered. "Just want to get there in one piece."

"Mal will be at the door, waiting."

Bree's fingers fished around the empty donut box for crumbs. "He left me a key at the front desk."

"Thought he'd throw confetti."

Bree laughed. "I'd prefer someone throwing hamburgers right now. I'm starving."

"Me too. First thing I'm doing is finding some place to eat."

She patted her growling tummy. "Tell me if you find a donut shop." She shifted her seat one position forward, to sit more upright. Her fingers hovered over the end call button.

"See you later, Bree."

"Goodbye." She hung up, exited the highway, and pulled onto the main strip.

***

With large eyes and a mouth held closed with effort, Bree stared at the blue suited attendant. "Seventy-five dollars for one night's valet parking?" She shook her head and closed the window.

She followed signs to the hotel's parking garage. One incorrect turn later and she was back on the Strip, weaving among the honking cars and swearing under her breath as her stomach rumbled its discontent. By the time she found the garage, she felt faint and couldn't believe her luck when, on the second floor near the elevator, someone backed out of a prime spot. She swerved in before an oncoming car could steal it and slumped, head on the steering wheel, wondering why she hadn't shelled out the money at the valet entrance. *Could've been halfway through a cheeseburger by now.*

Her bags fell to the concrete with multiple thuds. She slammed the SUV door shut with the last of her energy and threw a weary glance at the driver's seat. *I am* not *getting back in till I head back to San Francisco.*

Dragging her roller bag behind her, garment bag draped again over one arm, she trudged to the elevator and, after a swift ride down, followed vague signs that pointed to the lobby. On her left stretched an open area with a low ceiling and bright lights, blackjack tables, laughing groups, and shouting couples. The air smelled of smoke, perfume, and cologne. The thick maroon carpet beneath her pumps muffled noise from the multitude of pedestrians. The walls were gilt, the ceiling painted with what looked like replicas from Italian churches, and the wide hallway was adorned with enormous flower displays that meandered and twined into the heavens as though rooted in soil. It was overwhelming and beautiful, although somewhere in her mind still lingered a comparison between where she found herself now and her foray into the desert just a few hours earlier where lights of a different type had glittered. Her head turned this way and that as she walked, taking in jewelry shops and handbag stores between rows of slot machines, her face brightening as she absorbed the different retail therapy possibilities.

Suddenly, three signless hallways branched from where she stood. She accosted a woman in uniform balancing a tray of eight martini glasses.

"Where's the lobby?"

The woman pointed down the middle hallway.

"And where's the closest place I can grab something to eat?"

The woman tilted her head. "Tex-Mex, Japanese, California Pacific island fusion, Chilean…"

Bree held up her hand. "Hamburger."

The woman shifted her tray, a small furrow sprouting between her eyebrows. "Maybe the Tex-Mex place would have something."

"Point me in the right direction."

A few minutes later Bree stood in the restaurant's short line, wondering whether she should have ordered room service. The purse under her arm vibrated.

Ryder: Don't gamble your life away.

She frowned.

Bree: Getting Tex-Mex.

Ryder: Hi to Mal.

She rolled her eyes and dropped the phone back in her bag, muttering to herself. "Why doesn't he just leave well enough alone?"

At the table, the meat lover's burrito caught her eye on the menu. She turned to flag down the waitress and instead found Ryder's unshaven face and blue eyes smiling down at her. Without waiting for her to ask, he flopped into the chair opposite her.

"This is a table for one." She snapped shut her menu.

Ryder grinned. "Looks like it's for two."

"For all you know, Mal's in the bathroom. Could be back any minute."

Ryder glanced at her luggage, piled high next to her chair. "He would've taken it off your hands if he'd been here."

Her eyes narrowed. "You act like you're welcome anywhere."

He reached out his hand. She sighed and handed him the menu. He took one glance, closed it, and slapped it on the table.

Bree opened the menu again to double check her choice. "I can never make up my mind when I'm hungry."

Ryder shrugged. "Bean burrito and a beer and I'm happy." He leaned back in his chair.

The country music playing in the background praised a man's wife for sticking with him though he had strayed. Ryder tapped his foot and hummed along. Bree watched and marveled, not for the first time, about his chameleon-like ability to fit in wherever he found himself. When he fixed a tire, he looked like a mechanic. Here in this restaurant, he looked like a country music star escaping Nashville. In suit and tie at the prom he looked like the prep school son of a Wall Street gangster. And on his way to a locker room in a dirt-smeared football jersey he looked like a blue-collar jock. It wasn't, she thought, that he simply adapted to an environment; instead, what he brought to the mix blended well with whatever environment surrounded him. Except with her.

Ryder gestured at a six-foot trickling fountain in the center of the tables, with live trees growing from hidden planters. The high ceiling had a digital display that mimicked a rosy sunset. Hidden speakers projected bird calls over the music. "My hotel doesn't have this kind of restaurant."

"Don't tell me your assistant booked you into a dive."

Ryder laughed. "I've got a penthouse suite. So she keeps her job."

"Magnanimous of you."

The approaching waitress stopped in mid-stride. At her look, Bree bit back a chuckle. She hadn't seen a girl do that since high school—someone stopping to admire Ryder's arresting looks. The kind of looks that made people turn around for a second glance because they couldn't believe what they saw was true. The kind that caused store clerks to fall over each other, that brought conversations to a halt. And yet with all that handsomeness staring back at him every morning in the mirror, Ryder didn't seem to know his face was anything but average. He brushed off compliments, seemingly spent little time on his own appearance, and was unaware of the commotion his entrance into a room could create. All the more aggravating.

At that moment, he had a dazzling, thin brunette twenty-something flashing him an expansive smile, and he looked as though he was placing an order with a grizzled greasy spoon fry cook who had a cigarette dangling out of his mouth. The young woman tried to hide her disappointment and turned to Bree, giving her a look Bree had also often seen in high school, the look that said, "Why on earth is that gorgeous guy with *you*?" Bree raised her eyebrows as if to say, "It's not as great as you think it is," and ordered.

After Ryder finished his second beer and mopped the remains of his burrito with his fork, he clinked his empty bottle against Bree's second glass of wine. "I really admire you."

Bree stopped mid-chew. "Excuse me?" She thought back on their superficial conversation about microbreweries, foreign travel, and tech blogs.

"You're not afraid to give love a chance." He leaned back in his chair and stuffed the extra napkins from the table into his pants pocket, suddenly seeming less like a famous country singer and more like a confused metrosexual.

Bree pointed. "Why do you do that? Take extra napkins, pads of paper, anything that isn't nailed down? You've got more money than God."

The look Ryder gave her made him seem ten years younger. His lips pursed. "Wasn't rich growing up. Learned it from my mom, I guess. Thought everybody did it." He removed the crumpled napkins and smoothed them onto the table.

Bree shoved the pile back at him. "The casino won't miss them." She used her knife to slice deliberately through her burrito, like a saw cutting down a tree. "I remember your mother. She came to the games."

Ryder repocketed the material. "Knew how to embarrass her son. Yelled louder than our coach."

Bree flashed him an angry glance. "You don't appreciate love and enthusiasm when you see it."

Ryder's gaze dropped. "I loved my mom. When

I was a kid, I used to thank God she was so fat, because it gave me more to love.'

Bree stared at him. "You call your mom fat?"

Ryder smiled and shrugged. "She was beautiful. She was also smart, ambitious, and, yes, fat. A fantastic combination."

"For a linebacker." Bree watched his face fall as though he'd lost something precious. Her toes curled under the table. "I didn't mean it like that."

"What?" Ryder glanced at her. "Wasn't listening." He tilted his chin in the direction of a couple two tables over. "She looks like my ex."

Bree turned in her chair, grateful to change the subject. The woman Ryder indicated looked like a lingerie billboard ad. She was spilling over with B words: beauty, breasts, body-conscious, breathtaking. But, Bree thought, if she had been going out with Ryder, probably not brilliant. Still, the enormity of the disconnect between Ryder's life and hers overwhelmed her. He was dating models and she was stuffing her face with the remains of a tortilla chip bowl with her dog-wash store owner fiancé lying upstairs. One thing was for sure: Women who looked like his mother didn't attract him. She fumbled with her cutlery.

Ryder rubbed his nose. "She broke up with me."

"You said that before."

Ryder drew invisible pictures on the tablecloth with his fork. "Because I told her I didn't do messy."

Bree blinked. "You require cleaning people?"

"Messy relationships. She ran hot and cold. I never knew if I was in or out." He put down his fork. "I'm not good at complicated."

Bree motioned for the check, but the waitress ignored her. "I excel at complicated. Sometimes I think it's what I live for."

"Because you're good at sorting things out. I'm not." He laid his napkin on the table and raised a finger. Two waitresses came running. He nudged away Bree's proffered credit card. "This is on me."

"In your dreams." Bree laid down cash. "Maybe I like sorting things out because I'd rather be in the background."

"You and me both." Ryder seemed not to notice the increasing gaggle of waitresses standing at the periphery of the restaurant, staring at him.

"I'm tired and my butt hurts." Bree pushed back her chair. "And you have to get back to your lonely penthouse lifestyle."

Ryder insisted on taking her luggage and accompanying her to the check-in counter. He hovered in the background as the clerk handed her the key with a raised eyebrow.

Sorry to disappoint you, Bree thought as she stuffed the plastic card into the pocket of her skirt, *but he's not as great as you think.*

Ryder took her arm. "Let's get you to the elevator."

She shook herself free with enough violence to cause a wave of dizziness and had to hold onto a marble pillar to steady herself.

They wound their way across the slick marble floor under multicolored lights that shone from high above like gentle sea anemones arching their fingers toward the earth in an upside-down universe. She walked with half-closed eyes. "I shouldn't have had that second glass of wine."

"Almost there." He jogged ahead and pushed the elevator button.

The soft classical music in the background and the clicking of their heels on the floor reminded her of dances and weddings, of friends and champagne, of feeling giddy and grown up and in love. It reminded her of Mal. When the elevator door opened, she almost fell inside. She patted her cheeks, hoping to rouse herself.

"What floor?" Ryder leaned over the display.

She handed him the card with its envelope.

After pushing a button, he slipped it back into her hand, draped the garment bag over her shoulder, and propped the suitcase next to her. "You know," he leaned toward her, "today reminded me of going to the beach when I was in high school."

The alcohol instantaneously evaporated from her bloodstream. She froze and faced him with stone cold sober eyes. "I never went with you to the beach." Her finger punched a button. "And I never will." She glared at his shocked face until the doors closed.

The elevator rose so quickly that it almost knocked her off her feet. She gripped the railing behind her tightly, her mind spinning with rage. Just when she thought he wasn't the lowest scum at the bottom of the deepest ocean, he reminded her of how much lower he could go. *I hope you drown at your beach.*

On the twenty-sixth floor, she tugged her luggage down the endless hallway, squinting periodically at the small envelope containing her key. When she found it, the door clicked open and she pushed it with her knee, fumbling on the wall for a switch. A recessed string of lights ran along the edge of the ceiling and gradually illuminated the room in a gentle glow. Bree stared across a wide living room, beyond a sofa and chairs, at a set of floor to ceiling windows that showcased the sparkling city far below.

"Wow." She stumbled across the carpet and stood with her feet at the edge where marble met glass, where floor met sky. She felt as though she could jump out and fly over the scene before her, as though the soft desert air would carry her across the shining buildings, pulsing lights, and buzzing Strip, ferry her over the highway, to the mountains beyond. She put her hands against the glass and leaned one cheek on the smooth, cold surface. *This is what flying feels like*, she thought. *It's not so scary.*

She entered the dark bedroom and pulled off her clothing piece by piece as she made her way to the rectangle that beckoned her. This was the bed she had been dreaming of for hours. The fluffy pillows. The sateen sheets. The down comforter. She flopped into them with a sigh. And then she screamed.

The hand that touched her arm withdrew quickly and a second later a light on the far nightstand snapped on.

"What?" Mal stared at her, his eyes bleary but showing concern.

Bree blinked. "Sorry. I was somewhere else."

71

Mal laughed and kissed her nose. "Somewhere other than in bed with me?" He lay back down and held open his arms.

Bree lay beside him. He switched off the light and snuggled into her back. His arms felt comfortingly familiar as he held her close and nuzzled her ear.

"Welcome to Vegas, Bree."

CHAPTER 7

Bree awoke the next morning thinking of a puppy chewing toes. She giggled and yanked her foot away. The nibbling continued, working its way up her ankle.

"You little shit." She sat up in bed, smacked the blanket, and stared straight into the eyes of her future mother-in-law.

Faye took a step back, her hands trailing from beneath the covers. The slender woman gave her a smile even thinner than she was herself. "I was trying to remove your pantyhose."

Bree felt around her stomach and realized with dismay that Faye had lowered stockings from around her middle without waking her up. She sat up and clutched the blankets high around her neck. "What on earth…?"

Faye picked up a pile of Bree's clothing and held it in her arms. "I'm doing laundry."

Bree yanked the sheets higher. "Not with my pantyhose you're not." She looked around the room. "Where's Mal?"

"Our room. Everyone gathered there after breakfast."

Bree struggled to push the morning fog from her brain. Her gaze searched in vain for a clock. The long drapes over the window in the room gave no indication of the color of sky outside. She felt on the dresser for her cell phone. It wasn't there. Had she left it in her purse in her rush to fall into bed? "What time is it?"

Faye glanced at her watch. "Quarter of ten."

"Shi…I overslept." She was about to swing her legs out of the bed when she remembered the pantyhose dangling inelegantly around her ankles.

Faye folded one of Mal's polo shirts and replaced it in the dresser. "We knew we couldn't count on you this morning, dear."

Bree still pulled the covers over her chin, wondering when Faye would get the message that her help was not required. Her future mother-in-law was invasive, dictatorial, and strong-willed. But Bree also knew her soft spots. "I bet the hotel breakfast wasn't as good as yours."

Faye beamed. "You are correct. The eggs were overcooked and the bacon was rubbery."

Bree nodded. "So I didn't miss anything."

"Mal said you got an SUV. It must use a lot of gasoline. Soumil increased the numbers in his spreadsheet."

At the mention of her future father-in-law's spreadsheet, Bree suppressed a groan. Nothing about the engagement celebration or wedding plans escaped entry into a row or column of a mammoth Excel workbook with the accurate but slightly ominous title of "Mal's Future." Even things Bree insisted on paying for herself were listed, conspicuously highlighted in yellow as "donated." Soumil managed the spreadsheet, like he managed the accounts for the family hotel business. But Faye provided the data that populated it, determined price cutoffs, and scrutinized the bottom line. Early on, Bree asked Mal about talking to his parents openly regarding her financial situation, about her willingness to shoulder some of the expenses in lieu of her absent family, and about her eagerness to adopt a more flexible approach to the costs surrounding both the engagement and wedding. But each conversation lasted only a few sentences. With the mention of the spreadsheet, Mal's eyes iced over, and as Bree outlined techniques for broaching the matter, he stopped breathing. The spreadsheet, Bree realized, was there to stay. Her only hope was that his parents' meddling in their lives would end with the wedding.

"Mark it as donated." Bree used one hand to wriggle out of the remainder of her pantyhose. "And now, Faye, I could really use a shower."

The thin smile returned to Faye's lips. "I will unpack your belongings while you shower." She held up the pile of clothes in her arms. "Then I'll wash your clothes in the sink."

Bree shook her head. She had traveled enough with Mal's family to know to set boundaries or Faye would roam through Bree's life like a bloodhound on a scent. On the first trip, Bree was shocked and indignant upon returning from a hike in Yosemite National Park to find Faye not only in her bedroom but in her closet, rearranging her clothes. She protested, politely but firmly. Faye shrugged off Bree's distress, explaining that she had raised four children, understood how things should be organized, and knew Bree didn't have parents looking out for her. In the face of those arguments, Bree's resistance gradually crumbled. What did it matter, she told herself, how her clothes were arranged? If her boyfriend's mother wasn't embarrassed to go through a hotel nightstand and find condoms and other personal paraphernalia, then Bree wasn't going to be ashamed on her behalf.

On family vacations, her main battlefield lay elsewhere. She wanted Mal to stand up to his parents and get an official blessing to sleep in the same room. She was too old to tiptoe half naked through a hotel corridor twice a night. But getting Mal to stand up to his parents took time.

Bree yanked the top sheet from the bed and wrapped it around her like a toga. With her free hand she took the pile of clothes from Faye's arms. "Most of this is dry clean only. I'll grab some hangers and let the steam take the wrinkles out." She waddled across the large room with five feet of sheet trailing behind her like a walrus tail. Hangers in hand, she smiled at Faye and closed the bathroom door.

***

Faye sang quietly to herself as she emptied Bree's suitcase and hung the clothing in the bedroom closet, smoothing folds, positioning collars symmetrically, and aligning shoes neatly under skirts. She hefted Bree's suitcase onto a luggage stand, biceps bulging on lean arms like a geriatric weightlifter. Mal's empty bag already stood in a corner of the room. Faye pushed his underwear to the side as she deposited Bree's bras and panties in the dresser. At one point, she lay a pair of Mal's briefs on top of Bree's. Bree's stuck out on all sides. Faye sighed as she folded both pairs and returned them to the drawer, then raised clasped hands to the ceiling.

"Lord, grant her the strength to get her appetite under control."

After she disposed of all the clothing, she rummaged through the outside pockets of the suitcase, transferring a laptop and endless tangles of computer cords and other electronics to the floor.

She shook her head. "This can't stay in the bedroom." She returned all the items to the suitcase and rolled it to the living room's office area, where she spread the paraphernalia on the desk. She examined the devices, determining which plugs fit into which receptacles. As she picked up a silver cell phone, it rang, and she dropped it on the desk with a clatter.

Her eyes scowled at the screen, which displayed a woman's name with the subtitle "legal department."

Faye shook her head again. "Bree Acosta, you are *not* taking work calls on this trip." Faye looked around the room, walked to the sofa, and put the phone between the cushions. She bit her lip and stood back, hands on hips, gazing at the bulge. She sat near it, and the phone's corner popped out. She cocked her head in the direction of the bedroom, where noise from the shower was still audible. Faye picked up the phone and scooted silently across to the bedroom, where she opened a dresser drawer, wrapped the phone tightly in a pair of Bree's underwear, covered it with a T-shirt, and shoved the bundle to the back. The drawer rolled shut and she nodded.

"That's better."

"What's better?" Bree stood at the bathroom door, head wrapped in a towel, another around her torso, the shower still running in the background.

Faye turned slowly and eyed the steam billowing from behind Bree. "Shouldn't you shut off the water? We are in a desert."

Bree smiled. "Have you seen how they use water around here? There's an actual pirate ship show." She laughed. "My shower isn't going to make any difference."

Faye tilted her head. "It's never bad to set a good example."

Bree leered back with an impish grin. "Unless nobody is watching."

Faye stood at the door. "I put everything away." Her eyes flashed from the dresser to the desk in the living room. "Bree, dear, I see you brought your computer."

Bree strolled to the dresser, opened the top drawer, and removed a pair of panties and a bra. "Don't worry. This trip is all about Mal and me."

Faye sighed and nodded. "We leave for Uncle

Frank's for lunch in," she looked at her watch, "fifty minutes."

After escorting Faye to the door, Bree donned the underclothes and walked to the living room's window, comfortably certain that the glass was tinted and she wouldn't be visible from the outside. She stared at daytime Vegas, shimmering in the desert heat. Her feet skipped to the wet bar, where she found her purse. She fished out her pink cell phone and, back at the window, took a selfie of her head in the towel and the city in the background. After texting it to Stephanie, she got dressed, glad that Faye arranged shoes with outfits, so she wouldn't have to guess what would make her future mother-in-law happiest.

***

By the time Bree and the Patel family had walked the five blocks to Uncle Frank's restaurant for lunch, the underarms of Bree's sleeveless blouse were soaked in sweat and Mal's hand stuck to hers like a wet suction cup. A double set of electric glass sliding doors whooshed open and let them into the cool, darkened interior. The air smelled of turmeric, clove, cumin, and cardamom. Bree closed her eyes and inhaled it with a sense of relief after the stale and vaguely putrid odors of Vegas's side streets.

She whispered into Mal's ear as she tugged at her sticky blouse. "Remind me again why we didn't drive?"

"Decadence not allowed." He nudged her with his elbow and she giggled.

In front of them, an immense archway behind a hostess podium opened into the largest Indian restaurant Bree had ever seen. Colorful illuminated fabrics hung from the ceiling, lending depth to the light in the room. Torches flickered from holders on the walls and from strategically placed posts on the floor. Though cavernous, the room was inviting, with countless planters of tropical foliage creating separate sitting areas from which candles glowed on red tablecloths. A thick carpet patterned to mimic grass mats muffled the wait staff's movements and the chatter from the hundreds of customers.

Bree squeezed Mal's hand. "Absolutely perfect."

Mal squeezed back. "Mom thought you'd like it."

A large man sauntered through the archway, hands extended, like a hunter about to pluck animals from traps. "Sammy." He threw his arms wide in the direction of Mal's father.

"That's Uncle Frank." Mal took a slight step back.

Mal's father shook hands with his brother and Frank next moved to Faye, whom he squeezed tightly to his chest, enfolding her slim frame in the folds of a broad suit that stretched across his wide stomach. "Faye, my darling, so good to see you again." After releasing her, he beckoned to the four Patel sisters, who were standing behind Bree and Mal. "Come here, my little flowers."

The young women slunk toward him. As the youngest sister, Amy, passed Bree, she darted her eyes at her uncle and then back at Bree and whispered, "Watch out."

Before Bree could respond, she was out of polite earshot. After patting the sisters each on the head, Frank centered his welcome on her and Mal. He clapped Mal so hard on the shoulder that Mal stumbled forward. Then the restaurant owner solemnly surveyed Bree.

"So this is the young lady who stole my nephew's heart?"

She pulled her lips together and met his gaze, a smile playing at the corners of her eyes. If this was a test, she thought, she wouldn't let Mal down. It took more than a big man with an overbearing personality to make *her* blush. A grin began to stretch his thick jowls and a plump index finger beckoned her to him. She advanced. He nodded. "He chose well."

Bree tilted her head, threw Mal a wink, and stepped into the man's waiting arms. Her eyes scrunched shut and then popped open. She blinked. Had her uncle-to-be just pinched her behind? She flung a glance around the room. Had anyone else seen that? Amy's eyes riveted onto hers with an unmistakable message of, "I told you so."

As the others traipsed after Frank toward a secluded area of tables in the back of the room, Amy plucked at Bree's blouse, holding her back.

"We call him Shiva." The girl's voice, coming from a lowered head, was barely audible above the talk of nearby dining customers.

"The god of death and destruction?" Bree cocked her head.

Amy squinted at her. "Shiva has many arms."

Bree stopped in mid-stride. "But you're his

niece. He doesn't…"

Amy flashed her a look of disgust and hurried to catch up with her family. Bree stood, alone amid the myriad plants and tables, with a pounding heart and a light head.

When Mal told her about his parents' proposal to use his uncle's restaurant as their venue, it seemed like a dream come true: a Vegas location big enough to hold all their friends and family, at a price that wouldn't break the bank. What was not to like? But as with everything in the Patel family, the devil, she learned, was in the details.

Having a big venue, for one, did not mean there would be a long guest list. At least for the engagement party, for which Mal's parents were footing the bill, strict limits were enforced. The event was family only. Bree would be one of the few non-Patels present, since most of Mal's father's business associates were in some way connected by blood. Bree's initial frustration swelled in equal proportion to the length of the Patel list.

"I bet your father's never even met some of these people." She flapped a document in Mal's face one evening at her apartment over spaghetti with clam sauce. "Stephanie's family is the only real family I have. Why can't they come?"

He shrugged. "You agreed to family only."

"Sure, I agreed to the kind of family that is flexible, not to blood-test-at-the-door."

Mal looked at the floor.

Bree grimaced. "You have a ton of relatives. I've got hardly any."

Mal placed the paper on the table and took her

hand. His eyes beseeched her. "This is the way life with my parents goes, Bree. I pick my battles." He kissed her fingers. "We have the wedding. Let's just let the engagement party go."

In the end, Bree agreed it was wiser to focus on the wedding. That became their strategic plan, the battle for which they stocked their weapons and conspired behind enemy lines. They fought for a live band, a diverse menu, and a more equally distributed guest list. And Bree categorized the engagement party as the equivalent of a church trip. Vegas might be one of the most exciting cities in the world and one of the most decadent, but she was going to be seeing it through the eyes of a lay minister.

When she got to the table where the rest of the family was sitting, Frank pulled out her chair. "You sit next to Daadi, your to-be grandmother-in-law." His voice boomed and belly shook, but Bree never took an eye off his hands. She seated herself, flashed him a stern look, and leaned over to hug the tiny Indian woman next to her, who was wearing a fuzzy red sweater and a pound of gold jewelry.

"Juli, it's wonderful to see you again." Bree squeezed the shriveled woman carefully.

The old woman's face creased into a myriad of tiny folds around her eyes and mouth. Her deep set brown eyes sparkled. Her long, leathery fingers gripped Bree's small, plump hands tightly. "This family welcomes you." Her eyes darted around the large table. "You are a big help for us."

The heat of sudden tears pricked Bree's eyes. "I'm the lucky one. I've always wanted to be part of a large family." She unfolded a napkin and put it in her lap. "And watch." She handed the grandmother a menu from the middle of the table. "Point to any item. I can tell you what it is."

"No more thinking korma is corn?" She cocked her head.

"Try me."

Just as a spindly finger pointed at an item, Faye's voice shot across the table. "Bree?"

Bree looked up.

"Daadi's probably forgotten. But Soumil and I will order for everyone. No need to stuff ourselves, is there?"

Mal's knee pressed hard against Bree's under the table. She flashed him a quick grin, held up the menu to block her face from Faye's view, and lowered her voice. "Good thing we spied that ice cream shop in the hotel."

Mal coughed into his napkin to cover his laugh.

Juli took the menu from Bree's hands, folded it, and placed it softly back on the pile. "We will be trying that test again later." She winked at Bree. "Now, suggest me what I should be seeing in Sinful City."

An hour later, all evidence of the main course had disappeared from the table and Faye used the break to rearrange the seating. Her daughters and mother-in-law moved obediently to chairs across from Mal and Bree, while Soumil took a position to Mal's right. Faye daintily arranged herself to Bree's left, hemming the couple in. When a plate of sweets arrived, she pushed it to the center of the table. "No time for dessert." When the waiter offered sugar and cream for the coffees, she waved him away with the flick of her hand. She lent in toward Bree, her gold cross bumping Bree's arm. "Studies show black, no sugar coffee is better for you."

Bree took a sip of the dark liquid and grimaced. "It might be better for your body, but not for your taste buds." She nudged her cup toward Mal, who had already finished his.

Faye folded her hands on the table in the shape of a church, with index fingers clamped tightly together, pointing at the ceiling. "God put many things on this earth to tempt us into transgressions."

Bree laughed. "Like high fructose corn syrup?" She heard more coughing and swiveled to look at Mal and his father, but both faces wore indifferent expressions. She lay her hand on Faye's. "I know you wanted a chance to discuss the final details for the party."

Faye fiddled in her shoulder bag and emerged with a small spiral-bound notebook. "Soumil and I have had some disagreements…"

Bree glanced at Soumil, whose eyes remained fixed on the far wall of the room.

"…about alcohol." Faye lay her palm on the notebook as though it were a Bible.

Bree settled back in her chair. She knew the woman well enough by now to read the certain signs of a coming lecture. Triggering events abounded even in suburban California, to say nothing of downtown Las Vegas. Faye launched into the intricate details and scriptural foundation of her position on the wickedness of alcohol. Bree crossed her arms and listened.

Although it was Soumil who converted his family to the obscure Christian sect after the 9/11 atrocities, it was Faye who latched onto the new religion as a salvation from everything in the world that caused her grief. Bree sometimes wondered whether Soumil regretted his attempt to find comfort and answers in a more concrete view of the world. He chose the conversion as an embracing gesture toward the country that was the only home he had ever known. But did the rules and rationalizations of the unusual version of Christianity provide the answers he hoped for? Bree wasn't sure. It was clear, however, that Faye had found her calling. Faye was wrong that she should have been a doctor. The woman was a preacher at heart.

"...so I don't think we have a choice. The Lord's way is clear." Faye shut the notebook and placed her right hand over her heart, a beatific look on her face.

Soumil cleared his throat. "We can't get around the fact that this is a party in Las Vegas."

Faye's eyes enlarged and her chest puffed. "Are you saying God's rule should have limits?"

Soumil's gaze slid from the spot on the wall to the flowers in the middle of their table. "These are our relatives and our colleagues. None of them shares our religion. We should treat them with respect."

Bree sat up in her chair. Six sentences was more than Soumil usually uttered during an entire meal.

"Whose respect is it you seek?" The words hissed across the table, silencing all conversation.

Soumil's eyes rose to meet his wife's. "My self-respect. Respect for our family. Respect for our son and daughter-in-law to be."

Faye closed her eyes. "Lord, forgive this sinner."

Soumil sucked in a breath and held it, letting it escape bit by bit with his next words. "I do not sin."

The frail, white-haired Juli rose from her chair. She leaned forward holding out both hands, brown with age spots. "Enough."

Faye sprung from her seat so quickly that it fell back on the carpet with a dull thud. She waved her notebook at each person around the table in turn. "I fear you not, for I am with the Lord."

Bree slapped Mal's knee and stood up too. "Time to put the gloves back on and holster those shotguns." She smiled and took Faye's hand. Faye looked at Bree as though she had sprouted antennae. "I think we decided a long time ago," Bree said, holding Faye's icy stare, "that there would be wine and beer but no hard liquor. Am I lying?"

Faye shook her head. "I have prayed on this, and the Bible says…"

Through the planters that shielded their table, Bree saw Uncle Frank approaching. She righted Faye's chair and motioned for her to sit. "I'm sure Uncle Frank ordered everything already. Wasting is sinful too, isn't it?"

Faye's throat jiggled like a boa constrictor struggling to swallow. She choked out a strangled, "Yes," and let her head flop dramatically into her hands.

"Holy crap, Bree." Mal's whisper a few minutes later sounded more like a rebuke than a compliment.

She shrugged, raised her eyebrows, and gave him a half smile. "How could we sneak back to the hotel if I didn't make peace?"

"Why do we have to sneak back?"

Bree giggled. "The ice cream store, silly."

CHAPTER 8

A relentless sun from the clear mid-day sky fired onto the roof of the black Mercedes cruising the top floor of the hotel parking garage. Greenwood, bloodshot eyes hidden behind gold sunglasses, tapped the brake repeatedly as his head swiveled back and forth, checking the rows. His vehicle snaked slowly past the seemingly endless parade of cars' backsides while inside the air conditioning blasted, the cool draft competing with the stale odor of French fries and hamburgers, whose refuse littered the passenger seat and foot well.

At the exit ramp from the roof, he slammed his palms onto the steering wheel as the car rolled down to the floor below. There, he pulled into the first available spot and voice dialed the number he had entered as "Asshole #1" in his contact list.

Before the person on the other end had a chance to say hello, Greenwood spoke. "You sure it hasn't moved?"

The voice sounded tired over the car speakers and edged with static. "Still in same place."

Greenwood's hand fished a cold French fry from a nearby container and sucked on it like a cigarette. "I've been in this garage for the past eight hours. It's not here."

"With big buildings, reception sometimes bad."

Greenwood inhaled the French fry, then spat it into the foot well. "Disgusting."

"Not best quality tracker."

"Am I supposed to search every garage in Vegas?"

"Maybe one next door?"

"Hold on." Greenwood backed his car from the spot and sped back to the ramp for the roof. When he got there, he pulled to the row nearest the edge of the building, got out of the car with the engine running, and walked to the wall. Across the narrow alley stood another, bigger garage. He cursed and returned to his car. "You're telling me it could be there?"

"All I say is no move. Still in same place."

Greenwood growled. "You're damn lucky I'm so far away right now." He pushed the end call button on the dashboard's screen.

On the second floor of the next garage, near the elevator, between a utilitarian black sedan and a truck that looked as though it had driven from halfway across Texas, he spotted the white SUV. He jumped out, a crumpled piece of paper in one hand, and held the numbers on the paper near the license plate. Then he kicked the bumper with his loafer and trudged back to his car, where he sat for a long time in stillness. He was hungry, had to use the bathroom, and hadn't slept since the brief rest he'd allowed himself after he heard that his quarry had parked in Vegas, presumably for the night.

Eventually, he pulled forward and drove up and down the row, looking for an empty space. He followed the few hotel guests who emerged from the elevator bank but abandoned them one row over, when he lost sight of the SUV. After a frustrating hour, an older couple maneuvered an ancient Cadillac from a space about thirty yards from the SUV. Greenwood hovered behind them, took the spot, cut the engine, and popped his trunk. He jumped out and rushed to the back, where he pushed aside children's soccer gear and emerged with two sport water bottles. Back in the front seat, he opened his fly. While he peed into one of the bottles, he kept one eye riveted on the white dot of the SUV. When he finished, he screwed the bottle shut and threw it in the foot well, where it sloshed among empty soda cans. He twisted the key and redialed the last number on the dashboard screen.

"Can you deactivate the alarm?"

"Not possible."

Greenwood groaned and hung up. He looked at himself in the visor mirror and rubbed a few crumbs from his beard. "The casino must produce worse looking people," he said to himself and got out.

His footsteps echoed in the low roofed, concrete building. At the SUV, he scanned the ceiling for surveillance cameras. Three round white balls were clustered near the elevators where the vehicle was parked.

He shrugged, pushed his sunglasses closer to his face, and cupped his hands against the window. He took his time, moving gradually from window to window. He didn't hear the approaching footsteps.

"Lock your keys in?"

Greenwood spun around, his face a mask of mingled embarrassment, fear, and annoyance. "What's it to you?"

The man looped his thumbs under a leather belt with a gigantic Texas-shaped buckle and chuckled. "Try the doors?"

"What?" Greenwood threw a glance toward the surveillance cameras.

"Sounds stupid, but I can't tell you how many times I thought I locked my keys in and never locked the doors." The man stepped forward and tugged one of the back door handles. It clicked open.

Greenwood stared and then tried the driver's side, which swung easily toward him. The passerby thumped him on the arm. "Hope some of your luck rubs off on me at the tables." He ambled to the elevators.

Greenwood waited until the man disappeared, then began a systematic search of the SUV. In the glove box, he found the rental agreement. He snapped a photo with his phone.

"Brianna Acosta." He spat the words like a foodie spits out day old pizza. "You're going to give me my phone back if I have to wait all week." He scoured the doors, floors, seats, crevices, and compartments. When he finished one round, he began again. As his fingers scrambled and his body contorted, images from a previous night he spent in the car flooded his mind.

He'd picked Paulo up where he always picked him up, four blocks south of Paulo's home. Paulo stood in the shadows near the entrance of a boarded-up drug store and waited. Greenwood pulled the SUV close, leaned over, and unlatched the passenger door. Paulo clambered in, using the dashboard to hoist himself onto the seat. Greenwood moved one hand to Paulo's lap and kept it there as they drove wordlessly across the city, over a bridge, and to a small, dark one-story house with boards over the windows and an abandoned sofa on the front lawn. With darkened headlights, Greenwood maneuvered the SUV down the driveway to the back of the house and killed the engine. In the silence that followed, the only sounds were the unbuckling of Greenwood's belt and the faint breathing of the youth next to him.

***

The same afternoon that Greenwood found Bree's SUV in the garage in Vegas, his wife bent over a marble kitchen counter in downtown San Francisco going through a stack of legal documents, a cell phone clamped between ear and shoulder. A slick leather briefcase lay open on a barstool next to her.

"I understand, Angelina, but I have no idea where he is." She picked up a knife from the counter and sliced open a series of envelopes. "I'm sure he's cooked up some secret plan, as usual. Let's not panic until a couple of days have gone by. He's a grown boy." She hung up.

"Who's grown? Me?" A curly brown head came level with the countertop. Abigayle Thackeray-Greenwood smoothed her son's hair with French manicured fingers. He hopped on a stool and let his backpack slip to the floor with practiced ease.

His mother frowned. "Planning on picking that up?"

"If you get me some…" He rolled his eyes to the ceiling in thought. "Freshly baked chocolate chip cookies." He grinned.

His mother smiled. "What gave you that idea?"

The boy spun the knife like a pinwheel on the cool marble. "Toshi's mom bakes cookies."

"Toshi's mom doesn't have a law practice."

The boy jumped from the stool and walked to the built-in stainless steel refrigerator. "We can't eat your legal briefs. So I think Toshi's mom has a better job." He returned to the counter carrying a loaf of bread, a jar of peanut butter, and a container of organic, low-fat buttery spread.

His mother poured him a glass of sparkling water and handed him a porcelain plate. "No eating off the counter."

When he finished making his first sandwich, he handed her the thick, gooey slices. "You need a snack too."

She had just taken a bite when her phone rang again.

The boy wagged a reprimanding finger. "No talking with your mouth full."

She peered at the screen, hastily swallowed the sandwich bite, and motioned at him to pick up his backpack. She stepped over it and strolled into the next room.

"Hold on." With her hand cupped around the phone, she marched up the long flight of carpeted stairs. At the top, a wide hallway diverged. She ambled across the shiny wooden floorboards and turned the handle of a door at the end of the corridor. Something blocked it from the inside. She leaned her shoulder into it. The solid wood resisted. She thumped her hip against it rhythmically and it yielded slightly.

"I'm listening." Jamming the phone between her shoulder and ear with a practiced gesture, she squeezed through the opening. On the other side, she squatted to tug a stuffed elephant from under the door. The toy trumpeted its objection when she tossed it into a corner. "Just a little playroom cleanup."

One wall of the room comprised large bay floor-to-ceiling windows with a view of a grassy park across the street. The three other walls contained shelves and drawers that spilled over with toys and pastel coloring books. The floor was littered with the detritus of children's play. Abigayle held the phone to one ear and used her other hand to throw stuffed animals into a wooden footlocker, while her feet shoved plastic building blocks and miniature metal cars to the side of the room. "Uh-huh. That really stinks."

After bringing some order to the chaos, she fell with a sigh into an oblong suede beanbag facing the windows. Her body slid into the royal blue puff until her feet splayed out in front of her in a large V, her black A-line skirt riding up to mid-thigh, patent leather pumps pointing to the corners of the high ceiling. "Sure. Every board member has her own agenda."

She ran her fingers through her short curls and turned away from the outside glare. She scanned the thin spines of the bookshelf to her left, with titles that conjured images of children's bedtime, then let her gaze drift to the higher shelves, where the volumes thickened and titles grew longer, until, at adult eye height, the genres metamorphosed from trains and animals that talked into biography, outer space exploration, and simple engineering principles.

"Not tonight." She pushed a stray strand of hair behind an ear. "Griff's on one of his mysterious product searches." Her thumb absentmindedly spun the large diamond encircling her ring finger. "Don't feel like showing up by myself again."

She ended the call and closed her eyes, thinking of when she and Griff first designed the room, when she was eight months pregnant with their daughter. She remembered how his eyes sparkled as he spoke of their children having a space all to themselves, a hide-away from the world. It was no use her pointing out it would be years before their unborn daughter would be old enough to appreciate a playroom.

He patted her belly and leaned down, as he often did, talking to the child in her womb. "Little one, I'll make the world safe for you. Fun for you. Easy for you." He gazed up at Abigayle with the look of a young, lost boy. "We have to do this right."

That was the Griff she'd fallen in love with, the

one whose love was fiercely protective. The one who reveled in pitting himself against the world. The one who supported her ambitions while at the same time smoothing the way toward motherhood. When she told him she might be pregnant, he came home the next day and handed her a "Baby On Board" T-shirt with a large yellow arrow pointing to her stomach. She laughed as though it were a joke. But the look on his face made her bite the smile from her lips.

Griff was the proudest father she knew. Even though he valued neatness above almost all else, the trunk of his car was crammed with the children's play gear. Even though he devoted almost all his waking hours to work, he sometimes missed meetings to watch the children's games. Even when she hadn't seen or spoken to him in days, he would burst into the kitchen with a photo on his phone of the kids by the pool or in the yard. Maybe, she thought, it happened like this to all couples. They grew apart. They had different interests. They didn't feel comfortable with each other anymore. But their children kept them together.

A gentle smile lit her face as she rolled ungracefully from the yielding suede ball to the floor, landing on her hands and knees, her face inches from a bookshelf, where the just visible edge of a magazine fluttered. She reached behind a pile of volumes detailing the adventures of a caterpillar in the Amazon and pulled out the worn magazine, with its creased cover and well-thumbed pages. Her lips hardened. A muscular young man with one leg on the first rung of a ranch fence and the brim of a cowboy hat held over his privates, smiled up at her. Other than the hat, he wore nothing.

"Again?" She dropped the magazine and looked around the room, as though someone had put the offending periodical there while she was talking on the phone. Then she yanked the entire caterpillar series from the shelf. It tumbled to the floor. In the space it left, she found a tight roll of magazines held together by rubber band. Her brow furrowed. She stood and pulled a tuft of tissues from a box nearby and used them to lift the roll and the stray magazine. Carrying them in front of her like dirty diapers, she left the playroom and tramped down the hallway to an office, where she removed a key from under a laptop docking station, unlocked a set of polished wooden filing cabinets, and dropped the magazines inside.

After re-locking the cabinet and replacing the key, she bounced on the edge of the mesh office chair, her legs twitching restlessly. She bit her lip, her gaze riveted on a family photo in a steel frame on her desk. For minutes, she didn't move. Then her hand picked up the cell phone and scrolled through the contacts.

"Griff, we've got a problem. I found some more of…" Her free hand twisted the heavy gold necklace around her throat, tightening it gradually. "Those things." She held the necklace from her and let it spin freely. "You convinced me last time. But now I'm taking charge. It can't go on."

She hung up and straightened the papers on the desk, pushing the family photo to the side and edging the individual ones of her children forward.

"What can't go on?"

The voice made her jump. "Justin, honey, you scared Mommy." She spun in the chair to face him. "Mommy's going to…hire a new cleaning company. The one we're using leaves too much garbage around."

CHAPTER 9

Mal, his grandmother, and Bree reclined on an iron bench licking gelato from spoons in an alcove of the hotel where sunlight streamed from skylights three stories above and a six-foot cherub splashed water from a trumpet into a glittering silver fountain. Juli was sandwiched between the young couple, her short legs barely touching the travertine tiles. She put down her cup and rubbed her hands together.

Bree felt her fingers. "Maybe ice cream in air conditioning was a bad idea after all."

Juli patted Bree's knee. "When I was growing up in India, things were hot or room temperature only."

Bree licked the remainder from her cup and got to her feet. "Give me your room key. I'll run up and get you a shawl."

Juli tugged at her hand. "Don't be troubling yourself about me."

Mal transferred Juli's purse to his lap and began rummaging through it. "Grandma, why do you carry all this stuff with you?" He held up a small sewing kit. Next a mini screwdriver dangled between his fingers.

"You are never knowing when something might break." She pulled it from him and reached in an outside pocket. She handed Bree a plastic card.

Bree nodded. "I'll be back in a flash." She gave Mal a quick kiss on the lips.

She strode past the numerous shops that lined the main pathway to the hotel, avoiding the eyes of attendants who stood outside the stores with tempting free wares designed to lure customers through their doors. She fought a tide of people heading toward the sunlit piazza and aimed for a bank of elevators, where she found herself alone. The lights above the eight sparkling doors indicated floor numbers and she watched with crossed fingers, hoping her elevator would face the outside of the hotel. She loved the dizzying sensation of rising above the city, watching it disappear through the glass beneath her feet as she was conveyed into the heights. A door slid open with a bing. Bree stepped into the box. The floor was polished black marble, the ceiling a mosaic of mirrors, and the only thing separating her from the outside world was a round glass encasement with a golden bar at its middle.

She pushed the button for the twenty-sixth floor. Before the doors closed, an arm stuck itself between the steel. The doors froze for an instant and then reopened.

"You almost lost your arm." Bree stared at the slim, tall African-American woman who slipped into the elevator.

The woman grinned, her eyes sparkling. "No hotel in Vegas would give you a reason to sue." She tapped the button for the thirtieth floor and stood with her back to the door, like Bree, ready to watch the city slip away.

As the elevator whisked them upward, Bree's eyes fixed on a young girl and her mother on the sidewalk outside. The mother was kneeling and listening intently to a story the girl told with much animation of her arms. The two figures rapidly shrunk as the elevator rose in stillness. A moment later, Bree and her elevator companion grabbed the golden bar in unison as their conveyance lurched, shook, and groaned. It dropped. They screeched. After a few feet, it shuddered. Bree whimpered. Then it stopped moving.

Bree glanced at the woman next to her. She wanted to speak but found herself unable. Her mouth was clamped as tightly shut as her hands were clamped around the bar. The other woman spoke first.

"Should we let someone know?" She peered at the elevator's number panel and the emergency call box beneath it.

Bree was closer to the panel and edged toward it, never releasing the bar. When she reached the corner, she pried one hand free, punched the red emergency button, and whipped the hand back to the bar. She smiled sheepishly. "I feel like this bar is the only thing between me and the ground."

The other woman nodded. "You and me both, sister." She moved one hand to her stomach. "I really wish I hadn't eaten the crab dip for lunch."

Bree gave her a halfhearted smile. She looked at the panel again. "Isn't the bell supposed to ring?"

The woman shrugged by lifting her shoulders without letting her hands leave the bar. "Can't speak from experience."

Bree looked down at the ground. The mother and daughter had disappeared into the crowds that thronged the afternoon Vegas strip. "How high do you think we are?" Her voice cracked. She felt a clammy, cold sensation spread from her chest through her limbs. Her head felt light. Her stomach protested against its shaken contents.

Her companion edged toward her until they were standing together. She released one hand from the bar and turned to face the doors. "Let's pretend we're on the first floor."

"More like the twenty-first." But Bree turned and then sunk to the ground, her hands still on the bar above her head.

The woman smiled. "You look like you just scored a touchdown." She stomped her foot.

Bree glared at her. "What are you doing?"

"Testing." She released her grip on the bar. She stepped to the elevator panel and pressed the button under the speaker labeled, "Push for help."

After a few seconds, a woman's voice with a thick Midwestern accent crackled through the speaker. "How can I help you?"

Bree yelled from the floor. "We're stuck in an elevator. Hundreds of feet up."

The Midwestern woman replied. "Please stand next to the microphone so that I can hear you."

Bree's companion bent at the waist, revealing a

Chinese character tattoo on her lower back. Before the young woman spoke, she turned with a grin to Bree. "While I have her on the phone, want to order takeout?"

Bree could not control the giggle that followed. She released one hand from the bar to hold her shaking stomach. "Double cheeseburger."

The woman turned back to the holes in the panel. "We're stuck in an elevator. I hope you know where."

"Information is transmitted automatically. Someone will be there soon." The crackling stopped.

Bree's elevator buddy folded her arms. "So I guess we wait."

From her position on the floor, Bree admired first the woman's open toed violet pumps, then her short magenta skirt and finally the sleeveless, untucked flowing top. She look at her own utilitarian shoes, gray slacks, and clinging white blouse. She pushed herself off the floor, released her grip on the bar, and stuck out her hand. "Bree."

"Celine." Celine's grip was firm. "What brings you to Vegas?"

Bree massaged her shoulders. "What brought me was a car." She shut one eye to stop herself from peeking out the window behind her. She focused on the other woman's face. "Because I'm afraid of flying."

"And heights?"

"After today, pretty much."

Celine tilted her head and paused. "I'm here for my best friend's wedding."

Bree's face brightened. "I'm here for my engagement party."

Celine's eyes flew to Bree's left hand and she reached out. "What kind of rock did he get you?"

Bree showed off the deep blue sapphire set flat in a circle of tiny diamonds. She chuckled. "Blew the down payment for a condo in San Francisco. At this rate, we'll be eighty before we can afford anything."

Celine let her hand drop and pursed her lips. "I feel you." She looked around the elevator. "Wish we had chairs. This skirt wasn't meant for sitting down."

Bree dug through her purse. "Use this." She handed Celine a napkin from the Tex-Mex restaurant that had somehow ended up inside.

"It's the getting down that's the problem." With her knees locked together and the help of the bar, she maneuvered herself to the black tile and sat with her legs straight out in front of her, her back resting against the glass.

Bree joined her, sitting a few feet away and playing with a loose thread hanging from the seam of a buttonhole on her blouse. "When's the wedding?"

"Tomorrow. They're out scoping the location now."

Bree shifted to a cross legged position and tugged harder on the thread, watching the buttonhole slowly unravel. "Don't they know where it's going to be?"

Celine raised an eyebrow. "In the desert. They're just not sure exactly where."

"Because everything in the city was booked?"

"Because they're crazy." Celine laughed. "Long story. The short version is that they're thru-hikers."

Bree stopped fiddling. "What hikers?"

"Thru." Celine stretched her arms wide. "They hike thousands of miles to get through from point A to point B."

Bree examined her companion's footwear. "Do you?"

Celine brushed a piece of lint from her skirt. "Darling, do I look like I'd put myself through that?" She raised one eyebrow. "They met on a trail, so they want a trail wedding." Her eyes rolled. "I convinced them to have it near airports and bars. So here we are, in Vegas. Tonight, we party. Tomorrow, Red Rock Canyon."

Bree stared and thought of the desert walk with Ryder in the dark, the crisp air, the clear sky, the silence. In the confines of the elevator, it sounded delightful.

Celine shuddered. "Cacti, scorpions, and rattlesnakes. I hiked once. Saw a man fall down a mountainside to his death. Never again."

Bree's gaze turned to the floor. "Sounds like why I hate flying."

Celine's fingers tapped a rhythm on her thighs. "You mind pushing the button again to ask what's taking them so long?" She pointed at her skirt.

Bree got to her feet. A different but still Midwest-accented operator informed her that the call center responsible for their elevator's operations was in Nebraska. The woman said her company had notified the Las Vegas contractors, who had dispatched a technician to the site.

"In other words," Celine laid her head back against the glass and closed her eyes, "this could take hours."

"Why didn't I think of this earlier?" Bree lifted her purse from the floor and fumbled in it. She lifted her phone above her head in triumph. "I can call 911."

On the floor, Celine crossed her arms. "You think Vegas police are going to care about a stuck elevator?"

Bree's face fell. "I can call my fiancé. He can let the hotel know."

"What does this fiancé do for a living?"

"Runs a dog wash."

Celine groaned and reached out her hand. "Give me the phone. My boyfriend's a cop."

Twenty minutes and a lot of wedding conversation later, the golden doors of their cage squeaked open and a gloved hand reached in from five feet up and wiggled its fingers. "You ladies okay in there?"

Celine scuttled to regain a standing position. "Keep that thing shut until we're decent." She winked at Bree.

A grinning, tan face perched on a wide neck and shoulders poked through the opening. "If you're too busy, I can come back later."

Bree lunged toward the door. She laughed and grabbed the hand he offered her. "Be careful. I'm not as thin as Celine."

"Celine's heavier than she looks. Take it from me." The man heaved with two hands while Bree's feet scrabbled for traction. She rose slowly over the threshold and lay for an instant like a beached whale on the cool floor of an elevator lobby. "Sweet freedom." She rolled onto her back and two EMT personnel helped her to her feet.

In the elevator, Celine got up from her knees and turned to the man who held his arms wide, with a smile so large that his eyes almost disappeared. "What was that you said about my weight, K-Rao?"

K-Rao jerked his thumb over his shoulder. "Wasn't me. That was this guy."

"Bree." The name from the hallway behind her sounded like a reprimand. Bree's eyes moved from the embracing couple. Faye stood with hands on her hips next to Mal, who lifted his eyebrows as if to ask whether she was all right.

Bree skipped toward them. "*That* was an adventure." She embraced Mal.

He fingered the mole on his chin. "Grandma's lying down in my parents' room. Since you had her key, we couldn't get her into hers." He gave her a half grin.

"Do they know what caused the elevator to malfunction?" Faye asked Bree while staring at the EMTs.

Bree shrugged. "No matter what, it's going to be a while before I trust those things again."

Faye tapped her foot and gave Bree an exasperated look. "I certainly hope you won't use this as an excuse to start another phobia."

Suddenly, every muscle from Bree's toes to her forehead stiffened. She pressed her side teeth into her lower lip and breathed in carefully, afraid that if she did it too quickly, something in her would break. Although she could feel the blood rushing to her face, she willed her voice to maintain its equilibrium. If she had learned anything about fighting from the Patels, she'd learned that the only thing worse than being attacked without warning was showing that a thrust hit its mark.

"Let me say goodbye to my new friend." She extracted her hand from Mal's grasp, smiled with lips pressed tightly together, and turned her back on the mother and son.

A smile lit Celine's face as she approached. "Ready to hit the tables? After bad luck like that, I figure for the rest of the day we should be golden."

K-Rao clamped his hands over his pocket. "Vegas isn't getting one cent of my money. I work too hard to waste it."

Celine grinned. "That island in the Bahamas could be waiting for us."

K-Rao pulled her close to him. "I live in Hawaii. What do I want with the Bahamas?"

Bree rubbed her cheeks, hoping her face had lost some of its aggrieved expression.

Celine tilted her head. She glanced at Mal and his mother, who still stood nearby. "Maybe your fiancé should take you to go lie down." She rolled her eyes suggestively.

Bree smiled weakly. "Was the invitation when we were talking earlier for real?"

K-Rao looked up at the ceiling. "You obviously don't know her yet. *Everything* this girl says is for real."

Celine gave him a playful punch in the shoulder. "He means that as a compliment. The wedding reception tomorrow is open to all. Stop by. It's a chance to see Vegas's flip side."

"You left that in there." K-Rao handed Bree her purse. "You don't want to give up a chance to see crazy hikers getting married in the desert, yeah?"

Bree slung the bag over her shoulder.

Celine gave her a hug. "I'm a poor substitute for the girlfriends you left behind in San Francisco, but I'll give it my best shot."

K-Rao held up two fingers, then a third. "She's worth at least two, maybe three."

Bree told Mal and Faye she wanted a few minutes of fresh air and refused Mal's offer to accompany her, saying he should check on his grandmother instead. Outside, the hot Vegas air seared her lungs. The bright sunshine made her blink and shade her eyes. She shivered despite the heat and let the crowd push her along the sidewalk. As she passed the hotel garage, she turned in. Maybe a drive into the desert was what she needed? She hopped onto a low wall near the entrance. Anything seemed better than returning to her room.

She thought back over the past year with Mal and realized that until today she hadn't understood why he and his sisters cowered from their mother's wrath. To her it was a game. She could jostle Faye away from a target, calm her down, and, when necessary, step in front of someone else to take the bullet. She was good at it. Mal appreciated it. It gave her a valuable role, a way to fit in. Even Faye seemed to like having a competent adversary, someone to outmaneuver, to respect. And someone to see her good side.

But Bree couldn't laugh about flying. She sighed. That wasn't a phobia, she told herself. It was fact. If you flew, you could die.

She got up and traipsed past the rows of cars in the garage. Out of the sun, the air felt heavier, more musty and polluted. The vast space seemed to stretch for miles in front of her, car after car, of every shape and size, with license plates from every state. Gradually, she became aware that the only sounds she could hear was her heels on the concrete. She looked over her shoulder. Where was everyone?

She pulled her purse closer to her body and walked faster, head erect, as though she knew exactly where she was going. Three rows in, she thought she heard footsteps behind her. Four rows in, she turned to glance over her shoulder. She took the car keys from her bag and pushed the remote's unlock button, listening for the distinctive beep. When she heard nothing, she pushed lock and turned around. She could still hear the footsteps. She pulled out her phone and put it to her ear, talking to the black screen.

"That's right. Meet me halfway. I'm in the garage. Near the street. You can't miss me."

A car rolled through the entrance. Bree increased her pace, heading for it. By the time it passed her, she was nearly at the exit. When she stepped into the sunshine, she let out the breath she had been holding. When the phone in her hand rang, she almost dropped it in surprise.

"Catch you at a bad time?" Ryder's voice made it sound as though he was eating.

She came to a halt and pedestrians flowed around her in two streams. "What do you think?" Her voice snapped with strain. "I'm here for my engagement party."

"That's why I'm calling."

Bree waited, phone an inch from her ear.

"My sisters surprised me this morning with a visit." She heard him take another bite of whatever was he was eating. "Turns out they know me pretty well. Knew I'd have a suite and that they could use it as home base for doing all the things I won't have time to do."

She had a faint memory of two middle school girls rushing up to Ryder at graduation. "And this is relevant to me because?"

He took another bite. "We're hitting a club tonight. You and Mal could stop by."

A hundred images flashed through Bree's mind, mostly from the prom. But among them were scenes of a dress shopping spree, of dancing with Mal, and of Faye standing at a door with her hands on hips, shaking head, clasped hands, and eyes lifted to the ceiling. She headed back to the hotel. "Text me the details."

CHAPTER 10

As Celine and K-Rao drove farther away from Las Vegas, the suburban developments on either side of the highway changed in character. Closer to the city, houses proclaimed their individuality. Even when they were constructed using the same architectural template as their neighbors, they endeavored to stand out. Vegetation, window trim, and maintenance levels all differed. Some homes had brand-new roofs and siding, others languished with peeling paint and cracked driveways. Each exhibited its owner's foibles.

Farther from the center of the circle of small towns around Las Vegas, individual character belonged not to houses but to the development within which a house was located. The developer of each small area struggled to create a unique identity, hoping for a leg up in the housing market, scrambling for a reason a potential buyer should choose to live there and not across the street in a house with the same square footage, the same granite countertops, and the same basement man-cave equipped with Dolby speaker system. In some developments homes had brick fronts and bay windows, in others each dwelling boasted a front porch, and still others prided themselves on their eco-friendly landscaping. The impressions flashed past Celine as K-Rao sped in the fast lane toward the desert. She imagined what it might be like to live in that house with the pool, or that house with the gate.

But close to the end of civilization, chaos ruled. Before them shimmered the edge of the economic bubble, the remnant of a time when people had thought the towns and developments outside of Vegas would expand indefinitely. Occupied homes with cars in the driveway and tricycles on the grass stood next to empty lots and naked foundations. Sidewalks ended so abruptly that the transition from concrete to dust could catch a wool-gathering pedestrian in midstride. Celine stared from the passenger seat in the convertible and could almost hear the anguished howls of realtors, investors, and speculative buyers who lost their dreams when the housing market crashed. The desolation seemed recent, the wound raw. Only desiccated weeds that grew through piles of bricks, white plastic sewer tubes, and flopping wire fences indicated workers had abandoned these worksites years ago.

Celine felt like an intruder, a voyeur of the macabre, while driving through the final stretches of the developments. But as abruptly as civilization ended, nature reclaimed its space. A few turns in the road brought them into the true desert, where cacti, sand, and enormous, variegated boulders of cream, orange, and red lined the road. Amid the vast natural enclave, the colors, the hills in the distance, and a blue sky welcomed her. She reached for K-Rao's hand. "Now I know why they wanted to get married here."

His foot eased from the accelerator. "How does a rock get to look like that?" He pointed at a sloping two-story mound where cream, tangerine, and orange stripes flowed sideways through the stone as if created as part of a celestial sand art project.

Celine's head shook slowly. "Where's a geologist when you need one?"

K-Rao maneuvered the car onto a dirt side road. Dust billowed around them. He slowed it to a five mile an hour crawl as Celine fanned the clouds from her face, coughing.

He pulled to a stop. "This is where the GPS is telling me to park. You okay with trying to find them?" He gestured to the cacti and rough orange hills in the distance.

Celine glanced at her phone. "I still have reception."

K-Rao raised his eyebrows. They closed the car roof and strapped on hydration packs over their T-shirts. K-Rao examined a trail map app on his phone and pointed to the intersection of three trails. "I think that's where they might be."

Celine kicked the dirt at her feet. "Grace almost died in the desert. I wonder why she wants to get married in one."

"Closure?"

"That's like me wanting to get married in an elevator." Dust exploded from beneath her running

115

shoes with each step as she marched down a narrow footpath that paralleled the road. K-Rao kept a few paces behind her until, after a few minutes, the trail widened and he jogged to catch up.

"Didn't he find her there?"

His question snapped Celine from a reverie. "Who?"

"Lone Star. Didn't he rescue Grace in the desert at the beginning of her hike?" He took Celine's hand and swung it as they strode together.

"He gave her water when she didn't have any." She reached for the narrow hose and sipped from her hydration pack, letting the quiet around her sink into her soul, allowing her eyes to acclimate to the desert's limited color scheme, watching subtle differences emerge. Cream, she noticed, could manifest as ivory and eggshell. Orange ranged from tiger yellow to tangerine, sandstone, and amber. The dirt was brick red, but the hills had bands of mahogany and blood. Plants waved thin viridian stalks, moss-colored tentacles, and olive leaves. Scruffy desert shrubs dotted the earth around them and snagged her hiking skirt when she passed too close. Beaver tail cacti arched their broad pads threateningly across the trail. Yucca plants towered above their flora neighbors.

K-Rao's presence lent comfort in the rough environment. His easy-going Hawaiian style didn't fit in everywhere, but in the wilds, he blended in. It felt like walking with a guard dog at your side. You could kiss it on the muzzle and pat on its stomach secure in the knowledge that, when called on, it would rip off a mugger's arm. Places inside her always relaxed around K-Rao, places she didn't even know were tense. But what did that level of comfort mean, she wondered, for their future? Should he abandon his home in Hawaii and move to San Francisco? Should she uproot and follow him to the islands? Would things stay the same if they lived together, or would they fall apart?

"Does this wedding get you thinking?" K-Rao squeezed her hand.

Celine released her grip on his hand and stretched her arms overhead. "That I wouldn't want to get married here."

K-Rao slowed his pace. "Why don't you ask me what I'm thinking?"

Celine's stride narrowed to stay shoulder to shoulder with him. "How do you think we'll keep our clothes clean? Paid a lot for my dress."

K-Rao shoved his hands in his pockets. He halted and caught her eyes. "We should get married."

Her eyebrows lifted almost to her hairline. She took a step back. K-Rao pulled his hands slowly from his pockets and held them out to her. "Grace and Lone Star are doing it."

Celine bent over at the waist, her hands on her knees, laughing. "You've thought a lot about it? Ever since the car?"

He sunk to one knee and looked up at her.

She smiled. "Something might crawl up your shorts."

"Celine, I want to—"

"This conversation's over." Celine sprinted down the trail, her long legs flying easily across the dirt. His shoes spewed small stones in an effort to overtake her. She widened her stride, laughing. Then her legs broke into a run. He laughed too and passed her. She overtook him, her face lit with determination. Through a gully, over a dried stream, up the other side, and on for half a mile they ran, like two children playing leapfrog, passing each other and then slowing down to let the other pass until Celine staggered to a halt, hands on heaving ribs, out of breath.

"Let's…" She gasped. "Discuss it…later."

K-Rao leaned forward, panting. "Okay."

When she caught her breath, she looked around. "Where the heck are Grace and Lone Star?"

He removed his cell phone and studied the app.

She peered over his shoulder. "Don't you do this as a cop?"

K-Rao bit his lip. "Question isn't where they are, yeah? It's where we are."

Celine yanked the phone from his hands. Her fingers scrolled over the map. "Where's the car?"

"Thought I dropped a pin." K-Rao leaned closer.

Celine sucked in her breath, handed the phone back to him, and put her hands on her hips. She searched the ground for a place to sit down.

He gestured for her not to squat. "Something nasty might crawl up your skirt." He paced in a circle, holding the phone in front of him like a scanner from Star Trek.

Celine stuck out her tongue. She alternated standing on one leg and the other, interlacing her hands behind her back, bending forward, arching her back.

K-Rao grinned. "What are you doing?"

She ignored him. "Finding inner peace. Lost it right about when you forgot to pin the car."

***

K-Rao insisted on hunting for the car by moving in a perpendicular line away from the mountains. Celine followed a few yards behind his confident, upright shoulders. They had been lost together before, including once on Maui, when he took a wrong turn during a night walk. That half hour on the far side of the West Maui mountains was much more frightening than this daytime desert adventure. There, Celine started at every crunch of gravel, every creature in the bush, thinking it was a local pulling out a gun to warn trespassers off his property. K-Rao told her people might be more likely to shoot first and ask questions later. This stroll through a national conservation area was benign by comparison.

Hands behind her back, Celine hummed as she scanned the horizon, searching for the gleam of sunlight on a car windshield when two points in the distance caught her attention. They look like strangely shaped trees at first. As she approached, Celine recognized them as two hikers. "Hey, MacGyver." She tapped K-Rao on the shoulder. Her finger motioned to their right.

He raised his head and turned. "Is that...?"

Waving her hands, Celine leaped over cacti and skirted prickly bushes as she ran with a big grin toward the approaching woman and man. "This guy's trying to get me lost." As she neared the couple, the woman broke into a jog. When they met, they hugged and waited for the men to catch up with them.

Celine ruffled K-Rao's hair and linked her arm through her friend's.

K-Rao's eyes were still focused on the app. "Think I know where we are."

Lone Star pulled the phone from his hands and swept his arm across the wilderness in front of them. "*Amigo*, there's no better map than the land around you." His blue eyes sparkled under a long mane of red hair that he tucked back behind his ears. "It's called learning the country." He stuck out his hand. "*Que paso?*"

K-Rao fist bumped him and chuckled. "Guess I should leave desert hiking to the man from Texas." He took the phone and stuffed it into his back pocket. "But on Maui, I'll take you spearfishing."

Lone Star shuddered. "I'm fixing to live life without coming face-to-face with a shark."

Celine pulled them both in the direction of the nearest path. "Either of you *hombres* know the way back to the road?"

Lone Star bowed to Grace. "Follow my lady love."

Grace flipped her long hair under a floppy brimmed sun hat. "I'm cooking on a front burner today."

Celine's eyebrows arched and she shook her head. "Got to get you out of El Paso more often, girl. You sound more Texan than he does."

She and Grace loped ahead, leaving K-Rao and

Lone Star behind discussing the merits of electronic and paper maps. Celine quizzed Grace on the location for the next day's wedding. Grace pointed at a striped mound that rose in the land before the larger hills in the distance and explained that it hid a small natural amphitheater that she and Lone Star had decided was perfect.

Celine shook a finger at her friend. "Remember when you were prepping for your Pacific Crest Trail hike and I kept giving you all those books and you never read them? Don't you think maybe you're doing the same thing here?"

"Avoiding reality?" Grace wiped the sweat from her brow with a light blue bandanna.

"Letting the romance of the idea carry you away. You are seriously going to schlep to that hill wearing a wedding dress?" Celine whistled through her teeth dismissively. "You'll have armpit stains and red dirt kicked up your back. Sister, that's *not* how I want to look in *my* wedding photos."

Grace's eyes twinkled. She gestured to the small pack on her back. "My wrinkle free dress is going in there."

Celine slowed her pace. "So only your guests are going to look like crap?"

Grace laughed. "Lone Star's best man is bringing a baby stroller rigged up with a rod to hold garment bags. Your dress will be chauffeured to the location."

Celine shrugged. "Make sure that stroller has room for wet wipes and a makeup kit. And if the photographer takes pictures of me before I'm dressed, I'm going to bust his camera."

"I'll warn her."

The two women arrived at Grace and Lone Star's rental car a few minutes ahead of the men. Celine pulled Grace to the far side of the vehicle and told her about K-Rao's proposal.

"At least I think it was." She squirmed out of her hydration pack and twirled it in front of her.

Grace regarded her with large, serious eyes. "Did you say yes?"

Celine hooked the pack on one finger and slung it over her shoulder. "I told him I didn't want to talk about it."

"You think he's serious?"

Celine pursed her lips. "About something like that, K-Rao couldn't joke."

Grace opened the back passenger door, sat on the seat, and undid dusty gaiters from her hiking shoes. She glanced up at Celine. "You don't look very happy."

Celine looked into the distance. "It's going to make deciding what happens next a hell of a lot more complicated."

Lone Star poked his head from around the back of the car. "You ladies decent?"

Grace tossed him the gaiters. He caught them and jabbed K-Rao with an elbow. "You should have been aiming at this guy." He suspended the dirty nylon sock covers between thumb and forefinger. "A thru-hiker's gaiters are a lucky omen."

K-Rao snatched the gaiters. "I'll hold on to these." He turned to Celine and reached for her hand.

Celine evaded his grasp and hopped into the

back seat. "I could use a drink, and we could all use a party."

***

While a laughing couple strolled past him, Greenwood leaned deep into the trunk of his car, positioned his legs in front of the license plate, and held a child's tennis racquet in front of his face. When they disappeared into the elevator, he resumed digging through the cavernous interior, throwing tennis balls, children's sports gear, and an assortment of towels and picnic paraphernalia into various corners. In the depths of a small duffel stuffed to its limit with smelly soccer uniforms, his fingers massaged crinkled plastic and tugged a soiled convenience store bag into the dull light of late afternoon. After inspecting it for holes, he thrust it into a pocket and slammed the trunk shut. He glared at the white SUV, which, thanks to the exit of a few tired gamblers parked in a prime location, stood in the garage only ten yards from his own.

His nose wrinkled. "Making me use a bag as a toilet." He slid into the back seat. "You'll fucking pay for this, Brianna Acosta."

Minutes later, with the bag tightly tied and back in the trunk, he wiped his hands furiously with a fast food chain napkin. It shredded under the onslaught, showering his slacks and the leather seat with white confetti. He lifted his phone and scrolled through the past hour's voicemails, reading their transcribed contents and muttering. After deleting his administrative assistant's bi-hourly update that referred him to emails on his work phone, a message from the marketing director, the general counsel's request for a return call, and an unctuous request for an informational interview from the cousin of his college roommate, a single remaining call stared up at him from the screen.

"What does she mean, 'It can't go on'?" He reclined in the seat and set the phone on his stomach. "She's taking charge?" He pinched the bridge of his nose and tried to imagine Abigayle's face as she opened one of the magazines. Had she been puzzled, frightened, or outraged? Was her message simply venting? Or were the magazines the last push she needed to take him to court? His hands turned cold and he tucked them inside his waistband. A minute later, he pulled them out and his thumbs flew across the screen, trolling the Internet for the hundredth time for stories about his company and himself. His eyes focused on the terms reassuringly grayed out in strikethrough text: investigation, police, warrant, abuse. The YouTube video at the top of the list beckoned to him. He closed his eyes and mouthed the words of the one-and-a-half-minute story about a lonely young boy, lost until he found the perfect playmate. That lonely boy was Paulo. The playmate was Greenwood's company's new action series soldier.

But behind Greenwood's closed eyes, in the stale and slightly putrid air of the car, in the garage hundreds of miles from his home, Paulo's perfect playmate was not the soldier. It was Greenwood.

***

The tween-aged girl hip-checked her younger brother from his spot in front of the eighty-inch TV screen and jerked the virtual reality goggles from his hands while glancing at her mother's back. When her brother protested, she clamped her fingers over his mouth and whispered something in his ear. His shoulders dropped and he threw himself onto the corner of the L-shaped red suede sofa.

The girl shouted into the dining room. "Tell Daddy to bring home a special edition Walter the Walrus."

Abigayle's face peered through a hutch. "Why don't you ask him yourself, Gretchen?"

Gretchen poised the goggles over her face. "The last time I saw him was…" She shut her eyes and counted on fingers shiny with dark green manicure, "Saturday. He picked me up from tennis." She shoved the visor down and fumbled on the coffee table for the remote.

Her brother ambled into the kitchen and stood next to his mother, who was sorting paperwork on the long counter. "One of her friends has cancer."

Abigayle's fingers halted, poised over a stack of spiral binders. She stared at her son.

"She has blue keemia and wants the walrus." He climbed on a stool and sat, legs dangling, his expression questioning. "What's blue keemia?"

Abygale blinked, her glance shifting from the papers to Justin and back again. She sighed and twisted away from the counter, meeting his eyes. "Leukemia. It's a kind of blood cancer."

"Do you have it?"

"Buddy, what gives you that idea?" She cradled his chin in her hand and shook it gently back and forth.

The boy's blue eyes bored into hers. "Is it why Daddy's not here?"

His mother took off her glasses, placing them carefully on the marble, and rubbed her eyebrows. She wheeled on the heels of a pair of alligator pumps and strode to the kitchen sink, where she gazed out the window past the black and white pebbles of a Zen rock garden and elaborate hedges shaped to resemble the San Francisco skyline.

"Mommy?" The boy squirmed off the stool and tugged at her silk blouse. A tear rolled down his smooth cheek.

She turned to face him, rubbing the streaks from her own cheeks, and lifted him with a grunt onto the counter so his face was level with hers. "There *is* something wrong with Daddy. But it's not leukemia."

CHAPTER 11

The zipper of Bree's new sleeveless pink dress caught on the waistband of her shaping wear and no matter how she contorted herself to free it, it stayed put. She called Mal into the bathroom. He yanked while she watched her jiggling image in the mirror.

"It's a little tight, isn't it?" She gasped as he hauled it past the obstruction and the fabric slithered shut, compressing her ribs and chest. She tested a few breaths carefully, straining against the Lycra, listening for signs of ripping seams.

Mal gave her behind a squeeze. "Open or closed?" He pointed to the second button on his checked dress shirt.

Bree fingered the white undershirt that peeped from beneath the pale blue and green pattern. "It could get really hot."

Mal scowled. "I hate being cold."

Bree smiled gently. "It's a club, darling, with dancing. I give you permission to drag me to the floor whenever you're feeling chilly." She embraced him from the side, wiggling her hips

127

against his.

Mal laughed and pushed her away. "Don't start now." He untucked his shirt and slipped it over his head. "Grandma's waiting."

Bree smiled. In line for the buffet dinner earlier that evening, she whispered her idea of going to a nightclub to Mal and his sister, explaining she'd met a friend from high school in the lobby the night before who'd invited them to go with his sisters. Wouldn't it be fun? The twins pounced on the idea sotto voce while Val protested in hissed tones that it wasn't appropriate to split up the family. Amy, meanwhile, sulked because she wasn't old enough to go. When the dinner ended, lines were drawn. The twins were coming. Val would take Amy to a show, and Juli, the grandmother, would go to bed early. At least that was how Bree understood it until Juli grabbed her arm in front of the dessert sideboard.

"Many years before, I was going, you know." The older woman ladled a spoonful of fresh fruit onto her plate.

Bree stopped scooping, tiramisu dripping from her spatula. "To bed early?"

"Dancing."

Bree used tongs to transfer two chocolate chip cookies to the corner of her laden dish. "You went to nightclubs?" She tried to imagine the demure Juli in a sari under disco lights.

"I was taking many dancing classes. I was quite good." Her brown eyes sparkled and she rocked her head in the beguiling way Bree enjoyed watching.

Because the Patel family table was visible from

where they stood, Bree pulled Juli closer to the soup line, where they were partly hidden by an enormous bread display that rivaled that of Parisian bakeries. She balanced her plate on one hand and put the other on her hip. "I have no problem with your coming." She grinned. "But I'm not sure you know what you're getting into. These places are really loud. And it's not just women dancing. There are…" Her mind searched for an explanation of the suggestive moves on contemporary dance floors. Her eyes narrowed. "Have you seen young people dancing?"

"I've seen my granddaughters. They are sometimes practicing in the house." She wiggled her shoulders underneath her flowing, light green shift.

"So you've never seen young men and women…This is really embarrassing." Bree grit her teeth and glanced around them. She quickly gyrated her hips, mimicking thrusting movements, and cocked her head. "Know what I mean?"

The grandmother nodded. "I'm a seventy-year-old woman with children."

Bree blushed. "So you're okay with seeing stuff like that in public?"

The old woman regarded her seriously. "No one will be trying that with me, yes?"

Bree's eyes shone with amusement. She shifted her dish and patted Juli on the arm. "Not with you. And not with me."

An hour later, with Mal, the twins, and Juli in tow, Bree hailed a minivan taxicab. Inside, she texted Ryder.

Bree: I'm bringing Mal's grandmother.

Ryder: Sweet.

Bree: Can we get a quieter booth? Is there such a thing?

Ryder: Leave it to me.

Under the nightclub's neon flashing lights, Mal escorted the four women up numerous escalators to the entrance, where a dauntingly long line snaked along a path outlined by velvet corded posts. He herded them in to the back of the line and yelled to Bree in the already deafening din. "Did you say he was inside already?"

Bree jumped when a hand clamped on her shoulder. She turned to see Ryder beaming at her.

"So glad you came." His voice rose easily above the din without degrading into a shout. He undid the velvet cord near them and ushered them out of line.

Side-by-side, Mal and Ryder looked their high school parts, Ryder every bit the ex-football player and Mal the ex-cross-country star. Ryder was taller, with broader shoulders and muscles that filled out his clothing without any ostentation. Mal's untucked shirt billowed slightly around his spare frame. Bree noted that while Ryder looked like a country singer in a Tex-Mex restaurant, he now looked like a Hollywood celebrity, blending in perfectly with the young, pulsing crowd. Bree positioned her dress folds more flatteringly over her hips and quietly blessed the spandex contracting her middle like an unrelenting boa constrictor. She had no desire to look like his charity case. She peeped at herself in one of the ubiquitous mirrors and sucked in her tummy.

Ryder guided them to the entrance and, with a slight nod at the enormous gentleman standing guard at the door, into the vibrating interior. Bree felt Juli's hand slip into hers. She squeezed it. The twins glanced back at Bree with eyes and smiles larger and more genuine than Bree had yet seen. She nodded to herself. She had done right to bring everyone here. Ryder knew how to show people a good time.

Popular dance music thundered from speakers embedded in the walls, ceilings, and floors. Conversation was impossible. Bree peeked at the grandmother she was leading through the crowd. The wrinkled face bobbed above a black sweater and slacks Bree had chosen and registered both surprise and awe as she was jostled by the throng of expensively clad youths. Ryder pointed upstairs, indicating an escalator at the side of the gigantic hall.

Pink, purple, and blue spotlights roamed the dance floor, where the crowd was so thick that it was difficult to see where one set of movement ended and the next began. Ryder led them between the dance floor and a wall of lit glass that separated the dancers from two rows of leather couches and marble tables jammed with people and drinks. When a tall man with an exquisite tan, gold jewelry, and a skintight black T-shirt bounced off Juli and proceeded on his way without apology, Bree bent down and shouted into the old woman's ear. "Are you okay with this?"

Juli rocked her head enthusiastically and wiggled her thin shoulders in time to the music. Bree laughed. She needn't have worried, she guessed. There was no indication that the all-but-fornicating dancers on the floor shocked this woman.

They finally reached the bank of escalators lined with dark purple fluorescent lighting. Bree searched for an exit sign and wondered how the building passed the fire marshal's inspection. When the moving stairway deposited them on the floor above, Bree exhaled as though she released from a pressure cooker. After spending time on the floor below, the space in which they now moved seemed almost unnervingly still. Juli released her hand. Bree could hear the gushing chatter of the twins. Ryder called to them and motioned a table where two blonde women sat with wide martini glasses filled with a sea blue liquid.

Two benches faced a table that was situated perpendicular to another tall glass wall. Below stretched an expansive view of the Vegas Strip. After Ryder introduced his sisters and everyone slid into place, Bree found herself sitting between Mal and Ryder, with Juli on Ryder's right and the four young women across from them, already far past introductions and engaged in animated conversation.

Bree leaned back into the soft leather. "This is heaven." Mal leaned into her and put his arm around her shoulders.

"My mom would flip if she saw what was going

on down there."

Bree put her hand on his knee. "She's having a great time with your dad going through the menu one last time. I promise."

Mal squeezed her to him. "Why can't I stop talking about her?"

Bree tickled his knee and turned to Ryder, keeping her voice light and playful. "I feel like you should be sitting next to Mal. I know more about you than I care to. But you don't know each other."

Ryder leaned forward and flashed Mal a grin. "Dude, all you need to know about me is that my plan for tonight is to get these ladies drinks and then get them dancing."

A waitress in a golden halter top and sequined shorts arrived to take their orders. While Mal reviewed the menu, Bree leaned closer and cupped her hand to his ear. "Don't forget to ask Ryder how much we owe him."

Ryder waved at the waitress, who reacted to the gesture by leaning halfway across the table to stare into Ryder's eyes. Ryder pointed to himself. "Everything's on me tonight. Do you think you can help make that happen?" The woman looked as though she would jump into his lap to cement the arrangement.

Bree kicked Mal under the table. He looked at her quizzically.

"We should chip in." She glanced at Ryder and hoped her whisper hadn't carried.

Mal shrugged. "That's what he did at the entrance. I didn't have a chance. He seemed to know everybody."

"I don't want to take his charity."

Mal shrugged again. "Didn't you say he was loaded? I don't think he thinks about it like that."

After the drinks arrived, Bree found herself sweating despite the cool night air. Sitting between Mal and Ryder was even more uncomfortable than she had anticipated. She had pictured the two men standing in a corner, talking guy talk while she hung out with the twins and carefully introduced Juli to the realities of modern nightlife. Instead, the four young women across from her were swigging their drinks, showing every intention of abandoning their elderly relatives for the youthful action one story below. Ryder maintained an intense, running dialogue with Juli and seemed to be teaching her how to text. And Mal pulled into himself in a way that he often did in a crowd. His arm was still draped across her shoulders, but there was no life in it. When the four young women slid off the bench and waved their goodbyes, Bree felt an upheaval in the pit of her stomach. *No way am I going to be left alone with Ryder*.

"Mal, let's dance." She shifted his tumbler of whiskey away from him.

He threw down the remainder of his drink and leaned forward. "They're quite the couple." He waved at his grandmother who waved her cell phone before turning back to Ryder. When Bree moved to pass them, Ryder put his hand around her waist and held her back. Bree wiggled uncomfortably, but he pressed her and Juli firmly into either side of him. "Come on, Mal. Let's show these ladies a good time." Juli giggled and Bree frowned as Ryder swung them toward an elevator. Mal followed.

The glass elevator doors opened directly onto the floor and the mob in front of them seemed impenetrable as it gyrated and bounced to the beat of the rhythm that shook the floor. Bree was tempted for a second to hold her hands over her ears; the noise felt like such an assault. But the rhythm was familiar and her hips started moving of their own accord, the feeling in her stomach left somewhere on the floor above. There was a reason, she thought, they played music loud in places like this. It was like a drug.

Watching Ryder cut through the crowd, she grabbed Mal's hand and tramped after him, ignoring annoyed looks from dancers who effortlessly parted for Ryder and the small woman in black still attached to his hip, but were instantly eager to close ranks again. Ryder looked like a blond piece of metal drawn by an invisible magnet to the middle of the floor. Bree elbowed and apologized her way after him, dragging Mal behind her. By the time they reached a space that could accommodate the four of them, she was out of breath and laughing.

Ryder clasped Juli's hands and swayed with her in the practiced manner of an expert. People nearby nudged each other and pointed, but only with smiles and signs of encouragement. Bree felt overwhelmed with gratitude. If Mal, Juli, and she had come on their own, they would have been relegated to the edges of the floor, an awkward threesome, ignored and pushed to the side. Instead, Ryder lunged with Juli into the center of the action. His assurance rubbed off on the older woman. He was confident, she was confident. He belonged, she belonged. He was having fun, and it was clear from the expression on her face that she was having the time of her life. Bree's mouth hung open as she watched her grandmother-to-be learn to whip and nae nae, to cheers and nods from young dancers.

Not to be outdone, Bree turned to Mal, who swayed imperceptibly, the bending of his knees barely visible through his slacks. When they danced together, it was Bree who took the lead. She loved the throb of the rhythm and the freedom of semidarkness, the freedom to feel pretty because people's eyes were on their own partners or on themselves. If Mal had enough alcohol in his veins, she could get him moving, in an out of control, stick figure kind of way. But how much Mal moved usually it didn't matter to her. In the riotous exhilaration of the moment, he was just another dance partner, a body to flow with hers. Someone else to breathe the same electrified air. He could've been Stephanie or Juli or one of the twins. There were times when he left her on the dance floor by herself and she hardly noticed, absorbed in the music and the energy around her, unconscious of her looks, at one with the crowd.

As she danced she thought of her friends back in San Francisco. She flipped her hair and danced for them. She thought of Faye and the tight confines of the world she created for herself. She threw her arms above her head and danced for her. She thought of nights in bed with Mal and bumped against his hips and danced with him. Sweat ran down her temples and between her shoulder blades. Her dress inched higher up her thighs and she stopped pulling it back into place, content and eager to jump into the next song, and the next, and the next. When Juli motioned for Mal to be her partner, Bree waved him along and closed her eyes, letting the music take over. She let her head rock. Upstairs, she had been very wrong. Sitting on a bench was not heaven. Heaven was down here. The crowd became denser.

She opened her eyes and found herself staring at Ryder only a foot away. He thrust his hands in his pockets, moving his shoulders in a terrifyingly familiar way. She felt panic rise in her throat, felt as if there wasn't enough air. People shoved against them. The space between her and Ryder declined until she was moving against him more often than not. She stood still, no longer capable of dancing, wanting only to escape.

He reached for her hands and squeezed them. He held her hips, his palms against her chunky contours, and she wrenched away against the pressure of his arms. A woman knocked into her, forcing her to stumble forward into Ryder's arms. He propped her up, his face concerned.

He arched his eyebrows in the direction of the still flailing woman. "Out of control." He grabbed her elbow and jerked his chin, just as before, a fisherman reeling in a catch. Only this time, she wasn't biting.

He encircled her still form with both arms. His chest leaned in. His biceps framed her breasts. His breath tickled her neck. She stiffened and pushed away but he held her tightly. His lips touched hers, the merest flutter, like a dragonfly skimming a pond. But her skin felt as though a set of live wires were run across it. She raised her hand and, before she knew what she was doing, slapped him, hard, across the cheek.

Bree stepped back, only able to retreat an inch in the crowded space, but creating what felt like a mile between herself and Ryder. Out of breath and out of words, she stared, mouth slack, heart pounding, thoughts racing. *What just happened?*

Tears of frustration, anger, and shame welled in her eyes. Her face burned. She turned. The escalators beckoned and she dove into the crush around them, the dancers parting for her as though she had absorbed the patina of his aura.

You idiot. The words reverberated in her mind, drowning out the music. She held her hands to her cheeks as she stomped to the edge of the throng. *Why did you let him do it?* Her head reeled. The escalator, both directions packed with joyful partiers, loomed above her, all of a sudden terrifyingly high. She looked around for signs to a restroom. When she couldn't see one, she grabbed the arm of the nearest young woman and asked. Tucked in a shiny black wall was a discreet light over a wide hallway. Bree jostled her way toward it, elbowing and shoving her way, her shoulders slumped, her eyes blinking back tears.

If she had come to the club on her own, she thought, she would run past the exit and out on the street, away from the club, from the hotel, from Vegas. Only pictures of Mal and her future with him prevented her from rushing to the exit. At the back of the line that extended out the women's room door and into the hall, Bree ran her fingers through tangled hair. *Why does he like making a fool of me?* She wiped the back of her hand around the contours of her mouth and used her pinky to dab the corners of her eyes. She tugged her dress down and pulled the creases flat over her stomach. Around her, young women chatted, giddy, drunk, and excited. The anonymity of the darkness calmed her, like crawling into a cave. She leaned against the cool stone and closed her eyes.

"Bree?"

The question came out of nowhere. She squinted into the gloom but couldn't identify its source. Someone tapped her arm. She focused on a mass of gray hair floating above a dark, disembodied head. "Grandma?"

The head moved toward her. "I was imagining I would never find you again."

Bree rubbed the older woman's shoulder. "You could have called me. We'd never leave without you."

"Ryder is having my phone in his pocket. Have you seen him?"

The heat that rose instantly to Bree's cheeks felt as though it made them glow. She shook her head. She licked her lips, her voice trembling as she fumbled for a story that would tie together. "First, I had to go…" She nodded in the direction of the restroom door. "But then I was coming to look for you and Mal."

The older woman pulled on her arm, urging her

to lower her ear. Bree felt as though a police car behind her on a highway had switched on its lights. Guilt and shame rushed through her. She lowered her head. The woman's warm breath skimmed her ear. "It's not a clean loo."

Bree exhaled. "I'm sure I've seen worse."

"India has worse. But this is Vegas." Grandma smiled. "The home of Elvis."

"Elvis?"

The gray head nodded vigorously. "You know him? The King of Rock and Roll?" She wiggled her hips seductively and lowered her voice. "Elvis the Pelvis." She clapped her hand over her mouth. Above it, her eyes glimmered with mirth.

Bree laughed. "You used to like Elvis?"

"I am still liking him." She pointed to the dance floor. "I saw one."

"One what?"

"An Elvis impersonator. But too skinny. Not enough…" She pumped her hips again.

The line moved and Bree shuffled forward a few steps. "Juli, you just made my night."

"Ryder is finding information on an Elvis impersonator contest." She gazed wistfully past Bree. "I was never seeing the King in concert. Maybe now is my chance."

"Grabbing a chance doesn't always turn out well."

The gray head shook slowly. "I was never telling my husband about Elvis…" She looked around as though someone might be listening. "Passion." She peeked at Bree. "Maybe I was needing to live a secret life."

"I hate living a secret life."

Brown eyes stared up at her. "Something is happening?"

Bree shrugged. "A stupid work thing. Not worth talking about. We're here to have fun." She swung the older woman's hand to and fro but met with resistance and dropped her fingers.

The hand pulled her down again. "Your work is making you trouble?"

She forced a laugh. "Everything's fine."

But the older woman persisted. "A few days before, Faye was talking about you and Mal. I was overhearing something about her hiding your work cell phone."

Bree shook her head. "You must have misheard. I don't have a work cell phone." She pointed to the large door to the restroom that opened. "I'll just pop in."

The noisy bathroom, where piped in music from the dance floor, flushing toilets, and excited chatter reverberated off the mirrors, black tile, and high ceiling, provided a comparatively still background to the cacophony in her head. Bree examined herself askance in the ubiquitous mirrors. She ran her fingers through her hair and eyeballed her makeup, blotting her lids with a paper towel and correcting her smudged lipstick with a fingernail. Next to her, a model-thin woman in a skintight gold lame halter dress that ended centimeters below her rear reapplied her own cosmetics and gave Bree a knowing leer through the glass. "They want us to look beautiful, then kiss us and make us look a mess." She winked.

Bree looked away, blushing to the roots of her hair. Her hands wrenched at the back of her dress and hauled at the neckline. She couldn't remember what she looked like hours ago in the hotel bathroom but was sure she looked different now. She shook her arms, flapping her wrists as though to shake residue from them and raised her chin to meet her own eyes in the mirror, ignoring the desire to flinch and look away. *Get out of here. Then you never have to speak to him again.* She stepped back into the hallway and marched determinedly with Juli to the escalators.

In the open air lounge near where they had first sat, she saw the twins chatting with a pair of long-haired young men. Juli pulled Bree's arm and asked whether they should ignore or interrupt them when, in one movement, the twins answered her question by waving furiously in their direction. The two admirers aimed toward the bar, seemingly content with the phone numbers they had just entered into their cell phones and leaving only the scent of too eagerly applied cologne behind them. Bree studied the girls' eyes for a sign that they suspected her of wrongdoing but quickly realized they were preoccupied with their own evolving infatuations. The dance floor also sucked them in with its intoxicating embrace. They gushed about falling in love, their young heads spinning with fantasies to which their mouths gave voice.

Out of the hubbub below, Juli leaned against Bree, her eyes blinking with fatigue. Bree put her arm around the older woman's shoulders and scanned the area for an empty chair on which she

142

could deposit her. But the crowd had doubled in size and decreased exponentially in average age. Everyone around them looked through anyone over thirty as though they didn't exist. No one jumped from their seat to wave a gallant arm toward a senior citizen. "Mal has the keys and my ID, but we could ask Soumil and Faye to let you rest in their room."

The color had drained from Juli's face and under the intermittent lighting, her features looked blotchy. Bree explained the situation to the twins, who all but jumped up and down at the idea of "needing" to stay at the club to convey to Mal why his grandmother and fiancé had disappeared. Bree gave them a wan smile. Half of her wanted to escape before Mal arrived and the other half couldn't stand the suspense of not knowing what he would, or would not, read in her expression.

Juli's feet stumbled over each other, the wild dancing septuagenarian of an hour ago vanished. Bree propped her up with a sturdy arm under her shoulder. The cool night air was redolent with intermingled cologne, perfume, and alcohol. Bree steered Juli toward the bar, thinking a cold glass of water before they left the building might be in order. She left the older woman propped against a pillar and elbowed through the three-person deep crowd to the white marble counter. When the man to her right complained about her elbow in his ribs, she ignored him and waved at the bartender, who ignored her in turn. The aggrieved man turned. Bree stood face-to-face with Mal.

He threw his arms around her. She smelled the

whiskey that hung in a cloud around his face.

He kissed her sloppily on the lips. "Kept calling your cell. But I had it." He pulled a phone with a pink case from his pants pocket. "Ryder thought you'd be back here." He backed up to give her a glimpse of the man standing next to him, stepping on Bree's toes in the process. She yelped and looked down at her feet.

"I hurt you?" Mal stepped on them again.

Bree backed away. "Grandma's really tired. I left her over there." She pointed in the general direction of the post. "I think she needs some water before I take her home."

Mal fumbled in his back pocket for his wallet. "I'll…"

"I'll get it and bring it over." Ryder waved at a female bartender whizzing by who skidded to a halt and whirled to face him, her tight silver T-shirt sparkling only slightly more than her smile.

Bree hobbled more than she needed to as she and Mal fought their way from the bar.

Mal's mouth hovered near her ear. "Most fun I've had in years." His lips aimed for her cheek but missed and slobbered a kiss on her ear. "So glad we're getting married. Want lots more nights like this."

Bree felt a headache coming on. She slipped her arm through his. "Don't count on it, darling."

CHAPTER 12

For Greenwood, the second night in the car felt less like a punishment and more like a special assignment. After ten, the pedestrian traffic entering and exiting the garage increased, with couples in evening wear, noisy groups of men in cowboy hats and women in tight jeans, and families with dozing toddlers in strollers. Fantasies about what he planned to do to Brianna Acosta kept him alert. The prior evening, at two in the morning, he had double parked his car behind the SUV to keep it from moving and fallen asleep, waking at six with a heart-stopping start to the blast of a car horn. His eyes snapped open and he focused on the retreating white taillights of an impatient driver's car. He slumped at the wheel. He planned to adopt the same tactic every night when he could no longer keep his eyes open. But for the moment, he had no trouble focusing.

A pile of empty aluminum soda cans he had liberated from nearby trash cans rolled over the leather next to him in the back seat. His balled up suit jacket served as a pillow between his spine and the hard, wood paneled door. From where he sat, he had a clear view of the SUV when he raised his head.

The only sound was the tinkling of metal as he rhythmically bent a can until it broke in half. Then he crushed the pieces with the heel of his foot and bent the metal more, carefully folding section upon section. When he finished, he tossed the completed object on the front passenger seat and resumed the same pattern with the next can. The repetition and the slow building of tension to a final moment of creation and release reminded him of sex. When the memories grew too strong and the pressure within him built to an unbearable degree, he cut strips off the rubber floor mats and wrapped them around his wrists like handcuffs, twisting his arms over one another to tighten the loops until his hands tingled and his mind focused only on Paulo.

Paulo didn't want to wear handcuffs the first time Greenwood presented them. His face turned as pale at the dangling silver object that shone dully in the muted light of very distant streetlamps. He scooted his naked body across the rough carpet of the folded down minivan seatbacks, shaking his head. Handcuffs, he said, reminded him too much of the police, of people being arrested, of screaming and violence, of his half unconscious father being hauled down the access steps of their building, his boots banging their protest against the concrete. It took Greenwood half an hour to convince him that these handcuffs were different, that Greenwood would wear them as often as he, that they represented good things like trust and longing, and that they paradoxically freed them both from the nonsensical restrictions of the world. Paulo, as with everything, eventually assented.

In the garage, Greenwood closed his eyes and exhaled, slowly relaxing the rubber spirals until his focus returned and his hands were again flooded with blood. With these breaks to regain his equilibrium, assembling one knife took almost an hour.

**

The stillness of their Noe Valley mansion at night always calmed Abigayle. When she and Griff were first married, she delighted in his roaming the expansive halls, breaking into her bar exam studies with his gentle question, "Mrs. Greenwood, isn't it time to come to bed?" Later, the silence carried the breathing of sleeping babies through open doors. It hushed the incessant clamor of cell phones, muted the San Francisco hum, and lulled her brain from law firm and parenting overdrive into, if not serenity, then at least acceptance. But more recently, the quiet in the wee hours served to normalize the stupor of her marriage.

At some point, whether Griff came home at six in the evening or stayed away until four in the morning ceased to matter. They interacted through their children, because of them, and around them, but never anymore despite them or over them. It was as though the darkness of the night seeped into their days. The unsure, overwhelmed man she married gradually morphed into an irritable, arrogant chief executive with an administrative assistant turnover rate that rivaled the throughput of an assembly line. Early on, she worried their careers pushed them apart and hoped the children would cement them together. But after a while she understood that something darker lay at the root of their troubles. The separate bedrooms they had drifted into were simply a physical manifestation of their cold tangle of unexpressed resentments and fears. When she was honest with herself, she wasn't even sure who Griff was anymore.

She reclined in the middle of the king size bed, her bare legs shifting between the maroon silk sheets, her torso bolstered by oversize pillows. A lap desk propped a sleek silver notebook computer on her thighs. Her eyes flicked periodically to the closed bedroom door.

She rubbed her eyebrows and smiled at the Asian woman who wore purple metal glasses and looked up at her from the screen. "Insomnia. I'm used to it. What time is it there?"

"Seven tomorrow evening." The woman grinned. "I like being ahead of the curve."

Abigayle folded her hands around the back of her neck. "I never saw this coming."

"You're the only one who didn't." The face on the screen stared unblinking.

Abigayle plucked at the sheets. "And they won't come after me?"

The woman shook her head. "You're not the one they want."

"What if they never find him? What if he knew

148

and ran away?"

The woman shrugged and tucked a pen behind her ear. "All the better for everyone concerned, perhaps." The sound of paper shuffling crackled through the laptop speakers. "Start signing the paperwork. And for God's sake, get some sleep. I arrive the day after tomorrow. Then we'll get the ball rolling in earnest."

"What if he calls me?"

The woman arched an eyebrow. "Abigayle, sometimes I have a hard time believing you're a divorce lawyer."

Abigayle sniffed. "It's different from the inside."

"That's why I'm single. Marriage is a fucking mess, from the wedding planning right through to the divorce."

A tear dropped from Abigayle's eye onto the keyboard.

"Don't you have some Xanax lying around? Take a pill and get through. See you Saturday." The screen went black.

Abigayle shut the computer. She tucked her hair into her ponytail and slid off the bed. Her baby blue satin nightgown rippled around her long legs as she walked to the bathroom, where she shuffled through a small collection of prescription bottles, reading the labels. Not finding what she wanted, she slipped on a pair of Birkenstock sandals, wandered down the hall, and paused at the door to the master bedroom suite. Her fingers fiddled with the handle, as though she'd forgotten how to open it. She pushed it ajar. The rumpled bed looked as though someone had been sleeping on top of the duvet, not under it. On the nightstand at her former side of the bed, objects lay exactly as she had left them over a year ago, the outdated fashion magazine and upside down TV remote lying alongside a half-empty shatterproof glass water bottle and a sliver-framed photograph.

She approached and lifted the frame. Her fingers stroked the glass under which her and Griff's faces shone, red cheeked, with zinc oxide smeared noses, above the children's grins, with chairlifts in the background along with the lopsided smirk of a teenage ski instructor. Lake Tahoe. The last vacation Griff organized for the family. The final time he left work completely behind. Her face smiled back at her, relaxed and carefree in a way she hadn't seen in the mirror for a long time. Her son looked into the camera with eyes that transmitted contentment and joy even through goggles. Her daughter grinned in a way that indicated she'd momentarily forgotten that being seen with her parents was embarrassing at best and, at worst, threatening to life as she knew it. Abigayle held the picture closer. That morning was the last time she and Griff made love. Hours before Justin broke his leg on the intermediate slope and was transported back to San Francisco in a helicopter. Months before she began to question why every picture from that holiday included the ski instructor.

She replaced the photograph and turned her back on the bed. In the bathroom that was lit from recessed ceiling bulbs and a hidden fluorescent strip behind the contour of an enormous mirror, she rummaged through cabinets and drawers, digging with eyes half closed. What was she looking for again? All at once, she snatched her hand back from a drawer as though it had bitten her. She blinked. Her eyes narrowed and the corners of her mouth curled down. Slowly, her hand reentered the drawer and emerged clutching a fistful of condoms.

She hurled them at the mirror and they scattered, flapping lazily into the sink, behind the soap dispenser, and in a scatterplot pattern across the white marble counter top. The sobs burst from her chest like the rapid fire of a gun. She sank to the floor and rested her head against the cold gray tiles, one hand pressed to her belly. The other covered her eyes. "I tied my tubes for you."

Minutes later, she scooped a few condoms into her hand and, on her way out of the room, flung them onto the bed. "Have your fun. I'm not playing this game anymore."

She climbed back into her own bed as though she'd climbed fifty flights of stairs to reach it and switched off the lights. "From now on, Griff, you're on your goddamned own."

***

At the same time that evening, Mal fell laughing through the door of their hotel suite. "She thinks Ryder's a real angel." He tripped over his own shoes and fell against the light switch. "Get it? Angel investor." He bent over howling, holding his sides, and lurched to the sofa.

Bree dropped the room key on the minibar and rubbed her temples. "She was so tired she got confused."

He held his arms out to her.

Bree rifled through the bar refrigerator and handed him a personal size water bottle. "How much did you drink before I found you, honey?"

Mal unscrewed the cap and tossed it behind him. "What's an angel investor?"

Bree retrieved the small piece of plastic from under an armchair and placed it on an end table. "Someone with too much money." She reached behind her for her dress zipper. "I'm going to change."

Mal patted his lap. "Come sit here." He leered at her. "I'll help you with your zipper if you help me with mine."

Bree perched herself on the arm rest nearest him and crossed her arms, smiling. "Drink that first."

He gazed at the small bottle with dismay. "It'll make me pee."

Bree ran her fingers through his hair. "It'll save you from a hangover."

Mal took a sip and almost spat it out when his laughter resumed. "An angel." He wiped his lips with the back of his hand. "I have to tell Ryder when I see him."

Bree bit her lip and swallowed before she answered. She had tried, ever since they left the nightclub with Juli, to push the incident with Ryder farther and farther into the back of her mind, hoping to lock it into a box she would never have to open again. But Mal wouldn't stop talking about him.

Ryder met her eyes questioningly before they left the bar, but she laughed in his face at a joke that wasn't funny, mortified, and wishing she would never see him again. The entire night swung between extremes: the intoxication of the dance floor, the humiliation of the kiss, the relief of escape, the horror of potential exposure, the ignominious retreat from the seam, and now Mal's obsession with everything Ryder. When was the last time she had stood on solid ground? She could hardly remember.

Mal shook his head as though trying to steer clear of cobwebs. He tipped the bottle, drained it, and passed it to her. "Now come here, gorgeous."

Bree shifted to his lap and twined her arms around his neck. "You didn't turn out so badly." She kissed his nose and nibbled on his earlobe.

Mal nuzzled his face into her neck, tickling her with his stubble. "I'm no comparison to you, Bree."

She laughed, pushing him back from her and meeting his alcohol hazed eyes. "What *are* you talking about?"

"When I saw you out on the dance floor with Ryder…"

The hair on Bree's arms rose. She held her breath.

"…I said to myself, 'Mal, you're the luckiest guy here. You have a beautiful, smart fiancée who dances like Beyoncé.'"

Bree's fingers caressed his lips. Gratitude and relief melted into her like a draft of sweet nectar. This was the man she loved, the one who focused on her strengths and would always take her side. The one whose sticky whiskey breath smelled sweet and familiar. She closed her eyes and ran her fingers over the accustomed contours of his face, the mole on his chin, his long eyelashes, his thick eyebrows and perfect nose. Her tongue caressed his earlobes, sucked on his neck, avoiding his mouth. One kiss on the mouth tonight was all she could handle.

His hands explored her in familiar ways, cupping her breasts and kissing her nipples through her dress, massaging her buttocks, losing themselves in the tangles of her hair. He unzipped her and slipped the pink lycra from her shoulders, burying his face in her chest, showering her with tiny kisses that made her shiver.

Mal looked up, his face intent. "The window."

This was, she knew from experience, a statement of the only place Mal could imagine making love in this moment. To ask him to do it elsewhere would snap his spell. She had gently prodded many times as to why he avoided a bed, preferring the floor, a chair, a bathtub, a table, a wall, anything except the one place designed to make lovemaking comfortable. He never answered. But as her eyes roved to the massive sheet of glass, she knew she couldn't participate in the way he wanted her to. For one, she thought, that glass would never hold the two of them.

She pointed to the sofa. "How about here?"

He strained to lift her off him and stand.

She twisted off him and to her knees. "How about you against the glass and me like this, okay?"

His eyes focused on her with concern. "Want you to feel how much I love you."

She ran her hands over the bulge in his pants. "Don't worry. I feel it."

She stepped out of her dress and led him to the window in her underwear. He looked back at the city and suddenly reeled. "Long way down."

Bree led him by the hand into the bedroom. He looked at the bed with disappointment. She gave him a soft push. He flopped onto it, eyes half-closed. "Make it up to you."

Bree slipped into the other room and downed two ibuprofen with a bottle of water. When she returned and slipped into bed, he rolled over to face her, eyes closed.

"You're the hottest." He paused and she thought he'd fallen asleep. Then his eyes half opened. "Woman in Vegas."

She stared through the bedroom window at the twinkling, shimmering city. "I'm not, Mal." She closed her eyes. "But I promise to try to make you never stop thinking it."

CHAPTER 13

Bree's phone pinged from the nightstand at ten the next morning, waking her and Mal, who shifted in bed and thrust a pillow over his head. She wiped hair from her face and lifted the phone.

Celine: The best show in Vegas…about to start.

A photo showed Celine and K-Rao holding formal wear on hangers against a backdrop of reddish canyon hills.

Bree: Sweet. Hiking in heels?

Celine texted back a photo of dusty hiking shoes and formerly white anklet shocks turned orange.

Celine: No wedding's worth a broken ankle. See you at reception?

Bree: We'll try.

Celine: Lone Star throws a great barbeque.

Bree slipped out of bed. In the bathroom, hot water from the large rain shower rolled over her. She closed her eyes and breathed in the mingled scents of chlorine and verbena body wash. *Only a few hours ago we were still in the nightclub.* She dispelled the thought and concentrated on the reflection of her naked body in the anti-fog circle of the bathroom mirror.

No magazine would ever use me *for a lingerie ad, not even to appeal to heavy women.* She scrutinized herself. There were bumps where, she thought, no one should have them, and lumps and curves that drew attention to indentations and stretch marks on body parts she wished she could cover permanently with clothing. Why Mal found her sexy, she didn't understand.

She stepped out of the shower and toweled her hair, still turning this way and that in the mirror. With the right clothing and makeup, she thought, she minimized the deficits. She didn't turn heads, but it could be worse.

When she was using the blow dryer, Mal's hand poked through the door clutching her phone. She turned off the machine.

"Did I wake you?"

He shook his head. "Someone's texting." His voice croaked.

She took the phone and nudged the door open. She watched Mal leave the bedroom, return with two bottles of water, and crawl back under the sheets with a groan. She wrapped a towel around herself and tiptoed into the living room. From her purse, she extracted a bottle of ibuprofen liquid gels, tapped two into her palm, and slunk back to the bedroom. She lifted Mal's limp hand from the covers, laid the two pills inside it, and closed his fingers over them. "Take these when you're up for it." She kissed him on the wrist.

"Thanks." The mumble came from under a pillow.

"Want me to tell your mom you're not feeling well?"

The sheets undulated. "What time is it?"

Bree glanced at the bedside clock. "Ten."

Mal rolled on his side. "I'll be up and dressed by eleven."

She chose her clothes, a gray skort and a flowing rose-print blouse and dressed in the bathroom. As she brushed the final touches to her hair, she cocked her head. Something in the mirror looked off. Her hands. What was wrong with them?

"Oh my God." Her gaze dropped to her left hand. The finger where her engagement ring usually rested was bare. She scanned the counter. The thudding in her ears was violent. Her eyes and then her fingers methodically swept the counter. She overturned the wastepaper basket. She crawled on hands and knees, lifted every receptacle and towel, and used a washcloth to sweep the floor. Nothing.

She hoisted herself to the toilet seat and sat trying to remember details from the night before. Her hands felt cold and she jammed them between her legs. She remembered it catching on the refrigerator door when she got Mal the water bottle.

What about after that? They stood by the window. Then she'd helped Mal to bed.

She dashed to the living room. Her dress still lay in a heap by the sofa. She felt it, lifted it, and gently shook it, but nothing fell to the floor. Her mouth was dry. Her feet retraced their steps to the bedroom and she stood at the entrance, hands on her hips. She rubbed the top of the nightstand and the dresser. She fell to her knees again and crawled across the floor. Her fingers felt in the crevices and pockets of each item of clothing in the closet. She stood all her shoes on end.

Mal shifted in the bed. "What time is it?"

Bree glanced at the bedside clock. "Ten-forty."

Mal heaved himself to a sitting position, the pillow flopping from his face onto his lap. "Shower." He swung his legs out of bed, shuffled naked to the bathroom, and closed the door behind him.

Bree got off the floor and threw herself on the bed facedown, her heart thudding. She redid her previous search exactly, inch by inch, hoping she had missed something. All she found was a spool of dental floss under the bed and a business card behind the coffee maker. A knock from the other room stopped her with her hand on the dresser.

She trudged to the hallway door. Her face sank when she spied Faye through the peephole. She undid the lock.

"I wanted to let you two sleep in." Faye swept past her and glanced around the living room.

Bree let out a breath, thankful that exhibit A of what took place the night before was no longer lying on the floor near the sofa. She followed Faye into the room, squeezing her hands behind her back. Her bare finger pulsed its loss like a homing beacon.

Faye cocked an ear in the direction of the bedroom and inspected Bree. "You kept Mal up late?"

Bree tugged reflexively at the hem of her shirt.

Faye's eyes focused on Bree's hands and flashed as she bent slightly forward for a closer look, the large golden cross around her neck glinting accusingly. "You're not wearing your engagement ring."

Bree snatched her hand out of view again.

Faye straightened and locked her eyes onto Bree's. "Are you breaking up?"

Bree blinked. Was that eagerness she heard in Faye's tone? *Or do I still look guilty?* She shook her head. "Of course not. We were tired last night." She waved her arm in the general direction of the window. "I must've put it down somewhere." She walked to the mini bar and lifted the ice bucket. "I was looking for it when you knocked."

Faye pursed her lips and covered her heart with her hands, rolling her head back. "Then the Lord will help us. Does Mal know?"

Bree's thumb played with the empty space on her finger. "No."

Faye circled the living area furniture like a bloodhound, her eyes darting under twitching eyebrows. She sniffed the air. Bree grinned then swallowed her smile quickly, wondering whether odors from the previous night lingered in the room.

160

She tagged after her future mother-in-law, picking up things Faye lifted and replaced, playing the inept Watson to her Sherlock Holmes. After one circuit of the room, Faye lay her hands on her hips. "Tell me exactly what you did last night when you got home."

Bree coughed. Her face turned red. "We sat around for a while. We did some stuff. Then went to bed."

"On the sofa?" Faye placed her hand on its back.

Bree nodded. Faye snatched the seat cushions from the frame one by one, her slim fingers poking into tight spaces. Bree shuddered at what she might find. She knelt down by the window. Her gaze flicked quickly back to Faye, who was on her knees, only half visible, her body twisted so that she reached with one arm past her shoulder under the couch. When she turned back to the city below, her bare foot stepped on something sharp.

She bent over.

Faye extracted herself and raised her head above the coffee table. "Find it?"

Bree leaned on one foot against the windows and inspected her sole. "I think something bit me." She looked accusingly at the ground. A sparkle caught her eye. She lifted the ring and held it for Faye to see before kissing it and replacing it on her finger.

Faye clasped her hands. She leaned on the coffee table to rise. "Now Mal never needs to know."

"Know what?" Mal stood at the bedroom door, clean-shaven, with hair combed, and wearing a fresh dress shirt and slacks. He looked, Bree thought, as though he'd spent the previous night at a prayer meeting not a nightclub.

Faye beamed at her son. "That your father and I switched the menu again. Chicken instead of lamb." She flung up her hands in a helpless gesture. "I couldn't see bothering you with it."

Bree's mouth hung open. *Way to deflect attention, Faye.* She skipped to Mal and gave him a peck on the cheek. She used her left hand to unbutton the top button of his shirt, as an excuse to reassure herself the ring was actually on her finger again.

He eyeballed her phone on the edge of the dresser. "It was vibrating again."

Bree laughed and picked it up. "I completely forgot."

Mal looked at the sofa parts strewn about the room. "What's been happening here?"

Faye handed him a cushion. "Bree thought this was a sleeper sofa."

Bree shook her head. *Impressive comeback.* She wandered into the bedroom.

9:36AM ***Ryder: You all make it home okay?***

9:55AM ***Ryder: Nightclub called. They have Juli's cashmere sweater.***

10:43AM ***Ryder: Never mind. Picked it up for you. Text when you get this.***

She dropped to the corner of the bed.

Bree: How do you know it's hers?

Her phone vibrated with an instant response.

Ryder: They remembered me and her.

Of course they did.

Ryder: Want me to drop it off?

Bree sighed and peeked into the living room, where Mal's mother engaged him in a discussion about appetizers. She leaned the door shut. *Having Mal meet him again is not something I want to have happen.*

Bree: I'll be over.

***

Greenwood cut the idling engine of his car and unplugged his phone from the charging cord. He scrolled through the voicemails, searching for one from Abigayle amid the calls from his lawyer, his assistant, and various unidentified 415 numbers. But she hadn't called.

Whenever he disappeared in the past, she acted as though he'd stepped out for lunch. She updated him on news about the kids and asked him to pick up soy milk at the grocery store, even though they both knew he might not be home for days. He ground his teeth. The world never collapsed because he wasn't there. That wasn't how they played things. It wasn't how he had set things up. He deleted his entire voicemail file without listening to them. "Can't be there for everything. They can figure it out by their goddamned selves."

His stomach growled. He seized the youth-size baseball cap he'd found in the trunk and yanked the brim tightly over his forehead before exiting the car. Head low, face away from the surveillance cameras, he lifted the top from a nearby garbage can and dug through the contents. With a clear plastic container of Caesar salad and half empty soda bottle clutched to his chest, he jogged back to his vehicle with downcast eyes and almost ran into a young mother and her son. The terrified boy clung to his mother's hand. The mother pulled him close and kept walking.

A few feet past Greenwood, the mother stopped and squatted. "Don't be scared, honey. He's homeless. He probably used to live like us and then had bad luck. You want to give him your cookie? He might like that."

The boy buried his snack beneath her windbreaker and shook his head so hard his ear-length brown hair flopped around his head like helicopter blades.

"Remember, homeless people deserve our pity." She stared after Greenwood. But when he stopped and slowly turned toward her, she broke into a run, dragging her son by the arm and throwing anxious glances over her shoulder.

Greenwood glared after them. When he returned to his car, he peered at what he could see of himself in a side view mirror. He brushed fuzz from his lips and spat on his fingers and rubbed at smudges on his cheeks. He sniffed under his arms and wrinkled his nose. His fingers fondled the last remnant of a crease in his trousers. He looked again in the mirror.

A week ago he wore the same suit to a two-thousand dollars per plate charity gala. In the opulent palm courtyard of a downtown San Francisco hotel, a string quartet played Bach while photographers vied for a shot of him with his wife, and his hand balanced a crystal champagne flute of Veuve Clicquot La Grande Dame Rosé. He berated a waiter who knocked his arm, causing him to spill a pin-size drop of liquid onto his pants. Abigayle dabbed the spot with her napkin as he looked imperiously over her head, feeling like a king with his subjects. The room buzzed with his name. Doors were flung open when he approached. People stepped aside. Everyone wanted a chance to be seen with him, shake his hand, or beg for a donation.

At events like the gala, the ability, foresight, and ambition that spurred his rise to the top shone, he thought, with particular brilliance. His role fit him perfectly. His former self disappeared, rendered invisible by the adulation flashing at him from all angles. In such bright light, there was no room for a man who didn't understand who he truly was, who didn't know how to grab what he wanted. When the world told you how wonderful you were, you had to act as though you believed it, to prove they'd all been wrong when they'd said you were worthless, would amount to nothing. The people who said that wouldn't even recognize him now. Griff Greenwood took whatever pleased him. He made his own fantasies come true. He didn't hide from the law, he laid it down.

Wherever he went, kids ran after him, begging for a free toy, wanting his autograph, saying they hoped to be him when they grew up. Videos of his new toys went viral. Children's hospitals flooded him with requests. Kindergartens and elementary schools cancelled classes if he said he'd drop by at the holidays. There was no need to count the awards and certificates he received—all he had to do was look at his office walls to remind himself. He was adored. People loved him. Children loved him. And he loved children back. Because children, he knew, gave him everything. They made all his dreams, even the secret dreams that once shamed him, come true.

And Paulo was the culmination of that love. Paulo loved the gifts he gave him. He loved the money. But Paulo loved Greenwood more. Why else would he send naked pictures of himself from his bedroom? Call his work phone to tell him he wanted him? Sext him from the high school lavatory? Those were signs of love.

Greenwood knew exactly what those signs looked like. His stepfather had shown him. Now he was able to show Paulo. It was a circle completing itself. Starting a toy company was the only thing Greenwood ever wanted to do. It represented a way to children's hearts, to boys' hearts. And now he had Paulo's heart, the heart of a pure eighteen-year-old who looked five years younger than his age but was a consenting adult in the eyes of the law. It was too perfect to be anything but fate. In the space of a few weeks, Paulo had become the beginning and end of everything in Greenwood's life, his passion and his fate, his freedom and his prison, his heaven and his hell.

Before getting into the car in the garage, Greenwood bent to inspect the material of his pants that was flecked with caked French fries and stained with melted chocolate and burger juice. He scratched at it violently with his fingers.

"Go to hell, brat." He called after the child who was no longer visible, his voice echoing in the vast concrete hall. "Go fuck yourself."

He ripped open the top of the salad box. An ear-piercing car alarm screeched through the building. He lurched forward, spilling limp lettuce dripping with gooey dressing into his lap, his head almost colliding with the windshield. When he caught his breath, he swiveled in his seat just as a plump woman in a gray skirt was pulling herself into the white SUV.

***

Abigayle peered through the ten-foot sidelights framing the stainless steel door. The intricate frosted and clear glass pattern afforded her a kaleidoscopic view of the man shifting from one foot to another on the doorstep. She undid the latch and swung the door wide.

"Henry, come in."

The tall man slipped past her and stood in the entrance fidgeting with his car keys. "Can't stay. Illegally parked." His jaw shifted from side to side and, despite Abigayle's efforts to meet his eyes, they avoided hers with the determination of a suspect in police custody avoiding the eyes of his interrogator.

She interlaced her fingers and let her arms hang loosely. "How can I help?"

He darted her a glance then studied the abstract wooden sculpture on the pedestal to her right with the interest of an appraiser. "You know I owe Griff." He took a step toward the door and closed it, keeping his fingers on the handle. "But I shouldn't be here."

Abigayle took a deep breath and moved her hands to her hips. "Henry, when your kid had his rollerblading accident, when he was bleeding like a stuck pig, I carried him in my arms to the hospital." She flashed him a look like a teacher chiding a habitually tardy student. "For God's sake, just spit it out."

The man kicked the floorboards. "There've been rumors for a while." He stepped close enough for her to smell the latte on his breath and notice, through the amber colored aviator sunglasses, the dark circles under his eyes. "Some really nasty accusations."

Abigayle riveted her eyes on his, daring him to look away. "You mean the investigation's started."

He stared back. "You know?"

"I do now." She dropped her gaze and her mouth tightened with the resignation of someone who had stepped over an invisible threshold.

Henry shook his head. "If I were you…" He unlatched the door and stepped through to the outside, poking his head in for the final comment. "I'd start to distance."

Abigayle looked around the wide foyer with its American hardwood flooring, glass brick accent wall, and mauve Chihuly chandelier suspended from the twenty-foot ceiling. She sighed and screwed her eyes shut for a moment, When they opened, their recesses glinted in the reflected light like two polished bullets. She marched to the foot of the wide staircase.

"Hey, you two." She took the steps two at a time while scrolling through the contacts on her phone. "Get out your suitcases."

CHAPTER 14

The atmosphere as she walked through the casino on her way to the garage was only slightly less frenetic than the night before. The areas reserved for gambling, she noticed, were far from windows and doors. It was impossible to tell, just from the surroundings, whether it was eleven in the morning or eleven at night. The music and noise from the slot machines, the calls from the card and roulette tables, the ambient music, the carpeting, the low ceilings, the adequate but not overpowering lighting, and the attractively clad hostesses all contrived to create an intimate and alluring environment. The tables were less populated, but the patrons were equally eager. The pale skin of some indicated they had not stepped outside in days.

Bree passed an enormous hall filled with slot machines. The garish multicolored lights drew her eyes, together with the bells and bings. The flashing machines with their digital payouts in large numbers and enticing phrases, "triple cash" and "lucky seven," were mesmerizing, like the attraction of hard candy mixed with the temptation of an amusement park ride. She followed the Mosaic pattern on the carpet to the closest one, located under a glittering chandelier, and fished in her purse for the complimentary voucher from their room. She scanned the seats nearby. *All I need is Soumil or Faye to catch me gambling.*

She squeezed her purse tightly between her knees, inserted the ticket, and pushed the button, holding her breath as the wheels spun. Near misses flashed before her. Her fingers tightened into fists, willing the images to stop in a line. She knew it was a computer generating random numbers, and if she had been watching a screen of zeros and ones, she would have walked away after the first spin. But the designers knew how to draw her in. And she was willing. When her first adrenaline pumping win made her squeal when it disgorged a voucher for five more dollars, her eyes glazed. *The big winner today could be me.* Her eyes riveted on the circling pictures below the large purple sevens that spurred her on. *This machine is the one.*

When the woman two seats over beat her screen and cursed, the commotion snapped Bree out of her trance. The delinquent was small and innocuous, in a 1980s lavender dress with puffed sleeves and high frilly collar and a thin gold belt cinched at her waist. A cream colored vinyl handbag perched on her lap. Her tight gray curls bounced as tiny fists assaulted the machine. And from her mouth issued colorful language that made Bree blush.

Bree hastily ejected her ticket and, with a quick

171

squint at her neighbor, slid off her seat and jogged toward the garage entrance, feeling as though she had engineered a lucky escape.

Her heart still pounded slightly when she exited the elevator on the second floor and looked across the colossal expense of cars. *Where's the car?* She tried to conjure an image from two nights before, but when she closed her eyes all she remembered was a sense of hunger and her mind being occupied with thoughts of Ryder. She shook her head and found the unlock button on the remote. She strained her ears but heard no sound. The recessed red alarm button on the reverse side looked ominous. *Here goes nothing.* The whoop echoed obnoxiously in the low ceilinged environment. She could see the lights flashing from where she stood and hastily silenced the alarm.

The driver's seat was higher from the ground than she remembered. She used the handle by the front window to pull herself inside. The car smelled faintly of donuts in the sand, transporting her back again to the evening when she had arrived. She started the engine, rolled down the windows, and gunned the air conditioning. As she backed up, the rear camera monitor showed a glimpse of a homeless man rushing toward her car. Bree shuddered and pushed the shift lever into drive, leaving the gesturing man behind. She kept an eye on her rearview mirror, but the only thing on her tail near the exit was a black Mercedes.

When she pulled into the bright near noon sunlight of the strip, she reached into her hair for her sunglasses and was momentarily disoriented when she didn't find them there. The fleeting lack of concentration resulted in her again heading the wrong way down the congested, multilane road. She leaned back and let the traffic take her where it wanted, her mind busy. Should she have told Mal where she was going? Was it clear that Ryder thought nothing of yesterday's incident? Should she turn around and ask him to leave the sweater at the front desk for her to pick up later? At the edge of the city, she made a U-turn and drove slowly back to his hotel, where she pulled past the glitzy main entrance and halted by the middle island. When a white suited attendant in gloves yanked open the door, she jumped.

"Valet parking, miss?"

She struggled to the ground and handed him the key. "How long does it take to get the car when I come back?"

"No more than five minutes." The young man accepted her five dollars with a bow and hopped behind the wheel.

Bree hurried inside, weaving among the Jaguars, Cadillacs, and Mercedeses crowding the pavement at the entrance. The cool air of the hotel hit her like a wall. Her eyes searched the opulent check-in area for signs of Ryder, and when she didn't see him, she slipped along a side passage that led to an enormous, three-story, shopping gallery. She breathed easier. A little retail therapy was just the thing to take the edge off. She could feel her blood pressure dropping as she wandered past voluptuously curved escalators that transported throngs from floor to floor under glass domed ceilings. Marble Roman pillars and statuary lined a huge mosaic water feature. Scents of perfume and leather wafted from large glass doorways.

Bree's eyes roamed the displays, imagining herself wearing the scarves, the watches, the jewelry, and the bags. Her heels tapped reassuringly on the stone walkways. At a window dominated by a life-size pink Indian elephant on which sat a mannequin in a white fur coat, Bree closed one eye and cocked her head. An Asian couple asked her to take a picture of them in front of the display. She obliged and laughed away their profuse thanks. At the next shop, the mannequins wore next to nothing, sporting negligees, bras, and panties. On a whim, Bree stepped inside. White, spacious, partly opened drawers displayed merchandise according to size. Against the wall, at artistic intervals, hung silver rods with hangers of dainty goods. Bree fingered a blue lace of a silk nightgown with an ethereal lily pattern print.

"May I help you find something?" A waif-like attendant hovered in three-inch high heels at her elbow.

"Can you tell me where the larger sizes are?" Bree held the nightgown against her chest and smiled. It covered barely half her front.

The attendant nodded and Bree followed her stick-like figure to the back of the store. They rounded a corner, and in an alcove, invisible from the front windows, on racks with little room to maneuver between them stood another set of merchandise. Bree looked from the jumbled display to the museum-like interior of the rest of the store.

"Are these the same products?"

The waif shook her head. "Those lines don't go up to your size. For people like you, we carry these others."

Bree stared. "You mean…"

The woman scanned her from head to toe. "Plus-size." Another customer entered the store and she turned on her heel.

A picture of the woman who looked like Ryder's former girlfriend sitting in the Tex-Mex restaurant flashed through Bree's mind. That's the kind of customer who gets to shop in the *front* of the store, she thought. The joy of the chase only partly returned as she shuttled hangers from right to left, halfheartedly searching for something she liked. The colors were garish, the styles less sexy, the animal prints overdone. But she found a semi-sheer black lace teddy in her size she knew Mal would enjoy and had the frosty attendant pack it in a gift box.

Swinging the silver bag with ribbon handles, she strolled back to the lobby, feeling calm. The lingerie store had been just what she needed, equal parts retail therapy and reality check. She was happy with Mal. She was happy with herself. Crazy high school idiots had no business intruding on her current reality.

When Ryder answered her call on the first ring, her voice was friendly but unemotional. She explained where she was. He said he would meet her in five minutes. She leaned back on one of the round velvet benches, watching the hotel guests check in. There were Arab men in white thawbs next to multi-generational Asian families in tight Lycra and silk, a pale Midwestern man and woman behind a tanned pair of southern California men. In those few minutes, she heard Arabic, Chinese, German, French, and Thai. Predicting what type of person would next walk through the door was impossible. The magnetism of Vegas attracted all spectrums equally.

Bree focused on the sweater suddenly dangling in front of her.

"Are you mad at me?"

She stood and swiped the sweater from his grasp.

He tried to catch her eyes. "Vegas makes me do things I don't normally do."

"I don't believe that movie line." She tucked the sweater under her arm. "But let me make this clear: what happens in Vegas stays in Vegas."

Ryder rose and stuffed his hands in his pockets. "I had too much to drink."

Her eyes flashed. "You had a different excuse last time."

"Last time?" He regarded her quizzically.

She smirked. "I'm not getting into it."

Ryder gently grabbed her arm. "Seeing you again changed my life, Bree."

"Glad to hear it." She spun on her heel. "But I'm not going to let you change mine."

The automatic doors whooshed closed behind her and she handed the attendant her claim ticket, feeling the warm outside air bathe her. She closed her eyes and inhaled. It was good to have that behind her. She felt like she had stepped off a bobbing raft back onto dry land.

***

Greenwood peered from his car, parked at the side of the immense hotel drive where the uniformed attendant said he could wait. He muttered curses at Brianna Acosta for meandering through the city and followed her with his gaze as she entered the lobby. His engine idled, the air conditioning humming in the strong Vegas sun. He dared not open the windows, for fear the odors within would attract attention and result in his being forced off the property. The already pungent aroma was augmented by the spilled Caesar salad remains that stuck to his clothes and shoes. Standards at hotels in Vegas were more relaxed than elsewhere. But he'd already been mistaken for homeless once.

He spent over an hour waiting for her to reemerge, his engine burning precious fuel, thankful he'd filled his tank at a station before entering the city two nights ago. His head ached and heart pounded. His stomach rumbled and his hands trembled from fatigue, excess caffeine, and anticipation. When she finally exited, he gripped the shift lever, ready to pull into drive.

She took the keys from an attendant, handed him a tip, threw a shopping bag onto the front passenger seat, and hoisted herself inside. Greenwood eased his car behind her and stuck to her like a burr on a dog's coat when she pulled into the flow of traffic.

The hour gave him time to think of his response to various scenarios he envisioned. If she drove somewhere secluded, he would accost her. If she returned to the hotel, he would jump her before she entered the elevator. If she reacted in fear to his demands for the immediate return of his phone, he would force her at knife tip to comply. With a baseball hat and sunglasses covering his more distinguishing features, he was certain he was unrecognizable. The night before, he had taken the precaution of smearing excrement on his license plate. No one could pin whatever happened on him. Two days in a car eating trash and defecating into plastic bags could change a person. It served him well.

His fingers drummed his legs, restless like the curved, spindly legs of a crab, while he waited for lights to turn. He would get the phone, drive home, and sort things out with Abigayle. He'd clean himself up and return to the office. His life would return to normal, as though nothing had changed.

He grinned when she flashed her blinker and turned into the garage. One hand fingered his suit jacket and its pocketful of knives as he followed her around the snaking rows of parked cars. He cursed at her for passing numerous spots in secluded areas. Once, she braked and rolled down her window to question a wandering couple. Greenwood jerked to a halt and sunk low in his seat. The couple shook their heads and the SUV's taillights dimmed again as it continued its search. On the third floor, she found an empty space only yards from the elevator doors. She pulled in quickly and was out of the car and on the concrete before Greenwood could slam his car into park.

He jumped from his seat, leaving the driver's door flapping open and dashed toward her. His voice cracked from disuse. "Hey, lady."

As he approached, the hotel elevator doors slid open and released a crowd of raucous twenty-somethings. The woman slipped past them and into the waiting conveyance. But the young men stopped short upon seeing Greenwood. They glared at him and pushed the women in their group protectively to the rear. One of the men stepped forward, one foot in front of the other, body turned slightly to the side, hands held loosely at hip level. With upper arms the size of a man's thighs, he presented a formidable obstacle.

"Dude, better turn around." He nodded toward the exit to the garage. "Go back where you came from."

Greenwood took a step closer and pointed at the elevator. "I came from in there." He put his hands on his hips and scowled, the same scowl that reduced high-powered attorneys and belligerent businessmen to obsequiousness.

The man shook his head very slowly. When Greenwood didn't move, the man jerked his thumb at one of his compatriots. "Jessie, want to call security?"

Greenwood held his position until the second young man removed a cell phone from his pocket. Then he stepped back. After a few more seconds of the standoff, his shoulders slumped. By now, Brianna Acosta would have disappeared into the bowels of the hotel. He turned and shuffled back in the direction of his car. The group moved deeper into the garage, the men throwing dirty looks at him and the women giggling.

Greenwood flung himself into his vehicle. His jacket with the knives still lay on the passenger seat. He stared down at his shirt front, covered with lettuce. "I look like a fucking maniac."

***

Bree shivered in the chill of the elevator and rubbed her arms. The group that had exited left the scent of stale beer in the air. She wrinkled her nose and wished she had taken the stairs. After transferring elevators and returning to the twenty-sixth floor, she stuffed the lingerie shopping bag into the top of her purse before opening the door.

"Hi, honey." Four sets of eyes swiveled at her entrance.

Bree could hear in the utter silence of the room the echoes of a previously heated discussion. She could see the fight as clearly as if it had happened in front of her. It was evidenced in Mal's slouch, Faye and Val's flushed cheeks, and Soumil's stoic expression and physical distance from the other three family members.

"Let me just put my purse in the bedroom. Then we can all go to lunch." She smiled and tromped past them, actually pleased at the familiarity of the scene. She hid the lingerie box in her suitcase and grinned at herself in the mirror. *You can fix this.*

When she returned, Soumil sat in an armchair by himself, Mal stood with his hands in his pockets by the window, and Faye and Val whispered together by the minibar. Like a German shepherd hurting a flock of errant sheep, Bree circled the room, speaking with each in turn, coaxing them closer and closer together until she had the family standing at the entryway in a tight ball. They weren't smiling, but at least, through her, they were communicating. Mal's hand slipped into hers as they exited. She gave it a squeeze.

The procession stopped twice as it meandered down the hall, picking up Mal's other siblings and his grandmother. When on the seventeenth floor, a bubbly family of four squeezed into the elevator with them and immediately stopped talking when they met with Soumil's stony face, Bree revived their good mood and, by the time they all reached the lobby, had the family and three of her four sisters-to-be laughing.

"Where to?" She raised her eyebrows at Faye.

Faye shrugged. "Back to Uncle Frank's?" Faye threw Soumil a look that seemed to say, "I know that's exactly what you *don't* want, sweetie, so let's go there."

Mal crossed his arms and looked up. His sisters became suddenly very interested in the pattern of the marble floor.

She smiled inwardly as she remembered how, more than once, Stephanie asked her whether serving as the intermediary for Mal's family fighting gave her headaches. Bree smiled. "I love it."

"Don't you want them all to just get along?"

She shook her head. "I know how to do nice. My parents were nice. Your family is nice."

"That's what most people strive for."

Bree chewed on her lip. "That's what I'm

striving for with Mal's family too. Only it's an uphill battle."

Stephanie gave her a funny look. "Do you really want that for the rest of your life?"

Bree shrugged. "You mean a family that needs me? I'll take that."

In the lobby, she offered her usual solution to a two-way impasse: a third, more neutral route. Bree had been keeping it up her sleeve for just such an occasion. Even Faye couldn't argue with a five-hundred dish buffet, an international smorgasbord where everyone could eat what they wanted, in the quantities they wanted.

The family sat at a long set of tables push together, half on the white leather bench, half on the cushioned metal chairs. Bree sat next to Mal, with the twins opposite them. Bree procured a beer and enjoyed watching his shoulders relax. Now and then she slid her chair toward the end of the table and peered across the laden plates at Faye and Soumil, who sat across from other in silence. It wasn't ideal, she thought, but at least they weren't fighting. Her main concern was Mal. And for him she had a plan.

"Did I tell you about my texts from this morning?" She skated her phone across the smooth table.

Mal pulled a shrimp kebab off a skewer with his teeth and shook his head.

"Remember the woman from the elevator?"

Mal chewed and nodded.

"Her friend got married this morning at Red Rock Canyon."

One of the twins interrupted. "Somebody got

married in a canyon? Sweet." Bree showed her Celine's photos and she handed the phone back, shaking her head. "Or not. Sneakers will have no part in my wedding."

Bree winked at the twins. "The reception is this evening. I thought we could go."

"Mal, don't answer until she tells you where it is." The girls giggled.

Mal held the skewer upright, its one remaining prawn looking like the lost dot of an exclamation point. "Where is it?"

Bree smiled. "In a local park. No hiking involved."

He waved the stick like a baton. "Won't we be crashing?"

"It's not crashing if you're invited. Besides," Bree slipped her hand onto his knee under the table, "It's a barbecue."

"She's got you, Mal," his sister told him from across the table. "You'd crawl on your belly through live slugs for a barbeque."

Bree turned to her. "You watch *way* too much reality TV."

Her younger sister-to-be laughed. "After life with our parents, reality TV is tame."

***

Bree rolled down the window of the Uber. The twang of country music floated on the breeze that whipped her hair into a tangle. She laughed and closed it. "We're headed in the right direction."

The car wound its way up an incline and dropped

them off at the beginning of a parking lot overflowing with vehicles. Under wide floodlights, Bree and Mal strode hand-in-hand toward a big tent lit by rows of battery-operated lanterns. Enormous moths fluttered, confused and helpless, around the lights. Chatter from the party ebbed and flowed in southern cadences. Half the license plates on the cars were from Texas, and half of those belonged to pickups. Bree raised her eyebrows. "Lone Star's from El Paso, about a ten-hour drive."

"Then you should feel right at home." Mal swung her hand back and forth in time to the music. "Apparently El Paso folks don't like to fly either."

His nose led them directly to the food. Lone Star wore a smeared white apron and a ten gallon hat in the middle of a cluster of smoky barbecue grills. His face glowed a red that matched his hair, which dripped with sweat. He beamed at Mal, who admired the brisket from afar.

A young woman dashed up to Bree and looped her arm through hers.

"You made it."

Bree gave her a hug. "Celine, this is Mal."

He tore his eyes away from the grills and stuck out a hand.

"This is a wedding. We hug." Celine squeezed him. He returned the embrace by cupping his hands and laying his fingertips on her shoulders. "I can see where your true love lies." She yelled over the music and sizzling. "Lone Star, you got yourself a barbecue fan." She pointed at Mal.

Lone Star waved a pair of tongs and motioned for Mal to join him. Bree nudged him along, waving her phone, then strolled through the crowds with Celine. "Where's the bride?"

Celine's gaze roamed across the large hats and short dresses. "Used to be you could find Grace in a party. She'd be standing on the edge somewhere talking to one person. But these days…" She shook her head. "Love sure does change people."

Bree counted with her eyes. "There must be hundreds of guests."

Celine studied her. "You thinking about your own reception?"

Bree blushed. "My to-be parents-in-law have strict ideas about who should be invited and who should be kept out."

Celine raised her eyebrows. "Then you need to send your in-laws on a vacation."

"I don't want to get rid of them."

"I'm not suggesting you try to lose them. I'm suggesting they need an attitude adjustment." She pointed. "There she is."

An Asian woman with long black hair in a white halter dress danced on a picnic table in the middle of a throng of people. A crown of woven daisies teetered on her head. When she saw Celine, she jumped down with one hand on the flowers. She pulled her arm. "Come join me. I'm doing the PCT. I just invented it." She waved her arms above her head, hula style. "Get it. It's the sun on the Pacific Crest Trail."

Celine laughed. "Hold on there, hiker trash." She gestured to Bree. "This is my elevator buddy."

Grace hugged Bree and, before Bree was half through her congratulations, tugged both their hands, hauling them across the dry grass and onto the picnic table. Bree stood on the seat, eyeing the top with distrust. "If I get on there, it might collapse."

Celine yanked her arm. "It's just like an elevator, girl. If we're going down, we're going down together."

Bree clambered up and couldn't help but laugh when watching Celine and Grace gyrate to the applause of the dancing crowd. The two women's enthusiasm and abandon were infectious. Bree joined in and, the more she let herself go, the wilder Celine and Grace's moves became. It was a tight squeeze, and the two other women made ample use of the benches, but Bree stuck to the top, afraid she might lose her balance or cause the table to flip.

Three songs later, out of breath and chuckling, Bree waved goodbye and jumped down into the melee on the ground. K-Rao, Celine's boyfriend whom Bree remembered from the elevator, hopped up to replace her. Around Bree, people were eating, drinking, dancing, and talking. If Faye were standing beside her with a checklist, Bree thought, Faye would tick all boxes. There was the chef in charge of carving meat. Numerous people helped serve drinks. Flowers adorned tables and people's hair. A DJ matched music to mood. The guests mixed well, and the dance floor was crowded. Yet it was also something Bree hadn't imagined a wedding reception could be: liberating.

Where she had imagined tables of seated guests holding staid conversations, here fast flowing streams of individuals and discussions changed before her eyes. Her future mother-in-law's stingy portions gave way to a sensuous exhibition of indulgence and abundance. Dancing metamorphosed into reveling, with spontaneous bursts of movement, like flashes from lightning bugs.

Bree roamed. Strangers handed her a paper cup filled with champagne and a piece of wedding cake. Families at picnic tables invited her to join them. When a glow-in-the-dark Frisbee landed at her feet and she winged it like a shaking green comment to the long-haired man waving across the grass, he and the fellow players included her in the game and she played until her arm ached.

A cluster of Lone Star's older relatives from El Paso persuaded her to join them on a blue and white checkered blanket spread across the grass. The gray-haired men and women sat in collapsible chairs and were catered to by younger children running to and fro with paper cups, plates of meat, and bowls of dessert. When a young boy tripped and rolled into the mound of strawberry shortcake he had just spilled, everyone laughed, including the boy. An older woman relative led him, joking, to the bathrooms to get cleaned up. Bree inhaled the night air, filled with scents of meat, perfume, and beer.

Mal phoned for directions to where she stood. He arrived balancing two plates heaped to overflowing with brisket, baked beans, sliced pickles, raw onion rings, and white bread. He handed her one of the plates.

Bree nearly dropped it. "This weighs a ton."

187

Mal sank carefully into a cross-legged position.

A neighbor in a denim shirt with mother-of-pearl studs and deep brown cowboy boots passed Mal a stack of napkins. "Son, you and your little lady are going to need these." He chuckled in a deep baritone and held his jiggling belly. "Trust me."

Mal nodded, looking embarrassed.

Bree waved at the gentleman. She tucked a napkin into her blouse and spread another on her lap. Mal looked at her askance. She shook her head. "I know your mother wouldn't approve of my table manners. But I'm not ruining this blouse." She gave the older man a thumbs up and constructed a brisket sandwich from the assortment on her plate.

Mal extracted a spoon from his pocket and scooped baked beans. He kept his eyes on the food, ignoring the tumult around them.

"Does this give you any ideas?" Bree held her sandwich in one hand and gestured toward the party.

Mal looked up. "About what?"

"About what a wedding reception can look like. I feel like a mouse who's been stuck in a cage and somebody just opened the door."

"Don't want anything outdoors." Mal rubbed his nose. "Too many dogs running around."

"Doesn't this give you ideas about how to think out-of-the-box?" She finished the sandwich and wiped her fingers with a fresh napkin.

Mal rolled pieces of brisket into a white bread-style burrito, bit the end, and talked through his mouthful. "Mom doesn't like out-of-the-box."

Bree shrugged. "She's not running the whole

show." She pushed the plate away from her across the blanket. "If I don't get that out of my sight, I'm going to finish it all."

Mal nudged it back toward her. "He cooked it with mesquite." He rolled a second piece of bread. "Mom runs *every* show, whether she gets credit for it or not."

The corner of Bree's mouth twitched down for an instant and then she smiled. "Maybe."

When they finished their food, Mal stretched himself out on the blanket. Bree lay her head on his shoulder. The sky above them was gray with reflected light. Only one planet was faintly visible. A pair of bulldogs roamed past and sniffed at Mal's shoes. He jumped from the blanket yelling in fright. Bree rose, groaning. "Come on." She shooed the dogs away and tugged him down the hill, away from the lights. She showed him how to cup his hands and stare through them at a section of sky. They let their eyes adjust to the darkness until they could see a few previously hidden planets and stars.

"When I was driving here through the desert, I pulled over on the side of the road and looked up. You could see so much more than we can now."

He lowered his hands. "Isn't it scary?"

She continued looking. "It's full of possibilities."

Mal squinted at the bright lights of the celebration. Bree smiled and pushed his shoulders as he trudged up the hill. He laughed and leaned back against her. They were both out of breath when they reached the picnic blanket. The older couples swirled nearby on the grass to the old-time country music blaring from multiple sets of speakers. They motioned for Bree and Mal to join their line dance. Bree shook her head, but the denim shirted gentleman from before grabbed her elbow.

"Learn as you go along, darling."

Bree gawked at Mal, whom two matrons had lassoed. A grin split his face.

Her tutor jerked an elbow in his direction. "Them's two medal winners he's sandwiched between. They ain't gonna let him go." He yanked a bandanna from his pocket and wiped his brow. "They've got too much stamina for me."

Bree's eyes flicked momentarily from the older man's prancing cowboy boots to his face. "You're not doing badly."

He shook his head. "That man of yours got more guts than you could hang on a fence."

Bree giggled and bent her knees in time with his. The maneuvers felt like aerobics class mixed with basic training. The night before at the club she had thought she was dancing hard, but these octogenarians put her to shame. No matter how much she tried, she couldn't keep up. She stomped and kicked and tapped and flicked, but always slightly out of time with the music. Mal, stick figure-ish and clumsy, followed his dual instructors' leads with tongue clamped between teeth and an earnest expression that earned him multiple pats on the cheek and more than one on the behind. Bree's eyes lit up. These women saw in Mal what she saw: a gentle nerd who needed coaxing to come out of his shell.

When, after close to an hour, they excused themselves, the dancing had spread to most of the company. The only people not dancing were the children, who lay under the tent in rows of wiggling sleeping bags, with faces that evidenced little desire for sleep. Bree pointed to Grace, still on the picnic table, only now with Lone Star pressed tightly against her in a slow dance.

Mal pulled her against him. "Let's practice." He swayed with her gently across the grass.

Bree leaned into him. "Practice what?"

"For our wedding."

She lay her cheek against his shoulder. He kissed the top of her head. She closed her eyes. *This*, she thought, *is heaven.*

***

She didn't feel like talking on the drive back to the city. The sights, sounds, and scents of the party still lingered around her like a bubble she didn't want to burst. Her lap was warm with the brisket Lone Star had wrapped in aluminum foil and placed in her hands when they said their farewells.

"It's all got to go." He winked. "Am saving just enough leftovers to get us through the flight to Tahiti."

She didn't want to interrupt Grace, who was having a teary-eyed conversation with family members clustered around a framed photograph of someone who looked like a younger relative. Mal wanted to break in, but Bree pulled him away. "Celine will thank her for us."

In the sedan, she scooted to the middle of the back bench and refastened her seatbelt, so she could lean against Mal, letting his bubble augment hers, taking her back to the slow dance on the grass. He clasped his hands around her torso and pulled her tightly against him. She wiggled to get closer and let her eyes close as her thoughts swung in time to the remembered music. His hands caressed her neck. She took one in her own and kissed it. He rubbed her cheek and then moved his fingers down the front of her blouse, touching her as lightly as a feather would have floated. Her eyes flicked to the rearview mirror. The driver watched the road, seemingly engrossed in the steady stream of late-night talk show news emanating from the car's speakers. Mal's fingers gently untucked her blouse and crept up her stomach. She cringed, as she always did when anyone touched her muffin top. Then she drew in her breath as he cupped her breast. She shot another glance at the driver and squirmed to take a look at Mal's face. He stared straight ahead, his expression blank. She rolled her eyes and nudged him in the ribs. He pinched her nipple. The lengths he was willing to go to avoid romance in bed never failed to startle her.

When his hand trailed back down her torso and across her thigh, she grabbed it and shook her head. Color mounted to her cheeks, and she knew she could never present a poker face to the hotel staff who would open the door for her. How Mal would hide his own excitement she wondered. But hiding it was obviously not on his mind, for his hand then took her own and placed it between his legs. She gave the area a pat and struggled back to an upright position. They were already on the Strip. The plethora of multicolored neon lights around them illuminated the inside of the car. She re-tucked her blouse and peeked at his face, which to a stranger would have presented the same façade as before but in which she could now read a mood slightly tipped toward annoyance. She whispered, "Later, okay?"

He acted as though he hadn't heard her. She closed her eyes and tried to remember the party, but the bubble had burst.

The doormen who rushed to open both sides of their car seemed just as fresh as if they had been greeting visitors at one in the afternoon instead of one in the morning. Things in Vegas, she thought, must just be getting started. She reached for Mal's hand as they walked through the massive, marble columned entrance. It hung limply in hers. She sighed and squeezed it. "Should we get a quick drink?" His steps slowed. She watched his expression and pressed her advantage. "There's a bar on the top floor. Have a little engagement party of our own before tomorrow."

The corners of his mouth twitched up. "Okay."

She grinned and skipped beside him, her heels clicking on the marble.

"Mal?"

The voice froze them in unison. Bree felt her vision of the next few hours shatter with the single word.

Hands on hips, Faye appeared from the side. She maneuvered in front of them and paced back and forth. Soumil stood a few yards away, hands in pockets, eyes focused on the floor. "Our family had plans for this evening. Or did you forget?"

Bree felt rather than saw Mal flinch. He slowly withdrew his hand from hers and dug both deep into his pockets, his gaze dropping to his shoes.

Faye faced Bree. "We all expected you at dinner." She let out her breath. "Grandma was so disappointed."

Bree struggled not to let resentment show on her face. But she wasn't sure she won the fight. "Didn't the twins tell you we were going out?"

"Do you think it's right to have young girls do your dirty work for you?" Faye shook her head. "I expected better of you, Bree Acosta."

Bree bit her lip. *If you can't say something nice, don't say anything.* She paused and searched her mind. "I can see you're upset."

Faye raised her hands to the ceiling. "Lord, give me strength. You take my son away from his parents the night before his engagement party. One of the few evenings we have with him. How is a mother supposed to feel?"

The hyperbole made Bree smile. "I'm not dragging him off to Mexico."

Faye clasped her hands. "Lord help us if you move back to your relatives."

Unexpected anger crackled through Bree like a lightning bolt. She looked at Mal, who edged just perceptibly away from her side. She crossed her arms. "The next time we go out for the evening, we will be sure to let you know."

"Next time?" Faye looked at her as though she had received a slap in the face.

Bree uncrossed her arms. "This *is* Las Vegas." She forced a laugh and gestured at the milling groups around them.

Faye scrutinized Mal. "Was the whole thing her idea, honey?"

Bree reached out and stroked the back of Mal's hand, the same hand that minutes before was playing with her breast. Mal jumped away as though stung. He threw Bree a glance that clearly said, "Don't drag me into this," and shuffled to his father's side.

Bree's mouth dropped open. A sudden waft of cold hotel air made her shiver. She blinked once and locked eyes with Faye. "They were my friends." When Faye didn't respond, Bree wrapped her arms around herself and strode toward the elevator bank, Mal trudging several steps behind. Soumil soundlessly disappeared. And Faye remained alone in the lobby, lips parted in consternation, amid the swirl of excited guests.

In the elevator, Bree blinked back tears as the small, packed lift ascended. An amorous couple separated her and Mal. She turned away from their French kissing and concentrated on the yellow numbers that marked their passage to higher levels.

On the twenty-sixth floor, only she and Mal exited. When the doors closed behind them, she turned. "Why didn't you defend me to your mother?"

"Defend you?" He fingered the mole on his chin.

"You wanted to go too." The tears slid from underneath her eyelids, hot and disturbing. "It's supposed to be the two of us against the world."

Mal strode to a large window overlooking the bright skyline. His eyes focused in the distance.

"You don't need my help."

The hopelessness she read into his response moved her. She wiped her cheeks with the back of her hand and stepped to his side. She lay her fingers lightly over his heart. "Of course I do."

He shook his head.

She sniffed and rubbed her nose. "I know you think I'm strong."

He twisted away from the window and met her eyes. "Not strong. You're the same as my mother."

Bree felt like he'd punched her. She stared, trying to gain foothold in his eyes but failed. Her hand moved to take his but dropped before she touched him.

His lips barely moved. "She wants to make people miserable. You want to make them happy. But you both want control."

The elevator opened and expelled a gang of laughing teenagers who tumbled into the lobby and cantered down the hallway. In the echoes of their mirth trailed silence. Mal wandered into the empty elevator and Bree, unable to move, watched the doors shut behind him.

CHAPTER 15

A narrow shaft of the next morning's light peeked through a chink in the room darkening curtains and fell across the bed where Mal slept. Bree sat in an armchair opposite. Her hair fell in disorganized tangles. Dark circles rimmed her eyes.

Before Mal stumbled to bed at about two-thirty, Bree found sleep impossible. The mattress shook as he crawled in between the sheets. Bree pretended to be asleep, her back turned, her breathing regular. Minutes later, he snored gently. His twitching and nocturnal mumbling, which she usually found endearing, annoyed her. She wanted to fling a pillow at him. When he rolled over and exhaled deeply directly onto her neck, his warm breath mingled with the odor of recently consumed alcohol, she got up.

She tried sleeping on the sofa in the living room. She listened to a book on her phone. She launched a meditation app. But she couldn't stop the continuous playback of Mal's saying she was the same as his mother.

When his alarm went off, she climbed carefully back into bed and rolled over to greet him, not knowing what to expect, either of him or of herself. But his expression indicated nothing except the misery of waking up with a hangover. His bloodshot eyes blinked at her and his mouth cracked into a smile. He kissed her tenderly and pulled her into his arms for a hug.

"Stay put." She slipped out of bed. "I'll make you a cup of coffee."

She threw on a hotel robe and tiptoed into the living room, closing the door behind her. While the coffee was brewing, she threw the security lock into position on the hallway door. *No impromptu visits* this *morning.* Balancing the full mug in one hand and holding a water bottle and two ibuprofen in the other, she unlatched the bedroom door with her elbow and nudged it open with her hip, eyes on the coffee.

Mal coughed. Preoccupied with the level of liquid and expecting to find him in bed, she started when she looked up to find him instead in the middle of the floor, naked and aroused, with arms spread wide. She screamed and dropped the coffee. It spilled in an arc, landing across his left foot. The mug cracked and in her hurry to help him she stepped on the stoneware shards. For a moment, they both hopped on one foot through the room, Bree dripping blood and Mal watching an ugly red burn grow on his leg. She put both feet to the ground, touched one heel gingerly, and dragged him by the hand into the bathroom, where she helped him hobble onto the bathtub edge and let cold water run on his burn. She hoisted her own leg into the sink and turned on the tap. When their eyes met, Bree felt a tickling at the back of her throat. Her eyes sparkled. Mal's sparkled back.

He chuckled. "We're quite the pair."

She giggled. "Are you okay?"

He looked at his leg. "The water's helping. You?"

Her growing laughter made keeping her leg elevated difficult. She turned off the tap and examined the cut, her belly shaking. "It's hard to see." She snatched a hand towel from the rack and dabbed her eyes.

Mal patted the side of the tub. "Come over here."

She tottered on one foot across the smooth floor and plopped herself on the rim next to him. He bent and kissed her foot. "I wanted to surprise you." The confession sent them both into another convulsion.

"You managed that." She dried her eyes on her sleeve.

He rubbed the back of her head and pulled it toward him so that their foreheads were touching. "Sometimes I do stupid things." The words burst out as part of a chuckle, which he eventually subdued. He raised his head. "I didn't mean to hurt you."

When she caught her breath, she kissed him on the lips. "I know."

***

It was apparent to Bree that shopping was, for Mal's sisters, a unifying occupation. Val suggested a "girls only" lunchtime outing, the twins jumped at the opportunity, and Amy wasn't able to control her glee at being invited. Bree momentarily worried that Faye would spoil the party, but she was occupied in last-minute preparations for that evening's extravaganza. If Bree read her to-be mother-in-law's eyes correctly, relief at Bree's not interfering trumped fears of being excluded. She wished them off with a wave, only adjuring them not to be tempted to support "this city of sin and perdition."

At the sight of the shopping plaza designed to mimic the streets of Venice, four pairs of eyes lit up. Amy waved a hundred-dollar bill as she stood on the edge of the main water feature. "I can't wait to spend this."

Bree snatched it and stuffed it back in the girl's pocket. "Somebody will mug you." She put her arms around Amy's shoulders. "Where did you get that?"

Amy leaned in close, with one eye on her sisters ogling the gondolas. "Dad gave it to me." She raised one eyebrow and cast a knowing smile at the ceiling. Her next sentence was lost as the amazement at the sight of its realistically painted blue sky with clouds overwhelmed her. Bree led the still gawking teenager to the dock where her siblings clustered.

Val contemplated their group. "They can take up to four in a boat."

Bree raised her hand. "You guys are going." Inside her purse, her phone rang. She clasped it and waved at them. "It's fate. I'll be here when you get back."

Amy objected, saying they could split into two boats. But Bree shook her head. "Remember this as sisters." She helped Amy into the rocking conveyance. "Besides," she watched the gondolier push carefully away from the dock, "we're coming again for my wedding."

She leaned on the railing and took out the still ringing phone. It was Ryder. With a hand on one hip, she answered, watching the slowly receding boat. She gave up trying to keep the irritation out of her voice. "What about the words 'leave me alone' don't you understand?"

"Where are you?"

"At the gondolas. My *fiancé's* sisters are taking a ride."

"Are you alone?"

Bree raised her eyebrows. "What on earth does it matter to you?"

"I'll be there in ten minutes." He hung up.

She stared at the phone as though it had grown legs in her suddenly sweaty palms. She wandered from the dock. A marble one-story waterfall with vines growing on either side, made to look as though the passersby were strolling through an Italian arcade, splashed and gurgled nearby. But only when a mother yelled at her toddler not to climb into the basin at its base did Bree notice it. She watched water hit the marble, dance with reflected light, and disappear into the hidden drains and pipes that cycled it back to the top to endlessly repeat its fall.

Near the bathrooms by an entrance far from the gondolas, she found some benches and sat, wondering how long he would search for her before he gave up.

The tap on her shoulder made her jump. Ryder slid, slightly out of breath, into the space next to her, his face flushed, his wavy hair windblown.

"You were supposed to go to the gondolas."

He fidgeted with his cell phone as though it were too hot to touch. "This entrance is closest to my hotel."

"Just my luck." She pulled at her shirt and stood.

He laid a hand on her arm. "I get you, Bree."

"I don't get *you*, Ryder." She jerked her arm from under his hand. "Not your stupid high school tricks. Not your following me to Vegas. Not your kissing me last night." She ground her teeth at the sound of her own voice's quavering. "And least of all your showing up now."

He rubbed his tan shorts, his fingers tracing the outlines of his pockets. "I want you with me at the beach."

Bree exploded. "What's with the stupid beach?"

"It's what I was trying to tell you ten years ago, at prom."

Bree held her hands over her ears. "I heard loud and clear what you said ten years ago. A pity date." A tear slipped from beneath her lashes.

"Pity date?"

At his incredulity, her tears dried, as though evaporated by the heat of her anger. "You're a lying, selfish, heartless prick, Ryder Fitzgerald."

He raised his gaze to hers. "I swear, there was no other girl in the school I wanted to take."

Bree's eyes narrowed. "Is that what you came

here to tell me?"

"I thought…" He sat erect. "You should know."

She took a step backward. "I don't believe you."

Ryder's gaze shifted from her eyes to his lap. "I thought you were the most attractive girl in the school."

Bree licked her lips and spat out her words. "And what am I supposed to say to that? That I've spent ten years worrying and now I'm relieved? Poor fat Bree Acosta now has a happy high school memory?"

He pushed back an inch on the seat. "You're getting it all wrong."

"You called me heavy."

He shook his head. "I said my mother was heavy."

Bree ran her fingers through her hair. "Whatever."

He touched her arm. "I didn't come here to fight, Bree."

She flicked his hand away. "So why did you come?"

"It's not going the way I wanted it to."

The hand that had slapped him tingled. "It never does."

He rose slowly, pressing himself from the bench like a ninety-year-old. "You're engaged."

She turned. "I've got to pick up my sisters-in-law to-be at the boat dock."

"Take care, Bree."

She stomped away and then wheeled. "It's a nasty thing to do, you know. Try to rewrite history."

"Rewrite history?"

She glared at him, her fist clenched around her phone, her eyes burning into his. "Couldn't you let me believe that it was pity?"

"Thing is, Bree." He rose from the bench and brushed his shorts so the crease fell straight down his leg. "I couldn't."

She spun away. Her question came out in a whisper, though she wanted to scream it so loudly that the entire city would reverberate with her cry. "Why not?" But when she turned back, he was gone.

CHAPTER 16

Today was their one month anniversary, Greenwood thought, studying the cell phone photograph. A smiling youth posed on a lawn with a soldier action figure. It was a proof for an advertisement featuring Paulo. He zoomed in on the face and ran his stubby finger over the boy's lips.

The first few seconds of kissing Paulo always transformed Greenwood. The mingled rush from the risk of being caught, the feral scent of the boy's teenage body, the desire that burst in flaming simultaneous waves from Greenwood's crotch down to his feet and up to his head, transported him to an addictive place that constantly called him back.

Again and again, he would promise himself he would stop, cease running risks, gird his desires, climb into the cleansing light of normality and let the youth go free. But he couldn't. "It's your fault, Paulo," he would explain in the darkness. "If you weren't so fucking beautiful, I wouldn't have to sneak around. If you hadn't seduced me, I wouldn't have become the two-faced shit I am. I could get in trouble for having sex with my employee. People will think you're underage. So really, you control everything." He would take Paulo's face in one hand and raise a trembling fist. Paulo would flinch and close his eyes. The moment of transcendent vulnerability would douse Greenwood's fiery rage. He would shower the smooth skin with kisses. And the cycle would begin again.

At an audition a month before, Greenwood sensed the start of what he knew would be, if not his final end, the end of life as he knew it. Over the past year, photographs and videos grew increasingly unsatisfactory in quenching his desires. The two dimensionality of his longing became nauseating, repulsive. The images disgusted him and, in turn, made him disgusting. He needed a male of his own. He needed companionship. He needed victory. He needed to feel the warmth, the throbbing, the wetness. He needed the revenge.

Then, thirty days ago, the casting director introduced him to twenty boys selected as possibilities to feature in the new commando collection advertisements. Greenwood scrutinized them, prowling not for prey but for billboard possibilities. Yet something inside him tingled. Something unusual, something that told him that today there might be more. That a door might open and he could stride through, not by chance, but by asserting his will. He could use the power he spent his adult life accumulating to craft an ultimate act of defiance. The possibility shimmered in front of him like an enticing mirage.

Then, after sixteen handshakes, Paulo laid his pliant, soft, child-like hand in Greenwood's, meeting Greenwood's gaze with unfathomable brown eyes and long lashes, and holding Greenwood's grip more gently than any other boy. It was the sign he was waiting for, the invitation, the command.

Making contact with Paulo was easy. Paulo's mother was enthusiastic about their spending time together. Her son visiting the offices of the CEO of the company was an honor, she said. Her son being whisked away in a limousine was a miracle. Did she notice when things turned? Her son coming home later in the evening and finally not at all?

Why did mothers never notice the important things? His own mother never noticed when his stepfather spent more and more time in Greenwood's room. She never questioned why the door was locked from the inside. That's a mother for you, he told himself. Self-centered and preoccupied. And, in the end, he was grateful. His own bad mother helped him understand Paulo's situation. It gave him the opportunity to show Paulo how much he was truly worth.

A jiggle from the phone interrupted Greenwood's anniversary musings. He let the incoming call go to voicemail, then hovered, ready to swipe left to delete the message, but hesitated before completing the action. His company's chief legal counsel had never called before. Greenwood stared out the window beyond the avenues of cars to the spec of blue sky he could see in the distance. He looked at his hand, to his mind noticeably paler than two days ago, his carefully crafted suntan bleached by the constant exposure to neon light. How much longer would he have to sit here? She had to come back to the car soon. No one could stay locked up in a Vegas hotel forever.

He swiped back and skimmed through the written transcription of the attorney's message. Then he read it again.

He threw the phone into the foot well, where it plummeted through the ankle-deep detritus of his homeless existence and disappeared. "Why didn't you bar the police from my office, you ignorant shit? Did they have a warrant? Did you even ask?" He kicked the floorboards. "I owe you, my ass. They've got nothing. The only pictures are on my phone. Once I get it back, everything will be solved."

He leaned on the horn, letting the harsh reverberation drown out his curses. His fingers snatched one of the knives from the pocket of his jacket and stabbed it into the armrest. The leather and foam yielded as mouse flesh yields to a hawk's talon. The blade halted only when it made contact with hard plastic. He jerked the clumsy dagger out, raised his arm to the ceiling, and let it fall like an axe, heavy with purpose.

***

After the gondola ride and shopping trip, things were rushed. They returned later than expected, because Amy was unable to decide where to spend her father's money. In the end, she returned with a twenty-dollar tank top and her change crumpled tightly in the pocket of her shorts. With only an hour to spare before the family left the hotel, Bree had little time to get ready.

The meeting with Ryder left her preoccupied, confused, and irritable. And over the course of the afternoon, the feeling didn't lesson as she hoped it would. When Mal wanted to inspect her purchases, something she usually found endearing, she snapped at him for micromanaging. He retreated into the living room to finish getting dressed. She snatched her clothes from the closet and slammed the bathroom door.

In front of the mirror, she smoothed product into her hair, teasing it at the ends, her bad mood hanging over her like a fog. She shook a finger at herself. "You *love* him." She smoothed on lipstick, smacked her lips, and stepped into her dress.

A tentative knock on the door interrupted her eyeliner application. "Bree, honey? Are you ready?"

Bree shook her head but opened the door.

"You look beautiful." Mal kissed her on the lips.

"Did you have to do that?" Bree stepped back in front of the mirror, jerking a tissue from its box so violently that the whole container clattered to the floor. She dabbed at the edges of the smudged line.

Mal retrieved the box and set it gently on the counter. "I know you're nervous."

Bree presented him with her back. He zipped her dress. "Sorry. I'm a little on edge at the thought of being the center of attention tonight." She threw him a wan smile.

The zipper caught his finger. Mal winced. "This

is Mom and Dad's show anyway."

Bree patted his behind. "Our wedding will be *way* more fun."

Half an hour later, at Uncle Frank's restaurant, Mal's arm shook slightly when he looped it around Bree's. "I think I'm nervous too."

"Let's keep our eyes on the prize." Bree intertwined her fingers with his and kept her voice low. "Our wedding's what counts."

She peeked through at the guests and latched him against her side, making Stephanie's gift bracelets jangle playfully on her wrist. The subtle rose pattern woven in shiny black thread into her black matte cocktail dress shimmered. She sucked in her stomach, hoping she looked less wide from the side than she feared. She drew a deep breath. "Here we go."

They stepped through the archway.

In the hours between the end of the lunch rush and now, Uncle Frank and his staff had transformed the room by pushing planters into new configurations, creating the effect of a ballroom with strategic alcoves. The many circular and square tables were clustered at the back. As she and Mal walked down the center aisle, the guests gave them a standing ovation. Men in sport jackets and women in flowery dresses and saris stared. Bree winkled her nose and, out of the corner of her eye, assessed the crowd. The average age seemed close to sixty. Too much hairspray and heavy perfume, she thought. At the front of the room, opposite the entrance, was an open area and beyond that a low stage with a single microphone on a stand. Hidden speakers played a familiar classical tune Bree couldn't place.

At the first table near the front, Faye motioned them to two empty seats. Soumil pulled out her chair and edged it carefully under her, the back of the seat hitting her knees just at the right instant. He placed his hand briefly on her shoulder and gave it a squeeze. At the unexpected gesture, Bree turned to look at him, but he had already stepped away. The room quieted. Guests resumed their subdued chatter, mostly in English, but also in what Bree assumed was Gujarati.

Under her napkin lay a program of the evening's events. Bree felt her blood pressure rise. She nudged Mal. "This isn't the version I saw." Her finger rested on *Motivational talk by hotel chain marketing guru.* She focused on Soumil and Faye ambling through the company, shaking hands with the men and hugging the women. "Is this a party or promotional event?" She slapped the napkin across her thighs.

Mal sipped water before answering. "I think it's both."

"Did you know about the guru?"

Mal nodded. The waiter placed a small plate of appetizers in front of him.

Bree pushed the plate away. "When?"

"Sometime last week?" He lifted his fork.

Bree wadded up her napkin, threw it on the table, and pushed back her chair. "I'm going to the bathroom."

Mal's hand brushed her skirt. He peered up at her. "You're the one who said this is my parents' version of a good time."

"Order me a martini and have it here when I get back." She leaned down and kissed him lightly on the lips. "It'll help me pull myself together."

Mal cringed. "It's wine and beer only, remember?"

"Oh, Lord." Bree rubbed her forehead. "Just have a glass sitting here when I get back."

She gave Mal a thumbs up and marched in the direction of the restrooms. Near the recess that led to the men's and women's rooms stood Uncle Frank. Bree threw him a glance she hoped made clear she wasn't going to put up with any more of his hanky-panky. But when he opened his arms and boomed across the two tables near them, "Bree, my gorgeous niece, come let me give you a hug and welcome you into the family," the approving glances forced her into a brief embrace. How he managed to squeeze his upper arms suggestively into her breasts, she couldn't understand. But he did.

She recoiled and glared at him, with her back to the tables. Then she crooked her finger and called him into the darker hallway the way to the lavatories. He bounded toward her, his eyes glittering with anticipation. When they rounded the corner, she about faced, holding her arm out to stop him. He leered at her from arm's-length, out of breath from the few eager steps, his stomach jiggling.

"If you *ever* try something like that again with me," Bree hissed, "I'm going to take your arm…" She peered down the short hallway to make sure no one was looking and grabbed his thumb, twisting it unmercifully. His eyes widened. He held his other hand against the wall as she wrenched his forearm against his lower back. "And break it."

She released it and stepped back. He groaned and massaged his hand, regarding her with respect.

"That goes for Mal's sisters too." She wiped her hands on her dress. "My adopted brother was a Marine. Keep your slimy hands where they belong."

In the bathroom, she leaned against the wall, laughing.

Where did that come from? That move was the only one Kacey taught her after his basic training, thinking it might help her one day in a dark alley. But until a moment ago, all she thought she remembered was his "control the thumb and you control the person" mantra. She caught her breath and tugged her clothing back into position.

When she returned to the table, Mal eyed her inquisitively. "Were they serving drinks in the bathroom?"

Bree giggled and took a sip of her red wine. "Something like that."

An hour and thirty minutes into the event, they were a quarter of the way down the program. Bree's stomach growled. During the main course, Soumil and Faye escorted her and Mal from table to table, introducing her to hundreds of people she would never see again. They returned to their table to find their plates removed and the wait staff invisible. Bree twiddled her thumbs through Faye's long blessing and suppressed yawns during the toasts that spoke more about long-standing business relationships, future collaboration opportunities, and market growth than love, marriage, or even family. When the wait service finally started again, she ordered a second set of dinners to be delivered to her and Mal, only to be pulled to her feet by Faye.

"It's time for your dance." Faye shoved her and Mal toward the open space in front of the tables.

Bree cast a longing glance at the empty tablecloth. No DJ was evident, but the music suddenly switched to a romantic song from the 1970s, something, she guessed, likely to have been one of Faye's favorites when she was growing up. Mal wrapped an arm around her and shuffled across the carpeted floor. Spasmodic clapping issued from here and there in the large room above the hum of conversation. Bree's stiletto heels caught in the pile and she had to periodically yank them free, giving her motions a jerky, spasticity appearance.

She leaned close to Mal's ear. "We're going to need a wooden dance floor for the wedding."

A particularly strong carpet fiber strand snagged her shoe. In rescuing it, she accidentally kneed Mal in the groin. He released her and doubled over, his fists clenched at his thighs in a desperate attempt not to clutch at his privates. The room erupted in laughter. Even those who didn't witness the incident were soon told and joined in the mirth. Bree, unable to hold back her own amusement, chuckled and rubbed Mal's back.

"Are you okay, darling?" She covered her mouth, trying not to smudge her makeup.

Mal slowly righted himself, his face pale. He threw the audience a sheepish grin and hobbled to the microphone, Bree following. "We are actually a better fit than that." A few cheers erupted, along with shouts of encouragement. He paused between sentences. "We appreciate your coming. Enjoy the dancing. Watch out for those knees." After the laughter, the dance area slowly filled with older couples whose footwear was more amenable to the floor covering.

Mal limped in the direction of the restrooms. Bree returned to their table alone. Faye and Soumil were off schmoozing, the siblings had disappeared, and the only other person left was Juli. When Bree sat down, the older woman moved and took the chair beside her.

"I should have saved you some of my dinner." She pulled a basket with a forlorn, dry piece of Indian bread in it toward Bree.

Bree examined the bread and closed the cloth back over it. "I'm sure someone will bring me something."

The grandmother cocked her head at the dancers and smiled at Bree. "They should be playing Elvis."

Bree laughed. "Faye could have gotten one of your Elvis impersonators to come."

"Oh, that would not be possible. Tonight is the contest. They would all be busy."

A waiter deposited two laden plates on the table, one for Bree and one for Mal. Bree talked between bites. "I'm sorry you have to miss it."

"Nothing to worry. Ryder was texting me an Internet website location." She reached in her purse. "It is discussing about many contests." She pushed and scrolled on her phone.

Bree slowly put down her fork. "You're…texting with Ryder?"

"Oh, yes."

"When did he send you the website?"

The old woman's eyes scrutinized the screen. "That is being exactly twelve twenty-eight this afternoon." She looked up, blinking. "So accurate."

Bree fiddled with her napkin and chewed on the inside of her lip. "So…that's when Mal's sisters and I were at the shopping mall."

"Yes." She held the phone out to Bree.

Bree hesitated but then took the phone and read.

Ryder: Too bad about the contest timing. How's prep for tonight's party going?

Juli: Only I am here. Shopping mall is calling girls.

Ryder: Bree too?

Juli: Yes. Girls shopping. Parents planning. Grandmother taking nap.

This was followed by a sleeping face emoji.

Ryder: Mal went with the girls?

Juli: Mal is planning.

Ryder: Sleep well.

Juli: Please be wishing me dreams of Elvis.

Bree slid the phone back across the table, her eyes focused on the room's far wall. After a moment of silence, she picked up her fork and moved the food around her plate, trying to keep her voice neutral. "Do you text a lot with Ryder? Tell him what you're up to during the day."

The wrinkled fingers, slightly bent with arthritis, closed around the phone. "It's sometimes being lonely in my room."

Bree thought of the small room allotted to Mal's grandmother, how when they picked her up, she was often sitting cross-legged on the floor, leaning against the armchair, flipping through a magazine or staring at the TV. She was certain Mal's parents didn't include her in activities that didn't involve the rest of the family. And while the rest of the family had roommates, she had none. Of course she jumped at the chance to text with Ryder. Bree stabbed a piece of chicken. *And, of course, Ryder jumped at the chance to spy on me.*

CHAPTER 17

In their suite after the party, Mal threw himself fully clothed diagonally across the bed. He pulled a pillow over his head. Bree untied his shoes and wrenched them off his feet. She grabbed him by the ankles and slid his legs until he was lying relatively straight on his side. The pillow moved and half his face appeared.

"Come to bed." His hand flapped in midair, trying to grab her.

She evaded his attempts. "Not yet. I'm going to pack so I don't have to do it in the morning."

Mal removed the pillow, sat up, struggled out of his jacket, and tossed it to her. He flopped back, as though the effort had exhausted him.

Bree knelt by the edge of the bed. "Unzip me, would you?" She felt his cold hands fumble with the zipper and then undo her bra. "Hey, I was planning on keeping that on." She scooted the sagging shoulder straps back into position.

Mal laughed up at her. "I'm trying to help you pack."

Bree smiled. "Unless you want me arrested for indecent exposure tomorrow, I'm going to need at least one bra that stays *outside* the suitcase." She stepped out of her dress but re-fastened the bra closure. Wearing her bra and tummy shaper, she dragged their baggage out of the closet.

When, a few minutes later, gentle snoring issued from the bed, she propped her cell phone on the dresser and broadcast one of her favorite playlists at low volume. Her feet and hips kept time with the music as she folded blouses and skirts, depositing them in layers in a suitcase. At the party, she eschewed dancing after the incident with Mal's crotch, with the exception of one slow dance with Soumil in her bare feet, where his warm hand had encircled her waist and fingers with proper decorum.

Bree was surprised by his dexterity as he guided her carefully around the floor.

"Have you enjoyed yourself?" His large brown eyes glanced at her face before flitting away to resume contemplation of the far wall.

She bit her lip. "Everybody seems to be having a great time." Her eyes roamed across the still packed dance floor. "Whoever is in charge of the music certainly has their finger on the pulse of this guest list."

Soumil blushed, his cheeks darkening. "It was I."

Bree lost time with the music and stepped on his foot. "You chose the music?" Soumil lifted his arm and she twirled underneath it, while her mouth hung open in surprise. "You're a man of hidden talents."

The corner of his mouth edged up for an instant.

"You have to know your customers if you want to build a solid business. It's all about marketing."

"So you really *are* marketing your business here?" Bree whistled softly. "Strangely enough, I'm not insulted. I'm impressed."

Soumil dipped her, leaning forward and supporting her back in a gesture that was both practiced and effortless. "Please don't misunderstand. This party is about you and Mal. What I am marketing is the two of you. I'm drumming up support for your future happiness, making sure Mal has the contacts he needs to succeed, and advertising how special our family is because it can attract someone like you."

A warmth rose in Bree's chest. She squeezed his shoulder. "That's beautiful."

"In this family, sometimes you have to look for meaning *behind* words and actions. Things aren't always what they appear on the surface."

The bedroom's top dresser drawer screeched as she opened it. Bree peeped at her fiancé, but he didn't stir. She pulled out handfuls of underwear, piling them on the dresser. Her fingers searched the crevices at the back and encountered something silky but hard. She drew it out and unwrapped a pair of her panties tangled around a silver cell phone. She dropped the unfamiliar cell phone between the piles and stared at it.

She spoke softly as she pulled on a loose top and her only pair of shorts. "I've got to go downstairs to the lost and found. Somebody left their phone in a drawer. They're probably looking for it and going crazy."

***

Toward morning, Bree woke almost every hour, unable to sleep deeply, worried her alarm would fail and prevent her from driving the family to the airport. When she dozed, her mind wandered through scenes of dropping Mal and his family off, of driving alone through the desert and getting a flat tire with no other car in sight, and of drifting through Venice with Ryder in a gondola on a receding tide with no way to steer the boat. This final image erased all fantasies about sleeping soundly from her mind. An hour before she had planned to get up, she nudged the covers aside and slipped into the bathroom. By the time Mal awoke, she was dressed and had the suitcases lined up in front of the door. She sat sideways in the bedroom armchair, dangling her legs over the arm rest, kicking them back and forth through the air.

Mal kissed her on the forehead as he passed on his way to the bathroom. "You look nervous."

She smiled. "Just antsy."

He failed to shut the door behind him and his morning explosions and expulsions propelled her into the living room. She stood at the window, nose pressed against the glass, feet spread-eagled, arms bent at the elbow like goalposts. The city below crawled slowly from its Sunday morning bed. Helicopters circled a neighborhood in the distance, hovering low, predatory and expectant. Buildings threw long shadows across empty streets that until a few hours ago had pulsed with action and light. A few pedestrians peppered the sidewalks, like ticks searching for food on a hairless dog.

"I'm going to miss that window." The bedroom doorway framed Mal in his underwear. "You look like you're about to do a bungee jump."

Bree pried herself reluctantly from the glass. "It makes me feel like I could fly."

Mal retreated into the bedroom, but she could still hear his voice. "Flying's not like that. It's more like sitting in a big, slow bus." She heard him zipper his pants. "If you're not near a window, you don't even know you're moving." His dark haired head poked around the corner of the door frame and peered at her quizzically. "I didn't mean to go on about it."

Bree threw the city one more glance and pulled her pink phone from her purse. "It's almost time. Meet me at the elevators. I'll make sure everyone else is ready."

Walking down the hall, she hummed an old camp song. Gathering people for an outing always awakened memories of the summer after sophomore year in high school, when she and Stephanie volunteered as counselors at a rural day camp for children who would otherwise have spent the school vacation in the city. Stephanie called it their "summer spent herding sheep." The camp was located on a defunct strawberry farm, with acres of overgrown, dry grassy fields, a trickle of a river, an Olympic size concrete swimming pool surrounded by a creaking chain link fence, and an enormous wooden barn with swings hung from rafters, a small stage built in one corner, and ladders to an expansive loft where children sat on a railingless edge during sing-alongs, their sneakered feet swaying far above the counselors' heads, making Bree dizzy with fright. She was much happier on solid ground, racing after a wandering stray who had not heard—or pretended not to hear—the injunction to gather at the picnic tables under the cluster of broad oaks. On fiercely sunny afternoons when everyone retreated to the shade and relative coolness of the barn, she would entreat her colleagues to halt the steady flow of small bodies that clambered up the ladders to the loft, her arms wrapped around the children in her charge, holding them back, ignoring their pleas. "One mistake and somebody could fall," she would remind the young faces that stared after their friends with longing.

The merciless preteen camp attendees quickly nicknamed Bree's group the Bottom Feeders, reducing some of her more vulnerable kids to tears. After a few weeks of sobbing, fights, and attempted mutinies where one part of the group tried to distract her while the others dashed for the ladders, Bree shifted tactics, realizing that no single person could physically prevent fifteen children from climbing to dangerous heights. She decided to teach them to love the ground. She checked out library books on sharks and distributed them the next day during free time.

"When someone calls you a name because you're different, you have to embrace it and forge your own meaning." She held up a picture of a great white cruising, unconcerned, through Australian waters. "From now on, when they say bottom feeder." She bared her teeth and commanded all her children to do the same. "You think shark." That summer, every child in her group passed the swimming test and together they became the only group to enter the pool united and unafraid. They called themselves The Sharks.

In the hotel, she knocked on Mal's sisters' room first, then gathered Grandma from in front of the TV. Faye emerged just as Mal shut the door to their suite, pulling his suitcase behind him.

"Where's Dad?"

Faye narrowed her eyes and whispered. "He woke up in a bad mood, Lord help us."

From inside the room, Soumil's voice boomed. "For goodness sake, Faye, don't keep blaming it on a mood."

Mal and his siblings froze. Even their breathing seemed to stop. The hallway felt as though all the air had been sucked out of it. After a momentary pause, Juli pushed past Faye. "Let me talk with him."

Bree felt suddenly out of place. "How about I go get the car and meet you at the front entrance?" She didn't wait for a response but dragged her large carry-on and garment bag down the hall at a trot, feeling as though she were leaving the scene of an accident. In another family, Soumil's comment wouldn't have raised a single eyebrow. In Mal's family, it sent shivers down her spine.

In the garage, she stepped out of the elevator and hesitated, trying to remember where she parked the car. She pushed the remote and followed the familiar beep, her thoughts still very much on the drama being enacted on the twenty-sixth floor. She

224

flung her suitcase into the back and hauled herself into the driver's seat. Her foot pushed the break and she was about to put the key in the ignition when the passenger door flew open. She yelped as a man hurled himself into the seat. He punched the door lock button and held it down with a dirty finger while his left hand waved a glinting, metal object in her face.

"Give me my phone." His voice was harsh and raspy.

Bree stared at the crumpled blade the man wielded. Her heart raced. All she could think of was the edge of that blade cutting a vital artery or organ. She didn't care if she emerged with wounds. As long as she emerged.

"Don't move." The knife jerked forward. She evaded it by sliding back in her seat until her head rested against the window.

"I won't." She stared at the man, at the flecks of food caught in the deep stubble on his chin, the aviator sunglasses, his short but greasy hair. He reeked, filling the car with the odor of an abandoned public restroom. While her mind focused on the blade, her hand inched to the door.

"Give me my phone. That's all I want." He wiggled the knife.

Bree nodded. Her eyes flicked to her purse. "My phone's in there. My wallet. Take it all. Just let me go." Her fingers slowly tapped along the arm rest, searching for the door handle.

"Give it to me."

She pushed the purse toward him with her free hand.

"Get the phone."

She held her breath to get her breathing under control. Her hand scrambled in the deep pocket and she lifted her pink cell phone.

The man's face, which a moment ago she would have described as dark with fury, fell deeper into rage, as though into a black abyss. Only his sunglasses flashed frighteningly in the reflected light. "Not that. *My* phone."

Bree glanced at what she was holding. Her eyebrows drew together. "This is the only phone I have."

"What did you do with the one you found in the car?"

Bree racked her brain, but it was like trying to walk a straight line after four martinis. Everything was unbalanced. He wanted a phone. But he didn't want *her* phone. He said she found something in the car. But she hadn't found anything. She hadn't even looked. It was like her world and his existed on separate planes. She took a halting breath.

Maybe, she thought, she should enter his plane. "What did your phone look like?"

His lips parted, revealing not the chipped yellow teeth she was expecting but rather a row of flawless white. "Silver. No case." The words hissed through the immaculate incisors.

Silver? No case? Where had she seen a phone like that recently?

She willed herself to appear more relaxed. "I forgot. I found it. I brought it to the front desk." Behind her, the fingers that clasped the door handle relaxed their grip. If she could get him out of the car, it would make more sense to drive away.

He ran the blade of the crude knife along the edge of the steering wheel, slicing the plastic cover. "When?"

Bree bit her lip. "Last night. I took it to the lost and found. I'm sure they'll give it to you when you describe it." Bree hoped her tone hid the skepticism she felt about a front desk clerk handing this man anything.

He leaned forward. "Let's go." He swung a leg over the gear shift lever into the driver's side foot well, the thin wool of his trousers stretching at the seams. "Get out."

Bree opened the door and sucked in the fresh air as though she'd spent hours in the car. When she stepped out, the concrete under her feet felt reassuringly firm. She hid the sigh that escaped her lungs. Instead of murdering her in the isolated garage, this lunatic was going to march her back inside. To the front desk. Where she could get help. As the fear melted, confidence took its place. *I got this.*

The elevator pinged and liberated a crowd of people who milled for a few moments in the garage entrance then dispersed in various directions toward their cars. No one passed near them. She locked the car behind her and dropped the keys into her pocket.

She felt a push on her shoulder. "Knife's right here." A finger poked her belly. "I'm ready to use it." His hand grabbed hers. She resisted the urge to pull away and instead clasped it, trying to transmit calm.

They strode through the lobby, Bree setting a

brisk pace, keeping her head held high while her eyes swept the faces of passersby, trying to catch someone's gaze. But the goal of the casino, she realized, wasn't to have strangers mix with one another. It was to consume the attention of every human being inside. "Look at me. Look over here." That was the call transmitted by the glitter, the pulsing sounds, the flashy colors, the low ceilings, the provocatively dressed attendants. The longer you focused on the inside, the more money you were likely to spend. It was not the environment where a thin homeless man walking hand-in-hand with a plump, well-dressed woman garnered much attention. Stranger things than this, obviously, happened in Vegas.

At the entrance to the lobby, Bree paused. She saw Mal and his family clustered near the front, about thirty yards from the front desk. But in the middle of the room, between the Patels and the desk stood a four-foot-high circular marble vase, out of which billowed an assortment of tropical flora.

"Move it. The desk's over there." The man tugged her arm. Bree lagged. She dragged her feet and stumbled. He grabbed her under the elbow so tightly that she winced in pain.

"Watch your fucking step." He mumbled just loud enough for her to hear.

The eye-catching centerpiece appeared on her right and obscured her view of Mal. She shifted her gaze and riveted her eyes on the desk clerks, the uniformed attendants bouncing behind the counter like so many ping-pong balls in a lottery machine. She practiced what she would say. Thirty feet left to go. Her fingers tightened into fists. Twenty. She tensed her body, ready to rip away and run. Ten. She stared so hard at the face of the clerk nearest them that she was surprised the clerk didn't look up in wonder. Two feet from the desk her assailant stopped, his fingers still digging into her arm. He moved his other hand in front of him. She caught the flash of the knife in his palm.

They waited. The clerks ignored them. Guests standing in the snaking line to their right, waiting to check in, gave them dirty looks. Bree shifted her gaze to a woman attendant. Then a different man. She never before in her life been so studiously ignored. She felt like screaming but repressed the urge. The same inner voice admonished, as always, *Don't make a scene.*

But for once, the ridiculousness of the command appalled her. The enormity of her foolishness washed over her in such a sudden and staggering wave that she closed her eyes and would have fallen if her assailant hadn't maintained his grip on her arm. Her head drooped.

Mal, she realized, was right. She *did* want to make people happy at any cost. A lunatic homeless person was threatening her life with a knife. And she thought *she* had the situation under control. *Who am I kidding?*

The shriek that bubbled up from deep in her chest pierced the sedate lobby babble like a dagger. She twisted her arm free and fled, shouting at the top of her voice. "He has a knife. He's trying to kill me." People stared. She ignored them, hurtling toward the interior of the hotel, shoving astonished tourists out of her way. Her heels clattered on the marble. Behind her she heard footsteps and yelling. She didn't turn but bolted though the crowd, ignoring angry gestures as she bumped and stumbled against the tide.

At a four-way junction she turned right, keeping close to the wall, dragging her hand along the golden wallpaper for balance. The carpet beneath muffled the echoes of her footfall and slowed her sprint to a jog. The noise behind her faded. A blue suited man stepped in front of her, arms spread. She didn't have the strength to avoid him. He took one step back and caught her, holding her erect with his hands firmly on her shoulders.

"Whoa, there, ma'am." He flashed a badge by briefly opening his jacket. "Hotel security. I'm here to help."

Bree turned around. Unconcerned multitudes streamed by them. At nearby tables, dealers shuffled decks of cards. In the distance, slot machines played tinny music.

The security guard put his arm gently on her back. "Just got the message. That was quite a shock you had in the lobby. But everything's fine now."

She shook her head and burst into tears.

***

No one spoke during the twenty-minute drive to the airport. Potential icebreakers drifted through Bree's mind like a flotilla of Navy ships, but she sank each one with a shake of her head. Mal's family was preoccupied. No time for small talk.

Catching their flight was a touch and go endeavor due to the time lost at the hotel after Bree's recent incident. If the day wasn't going to end in total disaster, she'd have to get them to the departure terminal quickly and in one piece. Her hands gripped the wheel and her foot urged the accelerator to the floor. The car hurtled down the fast lane at eighty miles an hour, keeping easy pace with fellow vehicles on the highway. The day before, Faye's insistence that they arrive at the airport three hours early felt ridiculous. It meant they would leave the hotel earlier than most people with the same flight time got out of bed. But that all changed. First there was Bree's interrogation by hotel security, then the quick interview with the police, and finally a cursory inspection of the rental car, the entire set of procedures taking close to two hours.

Bree didn't press charges against the homeless man. Her attacker was, she thought, mentally ill. As soon as she was out of danger, she should have grabbed the first people she saw and had them call the police. Instead, she collapsed under pressure. Now there was a deranged man running around the streets of Las Vegas. The police officer's reassurance that, in Vegas, he wasn't the only one didn't help. If she had acted appropriately, he could have been in custody and gotten the psychiatric help he needed.

Throughout the two hours at the hotel, Bree's appeals for Mal's family to take a cab or Uber to the airport fell on deaf ears. Mal said he wouldn't leave her. The sisters refused to be ripped from the action. Soumil gently interceded on Bree's behalf with both the hotel staff and the police. And Faye was intractable. She jumped feet first into the martyr role and dug in her heels. "We couldn't possibly leave you here by yourself. It wouldn't be Christian." She clasped her hands over her purse. "Don't give a moment's thought to our catching our flight." She dabbed her eyes with a tissue. "We will pay for that extra day of parking. My physical therapy appointment for this afternoon can be rescheduled. And if Soumil runs out of medication, I'm certain nothing will happen. They must have a drug store here somewhere."

When the SUV finally rounded a corner and the white box-like structures of McCarran International Airport's departure terminals appeared in front of them, Bree released a breath that she felt like she had been holding since they left the hotel. She peered at the clock on the dash. "You've got almost forty-five minutes. I'm sure you'll make it." She jerked the car to a stop and swung open her door. By the time she reached the back, Mal was already unloading the luggage, flinging bags to the pavement where they toppled over one another.

"Take it easy." Bree reached in to help him.

"Don't tell him to take it easy. This is no time for slacking off." Faye looked at her watch as her daughters righted the cases and extended the carrying handles. "We only have twenty minutes." She glared at Bree with the fury of one whose martyrdom was about to be exposed as a sham.

She would have been happier if we'd missed the flight, Bree thought. She helped Mal hoist the final suitcase to the ground and slammed the door. "You have plenty of time."

Faye swung on her. "What do *you* know about airport travel?"

Soumil's fingers drummed on the handle of his bag. "Come on, Faye. Let's go."

"No." The last vestiges of martyrdom dropped from Faye's face. Underneath seethed a complex visage of anxiety, resentment, and fear.

"Mom," Mal called from the sidewalk. "You're making us even later."

But Faye stared at Bree with parted lips, as if she were holding back an explosion through sheer willpower.

Bree returned her future mother-in-law's gaze. It occurred to her that she beheld a woman who felt utterly out of control. It was as though the entire long weekend had been building up to this one instant, when Faye would let Bree have it for all the small ways Bree vied for dominance and won. Bree braced herself, wishing the attack could have come when she had more inner resources to muster, but feeling secure in her ability to weather Faye's rage. *It's not the first time. It won't be the last.* She put her hands on her hips and forced a smile.

Faye glared at Bree. "It's a sin to be dishonest." She threw a brief glance at her family, assembled around the cluster of luggage, then scrutinized her daughter-in-law to-be. "You, Bree, *made* us late. If you had flown with us in the first place, you never would have ended up with a rental car." She folded her hands and stared up at the sky. "When will you stop avoiding the truth? The Lord in his infinite wisdom has a reason for everything."

An inexplicable coldness gripped Bree's stomach. She shifted her feet and dropped her gaze. She didn't know what was coming, but she knew she wasn't going to like it.

Faye continued in full cry, her eyes closed, her folded hands shaking with force as she pressed them together and raised them above her head. "It's not flying that killed your parents. Why won't you understand? They had to die. The Lord willed it. That airplane had to crash."

"Faye!" Soumil jumped from the curb and yanked his wife's arm. "That's more than enough."

Faye, spent, allowed herself to be propelled toward the terminal. Her daughters followed, casting worried glances over their shoulders at Bree. In a few moments, Mal stood alone on the traffic island, arms limp at his side, gaping at Bree. "She didn't…"

Bree lifted her head. "Mean that?" She pulled on her blouse. "She's right, you know. I can't avoid accidents by not flying. That's not why I don't. It's because I never want to feel what my parents felt in their last moments. I know it seems crazy." She gave Mal a sad smile. "But it's my way of keeping them alive."

Mal stepped off the curb, his arms outstretched. Bree gestured for him to go back. She pressed her lips together, shook her head, and climbed into the car. Mal waved. She flicked her blinker and looked in the side view mirror for a gap in the passing traffic. A black Mercedes pulled up behind her and flashed its lights. She merged into the gap left for her and wove around the cars discharging passengers, following signs for the exit.

CHAPTER 18

Bree drove without noticing her surroundings. The part of her brain in charge of maneuvering the vehicle through the remaining city traffic and onto Route 15 could manage its tasks alone. She watched other cars without seeing them. Manipulated the accelerator without feeling it. Her mind slipped backward in time, to the crisp October day she stayed late at school for band practice. She remembered everything about that early evening. The last cicadas buzzed in the trees near the football field, their drone competing with the tubas and saxophones. The cold metal of her flute cooled her hands as she stood with the other ninth graders watching the older students practice. Shouts floated from football players occupying the other half of the field. Her fingers tapped the keys in time to the music, soundlessly rehearsing her part.

Those minutes were seared into her brain the way Stephanie's grandparents remembered what they were doing when Kennedy was shot. Or the way older friends remembered where they were on

9/11. It was in all other ways a normal evening. Band practice adhered rigidly to the same routine. The sky was clear, a deep blue that, with the approaching twilight, had begun to darken. She remembered jumping at the *thunk* the massive overhead electric spotlights made as they turned on. The sound of her friends laughing rang clear in the refreshing air.

At first, she didn't notice the teacher sprinting across the parking lot. Later she remembered it was her favorite teacher, the kind woman who taught ninth grade biology, who created acronyms to help students remember enzymes and didn't blush when the boys made jokes about reptilian reproduction. But when she first looked, she simply saw a teacher, someone who could run onto the field and interrupt practice with impunity. She gave the teacher one glance and continued talking with her friends.

Time only began to slow when the band director pointed to the ninth graders and conversation on the sidelines hushed. Bree leaned over to Stephanie and wondered what they had done, whether it was good or bad. So often, it seemed, Bree couldn't tell the difference when it came to band practice. When she thought she was on key, the director frequently yelled she was off. When her flute seemed straight, it was slanted down. When her feet felt in step with the others in her line, she would be called out for walking too quickly. Yet it was all worth it. Because the exhilaration of the music, the power of striding with the group, the unified spirit, and the roaring applause at game time diminished every misstep and embarrassment. She loved band with a passion. If she could choose to be anywhere on earth, she would be at home with her parents. But her second choice was band.

When the adults singled her out, she saw disaster in their faces. She remembered the clasp of the biology teacher's hand on her bare arm. The cold of the woman's fingers transmitting an uneasiness to Bree's heart. Later, she couldn't remember what they said. But she remembered not being able to breathe. She fell onto the grass, clutching at the cool blades. Adults bent over her. But the only face Bree ever remembered clearly was Stephanie's.

The memories before and after that razor-sharp turning point in her life differed in their quality. The scenes from before scrolled through her mind like a video, clear, uninterrupted, and smooth. The scenes from afterward were fuzzy, disjointed, and jarring. She remembered a shivering that wouldn't stop no matter how many blankets they piled on her. Bright lights of cars as someone drove her to Stephanie's house. Kacey's bedroom with its bunk beds, where they laid her. The phone calls to Mexico that ended with cries and screaming so loud Bree was never sure whether they came from the phone line or whether she heard them from across the continent.

Why did they go to Mexico? That question obsessed her for years after the event. That morning, her mother, dressed in a mauve suit, her long black hair carefully brushed back over her round shoulders, called it a quick business trip.

"You won't even know we're gone." Her necklace bumped Bree's chin, as it always did, when she leaned down to kiss her daughter. And

Bree joked, as she always did, about the small diamonds that rested on the intersecting platinum hearts scratching her skin. Her mother kissed her again, just to see Bree laugh one more time, and rattled her keychain at her husband, who was just entering the bright kitchen with its yellow curtains and deep blue tile backsplash.

"We'll be home before you get home from band practice." Her father lifted her off the ground, hugging her tightly to his ample chest and rubbing his beard against her cheek. She complained that she was too old to be lifted off the ground. "Someday you won't be so eager to grow up." He flashed his wide grin, looped his arm through his wife's, and stepped through the back door, letting the screen slam behind him. Bree didn't watch them drive away. She was preoccupied with something she could not remember later. What could have been worth not seeing her parents faces one last time? She cursed herself for her selfishness. But she cursed Mexico, the country that had murdered her parents, more.

The subsequent tumultuous battle to enable her to stay in the United States took place without her active participation. Her only living relatives resided in the one country Bree couldn't imagine ever visiting, to say nothing of living. But she was too weakened by her grief and shaken by anger to draw a line in the sand and refuse to go. In the end, Stephanie's parents did it for her. Stephanie's father, an attorney, negotiated the arrangement that eventually involved formally adopting Bree into his family.

From the outside, nothing much changed. She missed some weeks of school. She moved a few blocks. She dropped out of band for a while. People whispered about her in the hallways. Some friends—never Stephanie—avoided her. And for the remainder of ninth grade, no teacher ever yelled at her, not even the band director when she was so out of step that the tuba player tripped on her heels and nearly dropped his three-thousand-dollar instrument.

She remembered ninth grade as the year of silence. Silence in her heart. Silence at school. Silent wishes. She begged her parents to come visit her at night when she was sleeping. But for more than a year they never did. She willed herself to have a fatal accident and join them wherever they were. But instead, over time, she found herself having moments in which she laughed, or even forgot about them for hours at a time. She wished she could find someone who would understand her heart without her having to disclose its dark secrets and deep wounds. Stephanie tried, but the person who came closest was Ryder. It was as though that shining football star, the high school hero who lived in a stratosphere she couldn't touch, saw through a window in her soul everyone else ignored. He knew when she needed quiet companionship and when she needed jokes, when to sit next to her in the cafeteria and when simply to catch her eye in the hall. He buoyed her even when she couldn't tell she was drowning.

Until the prom.

On the highway outside Las Vegas, when the last

suburb gave way to the dry desert, Bree emerged from her fog, unclear how far she had driven and relieved she hadn't made a wrong turn. The GPS indicated another seven and a half hours until she could return the rental car. That, she thought, was enough time to get herself back to normal. She gritted her teeth. Faye unnerved her, but her future mother-in-law was correct to complain. Bree's obsession with control was unrealistic. Over a decade had passed since the accident. She was an adult, not a fourteen-year-old. Not flying wasn't preventing her from imagining her parents' last moments. And it wasn't suspending them in the air, halting them from crashing with the sixteen other passengers of the commuter plane into the side of a mountain.

Refusing to fly only enabled her to live in an illusion. It created a tiny bubble in the world where accidents like her parents' didn't happen. But they did. Pretending otherwise was make-believe, the escape used by children.

Time to grow up, Bree. Time to tell Faye she's right. Time to tell Mal I'll fly to Las Vegas for our wedding.

She pulled out of the fast lane. Biding her time, she navigated across highway markers and, at a spot where the breakdown lane merged relatively seamlessly with a wide, smooth expanse of desert, she rolled to a stop. With the car in park, she bent over her purse in the passenger seat, searching for her phone and headset.

A black Mercedes braked behind her in a cloud of dust, but Bree didn't notice. A man sprung into the dirt. Gravel flew as he dashed for her white SUV. He ripped open the driver's side door just as Bree was fiddling the headset onto her ear. At the sight of his face and the familiar knife she screamed.

The next second, her foot kicked his arm and dislodged the blade from his grip. It fell into the dirt. Her hand struggled to propel him away from the car and shut the door. She fought with a pent-up fury, her body rebelling with all the power she had repressed in the garage. But he jerked her by the blouse, his dirty fists balled around her lavender silk fabric, and wrenched her to the ground.

The cloth closed around her neck. Cars whooshed by. She felt the sides of her visual field go black. He lugged her, both hands tight on her collar, to the far side of the car. With one hand on the base of her neck, he pinned her against the vehicle. With his grip looser, she flailed against him, her blows landing on his face, neck, and torso. His thick arm pushed against her, unyielding. She screamed again and tried to jam her knee into his crotch.

"You should have given me my fucking phone when I asked." He raised his other arm. A new blade shone dully, level with her eyes.

Bree dropped her chin. She bit hard at the hand at her neck. The man yelped and released his grip. Bree careened through the scrub and cacti as footsteps pounded in close pursuit.

Her short legs pumped. She shot across the arid expanse. Thorns tore at her clothes. Her high heels threatened to trip her. She heard her assailant puffing. She pushed herself harder, swerving around yucca plants and Joshua trees.

Suddenly, she tumbled into and then over a creosote bush and landed painfully on her back. The man flung himself on top of her, pinned one of her hands and then the other. She butted her forehead against his until her head exploded in a blaze of white. She lay still.

When she opened her eyes, he sat astride her, panting. His stained white dress shirt expanded and contracted with his breathing. His dark gray eyes stared at her with an uncaring coldness. The glare frightened her. She looked away.

"Why didn't you give me my phone?" His voice mixed equal parts ferocity and incredulity. "This is all your fault, you know. If you hadn't stolen it, none of this would've happened."

Bree twisted her hips underneath him, trying to free herself. "I don't have your phone."

"You're lying." He leaned forward, his face an inch from hers. "Do you want money? Is that what this is all about?"

She jerked her head to the side. "You've got the wrong person."

He slowly righted himself. When she dared to peek at his face, she stopped moving. There was nothing human left in his eyes. They reminded her of stones. The desire to fight filtered out of her into the hot desert sand and left her body limp, resigned. Was this, she wondered, how her parents felt when they saw the mountainside approaching?

She screamed. He spat at her. But she didn't stop, her voice evaporating into the vast, deserted

243

expanse.

In a lightning movement, he closed one hand around her throat. The other joined it. He leaned his weight on her neck. Her cry faded, then stopped. She felt blackness close in from the sides.

"Let her go."

With her last strength, Bree opened an eye, sure that her assailant was giving voice to a second personality inside himself. But a moment later the grip on her throat relaxed. The weight on her stomach disappeared. The homeless man jumped to his feet and scampered across the dirt. She watched him dissolve into the desert landscape, as though he were mirage.

She coughed and fingered her neck, eyes closed. When a hand touched her arm, she shouted, sure the nightmare vision of the man had returned. But when she opened her eyes, the man before her regarded her with concern.

"Ryder?" She croaked out the name.

He fell to his knees. "Are you okay?"

Bree nodded. He lifted her, one hand under her head, the other supporting her back. His denim shirt felt smooth and smelled lightly of men's soap. She leaned her face briefly against his shoulder. He stroked her hair, picking burrs and leaves from it as he spoke. "Juli texted me about what happened at the hotel. So I thought…"

Bree pushed away and rubbed her face. "Do you never give up?"

Ryder shrugged. "I already planned to drive. I didn't think I'd actually see you. But then there was your car on the side of the road with the door open.

And that other car behind it."

Bree peered into the desert around them. There was no sign of her assailant. "Did you see where he went?"

Ryder shrugged. "He was running away from the road." He helped her to her feet. "Can you walk?"

Bree bent and examined her legs. "Besides scratches, I'm fine." She refused Ryder's offer of an arm and hobbled back to the three cars—hers, the black Mercedes, and Ryder's. Close to her SUV, something glittering in the sand caught her eye. She picked it up.

Ryder whistled. "Nice find." He held out his hand and inspected the frames. "Gold aviators. The person who lost these out here must be cursing himself."

Bree stared. "They belonged to that guy."

Ryder looked around the desert as though he expected the man to come back for them. "Why would a homeless person own sunglasses that cost four thousand dollars?"

Bree shook her head. "I saw them up close more than once. I'm sure they're his."

Ryder strode to the Mercedes and wiped his hand along the glossy black finish. "And this was his car? In most states you could buy a house for what this is worth. He couldn't have been homeless."

Bree shuddered. "I don't think he was sane. All that with the phone. It didn't make any sense. He probably lost his mind. After that, his life went downhill." She pulled herself into the driver's seat of her car. "My keys are still here." She held up the rental car agency's plastic fob.

Ryder returned from the other car dangling a different set of keys. "He left his too. But I take back what I said about his not being homeless." He held his nose. "That car smells like a toilet."

Bree leaned back, feeling suddenly faint. "What do we do?"

Ryder pushed the Mercedes's remote and the car locked itself with a subdued whoop. "We could call 911 and wait for the cops to show up. Or…" He twirled the keys on his finger. "We could just take off and leave the car and him here to fend for themselves."

Bree rubbed her temples. "It's not the first car left on the side of the road." She started her engine. "And somebody will pick him up." She shut her door and rolled down the window. "Let's get out of here."

Ryder wiped the keys on his pants and then hurled them into the desert. "Right behind you."

***

It took an hour for Bree to realize she never called Mal. Dropping him and his family off at the airport felt like something that had happened a week ago. She remembered she'd wanted to call him but couldn't remember about what.

What mattered to her at that moment was leaving insanity behind her. The trip to Vegas, while not entirely a mistake, felt in retrospect like the ride of a roller coaster car that jumped the tracks. Precipitous ups and downs, dizzying twists and turns, nothing like what she expected. The final crash in the desert symbolized the end. She miraculously escaped unharmed. But, she told herself, she wasn't exactly the same person who drove this highway in the other direction just a few days ago.

For one, there was Ryder, glued to her bumper like a tailgater from hell. Bree shrugged, reaching between the seats with one hand and feeling for the coffee that wasn't there. She sighed and kept an eye out for the next exit. What Ryder wanted, she decided, didn't matter. It was like the conversation with the homeless man about the cell phone. In the end, what made the most sense was for her to do what she needed to do and not worry about always being in control.

She slapped her leg. That *was what I was going to tell Mal.* And she suddenly felt strangely grateful to Ryder and Faye and the man she'd left running through the desert. *My fear of flying is over.*

The logos underneath the exit sign indicated only fast food restaurants and gas stations, but Bree eased down the ramp anyway, eager for a jolt of caffeine, no matter how bitter. At the junction, she tossed a mental coin and turned left on impulse. Just after the highway underpass, a bright yellow sign shone in the bright noon-day light. The golden circle with a hole in its middle beckoned like a beacon from heaven. Grinning from ear to ear, she swerved into the donut shop parking lot and maneuvered carefully into an empty space. She leaned back in her seat, rolled down the window and inhaled deeply. The aroma of frying dough, sweet glaze, and fruit filling drifted on the hot air.

Ryder tapped gently on the back passenger

247

window. "Want me to get you something?"

Bree rolled up the window, shut off the ignition, and climbed laboriously from the car. Her scratches smarted and her body ached. She winced with every step. But her heart felt lighter than it had in days. "No one is going to deny me this pleasure."

Ryder held out his hand to stop her. "You look like you've been rolling in the dust with an armadillo."

Bree glanced at herself in the side view mirror. She dusted off her clothing and passed her fingers through her hair, pulling out twigs and leaves. Then she shrugged. "Good enough." She tugged her blouse over her tummy and limped toward the entrance.

A few minutes later, on a bench under a scraggly shade tree opposite the shop, she and Ryder sat with a box of a dozen donuts between them. Bree munched with closed eyes, savoring the cloying sweetness as though she had never eaten a donut before. When she opened her eyes, she found Ryder gazing at her.

She blushed. "What?"

He reached out and touched her forehead lightly. "Does that hurt?"

Bree pulled back. She fingered the lump, remembered her head butt, and smiled. "A nice souvenir."

Ryder frowned. "It might be serious."

She shook her head and finished off the chocolate donut. She stretched her legs and slid down on the bench until her head hung lazily off the back. The ice coffee balanced on her stomach sloshed pleasantly with each breath. Sunlight filtered through the sparse leaves. She squinted through them at the clear blue sky. "Nothing's wrong with me."

In the middle of her third donut, her phone rang. It was Mal. She left her purse on the bench with Ryder and strolled across the dry grass, her sunglasses pulled tight over her eyes.

"We're home." His voice sounded strained and worn out.

She grinned and hoped her contentment carried through to him. "I've still got quite a ways to go. I had another little delay."

There was a long pause. "Are you okay?"

Bree smiled. "Nothing I couldn't handle."

Mal paused again. "I meant about what happened."

"Your mother? Tell her I'm grateful. Seriously. I needed to hear that. Next time we come to Vegas, I'll get on the airplane with you and your parents."

"Not likely."

Bree laughed. "Really. I'm..."

He interrupted her. "Not with Dad, anyway. He..."

The armor of warm contentment encircling Bree cracked slightly. She halted her stroll. "Is your father okay?"

Mal's voice, suddenly ripe with emotion, sounded angry. "He announced something on the flight home."

Bree resumed her perambulation.

Mal took a deep breath. "In front of all the other passengers, he stood up and told Mom he wants a divorce."

Bree dropped the phone. It bounced and came to a halt upside down on the dry grass.

***

Desert twilight whisked in quickly on the heels of the day. As the sun slid toward the horizon, the temperature dropped precipitously. Greenwood stumbled among the hills, feeling more lost than he had ever felt in his life. More than when a sudden blizzard enveloped the heli-ski lodge where he was staying and he, unable to see more than a few feet in front of him, trudged through knee-high snow toward what he hoped was the warm building and not the beginning of an icy slope. More than when his son disappeared under the water at the lake house and he dove into the frigid, clear water, his eyes straining through the silt for a glimpse of the boy's red swimsuit, his fingers groping for his warm flesh. And more than he felt the first morning after his stepfather forced himself upon him, when he looked into his mother's eyes and saw only denial and stood at the bus stop with his young friends, feeling suddenly as though he and they occupied separate universes and theirs was one into which he could never step foot again.

He lived, he considered as he floundered among the cacti, a lonely life. He hadn't always let himself feel alone. Abigayle helped. The children helped. Most of all, work helped him turn away from the emptiness the events of his youth carved into his soul. But the emptiness never fully disappeared.

Until Paulo. The celebration of union with that youth felt like fireworks exploding inside the Grand Canyon. When Paulo snuck out his window that first night to meet Greenwood in the parking lot, he knew. Paulo's tears that night were the kind he had seen his own son cry when he had made the soccer team or passed the entrance exam for private school. Greenwood held Paulo tightly to his chest, because he knew. They were not tears of sorrow but tears of relief, of release, of joy. Paulo was showing him that he had been lonely too. And Greenwood knew then that they had saved each other.

Night dropped in the desert like a final curtain across a stage, masking familiar objects, sucking away all vestiges of warmth, obliterating connections to the outside world. Nocturnal inhabitants crept, squirmed, and slithered from their hiding places. The starry sky morphed with the passage of clouds. Greenwood curled into a ball under a Joshua tree, his eyes scanning the darkness. If only Paulo were with him, he thought. Together they would make the night warm.

But he shivered uncontrollably. His limbs grew numb. And as he faded in and out of consciousness, the only image he could conjure was that of his stepfather's face. He closed his eyes a final time. A screech owl released its pent-up cry to the universe.

And after a few hours, a kangaroo rat scurried up to inspect his cold, rigid body.

***

Stephanie hunched over the steering wheel of her

electric car, driving as she always did, with her nose as close to the windshield as she could get. "It's not like Mal's parents ever got along."

Bree fidgeted in the passenger seat of the narrow car, trying to find a comfortable position for her bruised parts. "Mal said they always fought. But it got worse when she became more religious."

Stephanie glanced at her friend. "Does it make you reconsider?"

Bree blinked. "Flying?"

Stephanie laughed. "It's not the big happy family you thought it was."

Bree gazed out the window at the familiar San Francisco evening landscape, the tech billboards illuminated at the side of the road, the Teslas and hybrid cars jostling for position on the multilane highway, and the lights in the windows of the houses scrunched close together on the hillsides. "I'm not marrying them. I'm marrying Mal."

Stephanie's eyebrows shot up but she kept quiet, concentrating on fighting her way to an off ramp. "Are you sure you don't want to stop by urgent care somewhere, *amiga*?"

Bree's fingers touched the bump on her head. "What I need is a bath, some more ibuprofen, a bag of ice, and a cup of tea."

"And a donut?" Stephanie winked at her.

"Under normal circumstances, spot on." Bree rubbed her stomach and closed her eyes. "But I had a few on the way up."

"With Ryder." Stephanie drew out the name provocatively.

"With Ryder." Bree snapped the phrase to a

close as if it were a book she shut with a bang.

"Will you see him again?"

Bree thought about how she and Ryder pulled to the curb in front of the car rental agency with his car still close behind hers. She felt like she had towed his car all the way from Nevada. She exited wearily, aware that the long sitting had done nothing positive for her aches and pains. One hand leaned against the doorframe. With the other, she massaged her thighs. The overhead streetlights cast yellow shadows in the deepening dusk.

"The neighborhood seems kind of sketchy." He looked around.

Bree kneaded her upper arms. "I'll wait inside."

Ryder kicked at the pavement, for once looking awkward and out of place. "I…"

She interrupted him. "This is it. Not that I didn't appreciate your being there today."

Ryder nodded more with his eyes than his chin. "Straight."

She switched to massaging her shoulders. "All that crazy Vegas stuff is behind me now."

He raised his eyebrows. "Awesome."

"I'm feeling pretty good about myself."

"That's sick." He held out his arms. "You take care, Bree."

She embraced him quickly and stepped away. "Bye, Ryder."

Would she see him again? She didn't know. That was the real answer. But that wasn't Stephanie's real question in the first place.

"Right now I've got other things going on in my life."

Their car skirted a set of double parked vans and gained velocity as Stephanie drove it downhill. "Just wait till I tell Kacey you were attacked twice in one day." She rolled her eyes. "He's *so* going to regret not being there to see it all." She peeped at her friend out of the corner of her eye. But Bree was curled on the seat, arms crossed on her chest, fast asleep.

"Awesome, *mi hermana*," she whispered and eased off the accelerator. "You deserve some rest."

CHAPTER 19

Bree raised her fist to rap the wood. At the entrance to Stephanie's apartment, the hum of women's voices reverberated through the crack between door and frame. Bree lowered her hand without knocking, remembering her nervousness six months ago when she stood at this same doorway about to walk into a party with this same group of friends. She trotted back to the mirrors by the elevators and straightened her décolletage. Her eyes sparkled as she turned sideways, adjusting the hemline. As Mal pointed out when she debuted the tight fiery red outfit for him a few night before, it left little to the imagination. That, she had told him, was the point. He shrugged.

"Is he depressed?" Stephanie asked when Bree first remarked on Mal's plunge into extraordinary silence.

But Bree knew it was the divorce. Mal couldn't wrap his head around the rift in his family, his father and grandmother on one side, his mother on the other, and he and his sisters ricocheting between them like the puck in an ice hockey game. Usually taciturn, he pulled even more inside his shell. Even Bree had trouble prying him out. When she surprised him at a South Indian restaurant with her hair cut thirty-six inches shorter, he first walked by her, and when she ran after him and tapped him on the shoulder, stared at her without a word, kissed her on the cheek, and asked for a table away from the window. Her new penchant for bigger necklaces and striking earrings elicited no comments. Only when she asked whether he would join her in a park to work out with her twice a week did he demure. He preferred, he said, the dog-free environment of the treadmill and weights in his own apartment. Since they would soon be moving in together, he also pointed out, wouldn't it make more sense for her to save the money of a fitness class and simply use his equipment?

But these days Bree didn't like standing still, she didn't like waiting for things, and she especially didn't enjoy taking the easy route. Her first flight since the trip to Disneyland with her parents for her tenth birthday was to New England for the fifth reunion of her pharmacy school class. She took a Xanax, sat on the aisle, and blasted heavy metal through her headset on takeoff and landing. Besides grabbing the arm of the stranger next to her during an episode of particularly violent turbulence on the flight home, the trip was uneventful. When her supervisor implored someone in her workgroup to lead a teambuilding retreat to the Pasayten Wilderness in Eastern Washington state because the original director fell ill, she volunteered for the adventure that required flying, driving, horseback riding, and overnight camping, despite never having done two of the four prerequisites.

With Faye Patel focused gouging her soon-to-be former husband in the divorce settlement, Bree also had free reign over the wedding. That was handy, she told her friends, because a prior romantic weekend getaway with Mal in Puerto Rico unearthed the need to revise her honeymoon plans. It turned out that Mal's subcontinent genes gave him no immunity to the gastrointestinal onslaught of alien water. The first evening in San Juan, a fruit cocktail felled him, and he spent the following days crawling between bed and toilet. When he returned to Sacramento, he kissed the ground and subsequently refused to leave the country again for a year. The wedding would still take place in Vegas and an international honeymoon, she and Mal finally agreed, would take place on their first anniversary.

Bree skipped back from the elevators to the door and pushed it open without knocking. She yelled above the thrum of the music. "I'm here."

Celine leaned against the entrance wall, hands on hips. "I saw you hanging out at the elevators just now." She gave Bree a quick squeeze. "Don't get any ideas." She stepped back and surveyed her friend. "Girl, what have you been doing since I saw you last? And where can I get me some?"

Bree laughed. "Not telling. What happens in Vegas stays in Vegas."

"Well, if Vegas can do that..." She gestured from Bree's head to toes. "I sure am glad I'm going back."

Stephanie shoved aside the other guests who begun to crowd the entrance hallway. "Let me at her." She grabbed Bree's arm and towed her into the living room. "We've been waiting half the night for you. The bachelorette party can't start without the bachelorette."

Bree inspected the bottles of hard liquor on a narrow side table by a set of lace curtained French doors that led into the bedroom of the small apartment. "It doesn't seem to have stopped you."

A few minutes later, Bree stood on the sofa, her legs wobbling on the soft cushions, holding a martini glass, her arm raised high. She studied the upturned, smiling faces of the women crowded into Stephanie's cramped living room. She had been laughing, but as her eyes focused on each friend in turn, the laughter faded and she lowered her arm, at a loss for words.

Stephanie recognized the look and stepped onto the cushion beside her, teetering. "Let me go first, *chiquita*." She urged Bree back down to the floor.

Bree gazed up at this friend from her childhood, the thin blonde Caucasian who had always understood her plump brown Latina soul better than any person alive. Stephanie reached out her hand and another friend passed her a flat, rectangular package, beautifully wrapped in shiny lilac paper with a thick white ribbon.

"Tonight is about celebrating." Clapping interrupted her. She waited until it died down. "The flight to Vegas in two days will be about celebrating, even though your sorry ass is going to drive there again." A few people applauded. "And, of course, your wedding will be the biggest celebration of all." At this, cheering drowned out the music. But the expression on Stephanie's face shifted, and the room fell into silence. "But I know there's a part of you that abstains from celebration. It's grown smaller over the years. I've even seen it shrink these past few months. But I know it's still there." Stephanie's voice cracked and a tear rolled across her cheek and dropped, with a small splash, into her wine glass. Someone turned off the music. "Inside you is still a fourteen-year-old girl mourning the loss of her parents." She extended the gift. "I can't bring them back for you, *amiga*." A steady stream of tears now coursed down her face. "But I can bring them *to* you."

Bree unwrapped the large sliver-framed photo of herself and her parents at Stephanie's own fourteenth birthday party. Bree climbed onto the sofa and hugged her friend. Stephanie rubbed her tears. "The hotel will have a chair waiting for this picture at the ceremony and another at the reception. Wherever they are, Bree," she kissed Bree on the cheek, "I know there's nowhere they would rather be than with you." The silence that followed was broken only by repeated sniffling and blowing of noses.

It was an hour before Bree climbed onto the couch again, this time evidencing less stability and more inebriation. She held a glass in each hand, clutching them like invisible walking sticks, elbows tight at her side. "This will be short and sweet." She looked at the floor, her mind momentarily blank.

"Too short." Someone shouted from the back of the room.

"The Bombay Sapphire's got her sideways."

Bree raised a glass and swallowed. "The most important thing in my life is family. But things don't always work out the way you think." She blinked back a tear. "I got a firsthand lesson in ninth grade about how life isn't perfect. I don't expect a perfect marriage. I don't expect a perfect husband. But I expect to meet my challenges head on, to do the best I can do, and to be true to myself." She raised both glasses. "And I can't do any of that without my friends. So here's to you."

***

A day later, a stretch baseball cap with the brim to the rear kept her hair out of her face while she navigated a convertible through the easing congestion on Route five. The rushing wind whipped the last remnants of a hangover from her head.

"I reserved this just for you," Bree told Mal's grandmother earlier at the sleek rental car agency counter. "Wait till you see it."

The look on the old woman's face was worth the price. Her eyes widened and her mouth hung open. She ran tentative fingertips over the bright red paint, her hand trembling. "It's a Cadillac." She exhaled the words as someone else might say "It's a million dollars cash."

Bree's smile widened into a grin she couldn't repress. She opened a thick door and showed off the leather interior. "And you know who drove Cadillacs..."

Juli bit her lip and nodded. "The King."

"I wanted to get pink." Bree fanned herself with the rental car agreement papers. "He gave his mother a pink one. But that's a custom paint job."

Soumil pulled Bree aside while his mother peered into the trunk. "How did you know? Not even my father knew about her obsession."

Bree winked. "We girls have secrets. Isn't that right, Grandma?"

But the older woman didn't hear her. She nestled herself in the rear bucket seat behind the driver, her short legs demurely curled up under her green sari with its intricate border of silver flowers, her expression blissful.

Soumil shook his head, opened the rear door, and pointed at the pavement. "Get out." The wrinkled face clouded with dismay, like a child whose favorite toy was confiscated. Soumil placed her hand in the crook of his arm and led her to the other side of the car. "You're sitting in the front."

Bree saluted her soon-to-be father-in-law's gallant gesture. But Juli resisted her son's efforts to ensconce her in the wide passenger compartment. Women, she argued, wielding her purse as a shield, did not sit in the front and make men sit in the back. When Bree pointed out that a woman was driving, the older woman flicked the argument away like an annoying fly.

"You are American. It's different for me." Only after her son promised to switch seats halfway through the trip did she acquiesce, the twinkle in her eyes belying her former reticence.

On the highway, Bree initially hugged the breakdown lane, not wanting to frighten Mal's grandmother, who gripped the door armrest with one hand and the center island with the other. The car's speedometer hovered consistently at the speed limit. Cars overtook them in a constant stream. But Bree tapped the brake at the first sign of slowing traffic. Out of the corner of her eye, she watched Juli's face grow more and more rigid. Renting a convertible, she thought, had not been a good idea after all. Even though they couldn't fly on the same flight as Mal and his sisters and mother, they could still have flown. What made her insist on revisiting her first drive to Vegas?

After the flow of traffic temporarily forced her into the middle lanes, she turned on her blinker to merge right. A sudden outburst from the passenger seat surprised her.

"What are you doing?" Juli regarded her, eyes bulging.

Bree straightened the wheel and turned the blinker back off. "I'm getting back in the slow lane."

Juli held her face between her hands. "I am a seventy-year-old woman."

Bree's stomach sunk. This *had* been a bad idea. She took one hand off the wheel and fiddled in her purse. "Soumil, can you set the GPS to take on the back roads? That way we won't go over forty-five." She passed the phone to the back seat. The gray head beside her drooped. Bree's heart thumped. Was she giving Mal's grandmother a heart attack on the way to the wedding?

"Bree." Dainty eyelids fluttered as the wrinkled face leaned into the wind. "We are in a Cadillac like Elvis. But I am thinking you are trying to kill me." Her fingers quivered on the arm rests. "Stop driving like a grandmother. Give us some *speed*."

***

In the rest stop restaurant booth, Bree skipped ahead on the menu past the soups, salads, and main dishes, searching for the desserts. She flipped the clear laminated sheet back and forth and read all the entries twice but couldn't find the section she was looking for. Her eyes were unenthusiastically scanning the salad selection when Juli wordlessly slid a metal stand across the wood-grain plastic tabletop. It tapped Bree's elbow. She looked up. The corners of the older woman's mouth crinkled up slightly. Her brown eyes darted briefly to the stand and then resumed their perusal of her own menu. Bree picked up the hand-sized metal and glass display, which listed the day's fresh-baked pie selections. She grinned at Juli, who pretended not to notice.

They gave their orders to a friendly waitress with thick black eyeliner, a shaved head, and pewter-colored rings that pierced every facial feature except her eyes. Before the teenager was finished the notes on her pad, Soumil edged out of the booth and stood, hands in pockets, eyes focused vaguely out the window at an indiscriminate point in the parking lot.

"I'm going to the restroom." He sauntered toward the back of the crowded dining area.

Juli watched her son, shaking her head. "He is not going there. He is calling his girlfriend."

Bree blinked and leaned forward, hands on the table. "Soumil is seeing someone?" Her eyes followed the retreating back of her future father-in-law, unable to imagine him divulging his feelings about politics, to say nothing of mustering the emotional fortitude to maintain a new romantic relationship.

The deep eyes with their still dark lashes held Bree's gaze. "I am seeing things he doesn't think I'm seeing." She rocked her head in her characteristic fashion. "From me, he can't hide."

Bree nodded slowly. The idea of Soumil with another woman captivated her imagination. She wanted to ask what kind of person he chose after Faye. How he behaved when they were alone. And whether or not they fought. But she couldn't ask his mother. And Mal never even hinted at his father having any interest in life outside his job. The true story would have to wait.

The waitress propelled a basket of rolls in a small dish of butter patties across the table in a fluid motion, hardly breaking her stride on her way to another set of customers.

Juli carefully extracted the largest roll and placed it on the bread plate by Bree. "You can't be hiding from me either, Bree."

At first Bree thought she was talking about the bread. She looked up, ready to smile at a joke. But an intense, almost haunted look in the eyes of the older woman across from her gave her pause. "What do you mean?"

"Your secret with Ryder."

Bree leaned back against the red vinyl cushion of the booth. She felt her face flush even as she told herself there was nothing to be embarrassed about, nothing to hide. "It's not a secret." She reached for the butter, tore the roll in half, and slapped the bright yellow patty on one side without spreading it. "After Vegas we've kept in touch."

"I am not saying it is bad." Juli adjusted her fork with the fingernail of her index finger. "Only that it is secret. Like Elvis."

Background chatter and the karaoke version of a popular song on the overhead speakers filled the pause between the two women. Bree recombined the two halves of the roll and pressed down until the soft butter oozed out the sides. She thought about how to explain her friendship with Ryder, trying to remember how things started. But in her mind there was no clear beginning. It was as though their series of meaningless goodbyes in Las Vegas had created an opening through which it became natural to step. The texts between them when they returned to San Francisco simply extended something that never really started or ended. And when she called him that first time with a question about a situation at work, she didn't think much about it. Mal wasn't someone to go to with management problems. He'd always worked for his family. Finding creative solutions wasn't his forte. But Ryder excelled at seeing the big picture. His experience with startups enabled him to think outside the box. And at some point in the past months, it became routine to pick up the phone and call Ryder on the drive home. And sometime after that, it didn't feel strange when he showed up to take her out to lunch.

Just a few days ago, they met downtown, he looking every inch the hip young business man at the pour over coffee bar, even though he confessed to Bree that he hadn't worked in months.

"It's tough listening nonstop to people trying to convince me that theirs is the best idea since Steve put the bite in the apple." He lifted his cup and twirled his saucer. "I've decided to sit out for a while. My heart's not in it these days."

Bree ladled whipped cream from her cup and licked the spoon. "So what do you do with your money?"

Ryder laughed. "Invest it in property, like all the other dudes in San Francisco."

Bree rolled her eyes. "Mal and I pay rent to you dudes."

A woman passing their stand up table dropped her napkin. Ryder picked it up and reached it to her. She looked as though he had just handed her a thousand dollar bill. Then she took in Bree and swung her chin dismissively toward the bar.

Bree chuckled. "You don't even see it, do you? The way women think you're a god who's dropped in from heaven?"

Ryder pulled his hair back from his face, letting it feather over the nape of his neck. "Women?" He looked around him. "What women?"

"Never mind. Some things don't change."

Ryder drained his cup. "I nearly forgot." He

removed a thin, oblong box wrapped in silver paper from his pants pocket. "An early wedding present."

Bree wiped her hands on a napkin.

"Open it."

She ripped the paper and paused when she encountered a velvet box. She raised an eyebrow but said nothing and opened the lid. Inside lay a delicate platinum chain on which dangled two intertwined hearts with two diamonds in the center. Bree covered her mouth. The air in the coffee bar felt suddenly close. She raised it from its case and spoke in a voice barely audible above the insistent chatter. "It's like my mother's."

"I remembered it from back then. Checked with Kacey and Stephanie to make sure I had it right." He reached for it.

Bree turned her back to Ryder and tears fell silently from her eyes as he clasped it around her neck.

She fingered the pendant. "It must have cost…"

"Screw that." Ryder went back to twirling his saucer. "Thought you could use something from your family."

Bree retrieved a stack of unused napkins from a nearby table. "I've been missing them so much recently." She blew her nose. "It's nuts, I know."

He grabbed the top of the stack and thrust the napkins into his pocket. "Makes a world of sense." He glanced at the necklace. "It suits you."

She raised it to her lips and kissed it lightly. "It was supposed to be one heart for my mom and one for my dad."

Ryder guided her to the door with his arm resting

gently on her back. For once, Bree didn't notice the swarm of envious glares from the women left behind. Her fist was still clasped tightly around the two hearts, as though she could feel them beating. When they stepped onto the sidewalk, she pulled on her sweater. They stood facing each other for a moment. Then Bree balanced on tiptoe and gave him a light kiss on the lips.

"Thank you, Ryder." She turned to go but he touched her arm.

"Remember, Bree." He bent and kissed her just as lightly back. "Family isn't what you're given. Family is something you have to create."

Back in the restaurant, Bree held the roll to her mouth, noting the butter dripping down her fingers. "Mal knows he's my friend."

Juli began arranging Soumil's silverware. "My son's girlfriend was his friend before. What he wasn't knowing was that his feelings were growing."

"My feelings aren't growing. Ryder's like…a brother." She bit into the roll.

The old woman's eyes snapped up. "And your brother is kissing you like that on the dance floor and you are slapping him?"

Bree choked on the dry bread, coughing until her face turned beet red and the crumbs finally dislodged from her windpipe. She wiped her eyes and lips with a napkin before she looked again at Juli. "You saw?"

"At the nightclub." Again she rocked her head.

The bench on which Bree sat felt as though it were levitating. She clutched the tableside to ground herself as a thought worse than the one Juli had just put in her mind gripped her. "Did Mal see?"

Juli pursed her lips. "He was going to the bathroom. Like his father."

Bree hardly knew which way was up. In the space of a few minutes, this woman had upended three stories Bree had accepted as truth. Her father-in-law to-be was an unromantic, mostly unfeeling man. Her friendship with Ryder was not something to cause anyone shame. And that kiss on the dancefloor had passed into ancient history, never to be spoken of again.

"You are thinking that I am punishing you. Accusing you." A light brown, heavily creased palm glided across the table top and motioned toward Bree.

Bree laid her plump hand over the thin fingers. "I feel horrible."

"My marriage was arranged." Her gray head fell to one side and her eyes gazed at the ceiling, as though trying to extract long buried memories. "I was not having the choice of a love marriage like you. Soumil's father was not…" The deep brown glittered with a thin film of tears. "He was having much anger inside him. It was not good for the children. Bad emotions were leading to many terrible things. Many secrets. And now I am having many regrets."

Bree released her hand and shifted out of the booth. She slid in beside the thin woman in the sari and reached for her hand again. "I'm not going to have regrets. I know what I'm doing."

Juli's fingers clasped Bree's. "We aren't always

knowing when we are making mistakes, Bree. Sometimes we are realizing too late."

"But Mal and I aren't..." The shadow of someone close to the table caught her attention and stopped her midsentence.

Soumil glanced uncertainly at the empty side of the booth, his hand still in his pockets, as though he had never left. "Are we switching seats?"

Bree felt Juli's elbow tap lightly against her ribs and rose.

"Come here, my son." The older woman patted the now empty seat next to her. "I am wanting to keep an eye on you."

CHAPTER 20

The morning of her wedding, Bree's eyes popped open before the six a.m. alarm. For a moment, she couldn't remember where she was. The vastness of her surroundings disoriented her. She was used to her tiny San Francisco apartment and the queen-size bed that occupied most of the floor space. Instead she lay in the middle of an enormous circular bed, her legs seizing in cramps because she had been afraid she would roll off the strange configuration in the middle of the night. Who, she thought, thought curved sides on a bed was a good idea? It looked like a flying saucer. She felt like an alien in the middle.

The room was silent without Mal's snoring. She stretched, luxuriating in the wide space now that she was awake and aware. Her calf muscles relaxed. She turned on her phone, which she had connected the previous night to the room's overhead speaker system. She turned up the volume on the kind of music Mal couldn't stand. It was nice, she thought, to have some time to herself.

When Faye insisted the night before that Mal sleep on the pullout sofa in his mother's room, Bree's mouth fell open. Now *she's going to stand on ceremony and say we can't sleep together?* It seemed ridiculous, and she expected Mal to put up a fight. But he acquiesced immediately, sweeping his half-unpacked clothes back into his suitcase and zipping it shut without a word. Maybe, Bree thought later that night, as she lay in the room's Jacuzzi under dim lights, he didn't fight because it didn't matter. They hadn't slept together in the biblical sense for months. First there was his over-the-top reaction to his parents' divorce that completely sapped his libido. Then her attempt at reigniting the romantic spark through a trip to Puerto Rico resulted in the opposite effect when he spent half the vacation hunkered over a toilet. And her work group's trip to Eastern Washington fell, unfortunately, at a point when Mal wasn't yet fully recovered. He asked her to remain in San Francisco so she could help him at the dog wash in the evenings, because he still felt weak. But in her mind the opportunity to advance her own career took precedence.

After that decision, it seemed as though he didn't quite trust her anymore. Their previously smooth relationship bounced off its tracks. It wasn't anything she could point at, but he frequently took the negative view on things she said. On her side, with the wedding to plan for and Mal not helping much, she felt righteous in her irritation. She fought against it, trying to remain upbeat, but eventually something snapped. The rupture was small but painful. Neither of them talked about it. And Bree guessed that Mal, like her, understood it was temporary. Hang on until the wedding, and everything will be all right. That was her mantra, and in the moments in which their relationship bumped temporarily back on track, Bree felt it was Mal's mantra too.

She rolled on her side, lifted her phone, and called room service on her way to the bathroom. She and Mal had a date at seven that morning. She ordered banana pancakes, maple syrup, orange juice, Earl Grey tea, and a bowl of fresh blueberries for him. Her entrée choice was Belgian waffles with whipped cream, strawberries, and powdered sugar. She chose strong black coffee with heavy cream on the side. "And a papaya with lime wedges," she added before hanging up.

She used to eat papaya with lime with her parents on birthday mornings. Lime juice would squirt across the table as the three squeezed together and laughed.

"A papaya without lime is like a marriage without love," her father used to say.

She slipped on a brand new negligée, pulling the neckline down so her full cleavage showed. She caressed the front of the smooth silk, feeling the pent-up longing in her body. She bit her lip, trying to tamp down her expectations. *If not now, then tonight*, she told herself. *When the stress is all over, things will get back to normal.*

She threw a hotel terrycloth robe on when room service knocked at the door. A young woman in a dark gray bellhop outfit with gold buttons maneuvered a white tablecloth bedecked cart to the living area and, in fewer than five minutes, created an appetizing display framed by two chairs. When she was finished, she reached under the cart and extracted a large bouquet of red roses in a fluted porcelain vase, which she placed at the edge of the tableau.

Bree stared at the flowers. "Part of your usual room service?"

The woman's blonde bob cut bounced around her ears. "A gift. There's a card." She proffered an open palm toward the base of the snow white vase and backed away. Bree slipped her a tip before leaning the door ajar. The envelope of the card read simply, "Ms. Acosta" with her room number scrawled below. Inside were computer-printed words, "With love on your wedding day." There was no signature, no name. The handwriting on the envelope was unremarkable. Bree was still standing with the card in her hand when Mal entered the room.

"What's that?" He latched the door quietly behind him.

"Nothing." Bree slipped the envelope and card into the pocket of her robe and, upon seeing his face, immediately realized she had done the wrong thing. She pulled the card back out and handed it to him. "Stephanie and Kacey sent some roses."

He handed it back to her without reading it. "Nice."

Mal was wearing slacks and a dress shirt and had obviously showered. She tugged the neckline of the robe closed and tightened its belt. "I'm starving."

Mal peered at the display. "Had something with Mom."

Bree willed herself not to look disappointed but knew she failed. "I got your favorite tea." She pulled out a chair for him.

Mal laid his hand on hers. "And blueberries." He lifted the silver lid covering his plate. "And pancakes. Maybe I'll force them down." He grinned.

Bree sighed with relief and sat opposite him. "Banana pancakes."

"Didn't eat much with Mom anyway." He poured syrup until the stack of golden cakes was swimming in a sea of amber liquid that threatened to wash over the sides of the plate. "She kept quizzing me on people's names for today."

Bree spread the whipped cream in a smooth layer, nestled a row of strawberry slices on top, and covered her creation with a second waffle. She sliced slowly, dislodging as little cream as possible, and skewered a morsel.

Mal glanced at the papaya and limes. "Mind if I put that over by the minibar?" He gestured across the room.

Bree stopped chewing. "Why?"

Mal shoved his chair back and lifted the plate, the orange fruit with green citrus slices arranged in a band around its sides jiggling. "You know I can't stand this since the Puerto Rico trip."

Bree put down her fork. "Give it to me." Her voice was harsher than she intended. "I'll put it here." She pointed at a small end table near her.

Mal strolled toward the bar. "Over there's better.

I don't like the smell."

Bree stepped after him. "I'll cover it with one of the lids." She reached for the plate, expecting him to let go. He didn't. She pulled harder.

Mal wrinkled his brow.

"I'll keep it away from your precious nose." She jerked the plate.

The dish slipped from both their grasps. The papaya sailed in an orange arch to the floor, in a fluttering cascade of green. Bree stared at the mess, blinking back tears. Mal kicked a lime that had fallen near his foot. She bent and scooped it up, cupping it as though it were a baby bird with an injured wing. She peered up at him, her cheeks wet.

He focused on her face. "You're crying." His voice sounded astonished.

She wiped her eyes with her sleeve, still cradling the lime. "Why does this have to be so hard?"

"It's just some fruit."

Her eyes fixed on his. "Don't you remember why I like papaya so much?"

He shook his head. "I didn't know you liked it." He shrugged.

Bree squatted and picked the remaining fruit off the floor, depositing it onto the plate.

Mal looked around the room. "Where's the phone? I'll order you some more."

Bree didn't say anything. By the time he returned to the table, she was back at her place, sawing gingerly at the waffle, the makeup she applied in anticipation of a potential pre-or post-breakfast romantic interlude smeared. She carefully settled her fork next to her plate.

Mal covered his sodden pancakes with a silver lid, edging it into position. "Things don't fit like they used to."

Bree draped her napkin over the waffles. "Maybe we're not trying hard enough."

Mal picked up a blueberry. "People say you grow into marriage. Like my parents…" The blue orb slipped from his fingers and dropped to the floor. "Or my grandparents, anyway. That was an arranged marriage, but they were together till he died. They were happy."

Bree felt tears stinging her eyes again. She poured herself a cup of coffee. When she had finished doctoring it with cream, Mal was standing.

"Mom's kind of a wreck. See you at nine?"

Bree nodded and walked him to the door.

Don't go. She wanted to say it aloud, but couldn't.

He scanned her face, trying unsuccessfully to catch her eyes.

A few minutes after he left, someone knocked. She ran to the peephole. A bent man in a wrinkled gray uniform stared at the door through thick rimless glasses. She hid behind the door, not wanting him to see her tear stained face and held out her hand. He handed her a plate with a fresh papaya. Only after he retreated down the hall did she notice there were no limes.

***

Early that afternoon, in the dressing room outside the hotel's wedding chapel, there was a moment when she thought her dress wasn't going to zip closed. She felt Stephanie hauling two sides of the material together with one hand and clutching the fastener with the other.

Bree tugged at her neckline and hoped the seamstress who had refashioned her mother's dress had added enough new material.

"Suck it in, *amiga*." Stephanie grunted as the closure inched higher. "More."

The zipper finally reached the top and Stephanie let out a cry of triumph. Bree exhaled in a burst of laughter. "I thought last night's key lime pie was going to do me in." She tested the dress seams by gently inhaling and exhaling. "Looks like it'll hold. Thank God for Lycra."

Her jaw dropped when she turned to face herself in the set of floor to ceiling mirrors. The recessed ceiling lights and tasteful wall sconces cast hardly a shadow on her white gown. Overlapping layers of crepe flowed downward from the waistline at a sassy angle, creating an effect somewhat reminiscent of a flamenco dress. A multitude of ruffles flounced around her like a bell. But while the bottom of the modified A-line dress cascaded out in a design that evoked movement, energy, and uninhibited joy, the top layers wound tightly around her chest and overlapped across her breasts in bands of crumpled silk that reminded Bree of a comforting cocoon. While anyone who saw her mother's wedding photograph would recognize the dress in an instant, the new creation was unmistakably her own. There were no more pearls sown into the fabric. The lace sleeves had disappeared. Where her mother wore a veil, Bree wore a tulle bow on the left side of her head that complemented the flow of her hair, which was curled and tumbled across her left shoulder.

Stephanie peered over her shoulder and fussed with the bow. "I think she put this in upside down." Her hands disappeared under the gossamer fabric.

Bree laughed. "Leave it. It's symbolic of how I'm feeling right now." Her eyes swept the room. "These places think of everything. Do you think they have an airsick bag tucked into a corner?"

Stephanie slapped Bree's wrist playfully. "You'll be fine when you get out there."

Bree's heart was pounding so quickly she couldn't keep track of the beats. Her hands were cold and her head felt light enough to float off her body. "Seriously. I feel nauseated." Her dress rustled as she stepped toward the bathroom.

Stephanie hiked up her pale orange bridesmaid dress and dashed to block the entrance. She raised her arms against the doorframe. "I am *not* putting you back into that."

Bree tugged at the flounces near her tummy. "I can't even sit down."

"Tough." Stephanie led her back to the mirrors, then dug in her purse that stood on a glass table nearby. "Almost forgot. You told me to put this on you." Her hand emerged with an oblong box. She removed a necklace. Its intertwined hearts sparkled in the light. Bree held her hair out of the way while Stephanie fastened the clasp.

Bree let out a sigh. "That's better." She fingered the design. "Forget all this borrowed and blue stuff.

At a time like this, you need your family." She kissed Stephanie lightly on the cheek then checked her lipstick in the mirror. "Tell the troops I'm ready."

After Stephanie left, Bree pressed her hands over the necklace. "I wish you were here to tell me how you made your marriage work. Things don't have to be perfect." She peered at the ceiling. "But close would be nice." She smiled in the mirror just as Stephanie popped her head in.

"Ready when you are, *mi hermana*." Strains of Albinoni's Concerto in D Minor filtered through behind her. She held the door wide as Bree tiptoed through to avoid getting the dress caught on her high heels.

Bree looked up and down the short hallway. "Where's Kacey? Don't tell me the guy who's supposed to give the bride away is late."

Stephanie winked. "He'll be here in a second. I'll scoot inside to give the all clear." The padded door fell closed behind her without a sound.

Stephanie's father had offered to give Bree away, but Bree couldn't make peace with the idea of an older man walking her down the aisle in place of her father. Kacey stepped in as the perfect imperfect solution. She stood in the hallway examining the door's leather upholstery. Inside the chapel, she thought, were her friends on one side of the salon and as many of Mal's relatives as they could cram onto cushioned benches on the other.

She heard the pat of men's shoes on the carpeted hallway only when they almost reached her. She stretched out her hand without looking. A firm, warm grasp greeted hers. She squeezed the fingers, still averting her gaze.

"Are you ready?" Kacey's voice sounded hoarse and off-key.

Bree nodded.

He tucked her arm under his. "I'm glad you're not mad."

She raised her eyes questioningly just as the chapel doors swung open before them. The guests turned as one in their seats, staring at Bree, who stared, in turn, open mouthed, at the man escorting her with slow steps down the aisle. The wedding march echoed through the chamber. But in Bree's head, the white noise of confusion drowned out every sound. The man whose hand clasped hers tightly was Ryder.

She resisted the urge to stop in midstride. Her steps shortened. "Where's Kacey?" She whispered through clenched teeth, aware of the cell phones thrust into the aisle to capture the moment and, presumably, post it quickly on Facebook.

"Ask your friends." Ryder spoke in hushed tones, his mouth turned up at the corners in, as far as she could tell, a realistic smile.

Bree turned her head to search for Stephanie and Kacey among the assembled individuals. Her gaze fell on Mal. She scanned him for signs of confusion, annoyance, or even jealousy. But he looked past her, his face preoccupied with a seemingly uncomfortable internal struggle. She wasn't even sure he was aware the ceremony had begun.

They traversed half the floor length. She slowed their procession to a crawl.

"You're giving me away." The words jumped out of her mouth as though they had a will of their own.

His voice floated softly on the air. "Only if you want." He gripped her arm tighter to his side.

Her lips were growing tired from being stretched in a grin she knew must look horrible but was the best she could do. "Mal's waiting for me." She elongated her pace. He matched her stride and after a few seconds of silence they reached the altar.

Bree tried to catch Mal's eyes again, but they remained focused on a spot by the far wall. She felt as disoriented as he looked. All the nervousness from the dressing room returned, now coupled with a growing sense of unease. What was she doing in her mother's wedding dress? Who was this man in a white tuxedo who wouldn't look at her? How could she make her marriage even half as good as what her parents had? Shouldn't she give up now? Before it was too late? Or was it already too late?

Ryder's tanned face leaned toward her cheek and brushed it with his lips. "Sometimes, Bree, you need to grab what's waiting for you."

He released her arm and edged into the second bench on Bree's side of the aisle, behind Stephanie's family. Kacey turned around and fist bumped him, grinning. Mal's father and Juli scooted closer together to give Ryder more space. The remainder of the benches on her side were occupied by an eclectic mixture of Mexican relatives and San Francisco friends.

The Patel half of the salon was packed to the gills with brown haired men and women, some in traditional Indian clothes and some in expensive Western suits and elegant dresses. Faye occupied the front row, with two daughters on either side. Her face looked pinched. She threw periodic glances in the direction of her soon-to-be ex-husband, as though hoping to extinguish him from the ceremony with her vitriol.

The music faded and the guests hushed. The hotel-provided minister stepped forward from a recess. Bree closed her eyes and focused her attention on the weight of the necklace that rose and fell with her breathing. She turned to Mal. The minister cleared his throat.

Mal held up his hand. "I can't do this." He peered at Bree from under lowered eyelashes and shifted from one foot to the other. A mumbling issued from the guests in the front rows.

"Excuse me?" The minister leaned in.

Mal shook his head. "It's not going to work." A pallor tinged his face.

Bree took his hand. It was clammy and cold. She waved back the minister, who had begun to speak again. "Mal, it'll be over in a few minutes."

Mal's stomach heaved visibly. He held his hand to his mouth. He stared at her, his look both frightened and accusing. "I think it was the banana pancakes." His voice gurgled. He cast a desperate glance at the minister, who pointed down the aisle. Mal dashed past the assemblage, careened into the padded doors, and disappeared. A flower stand tottered in his wake, threatening to fall, before a lithe guest jumped from a bench and righted it.

The atmosphere disintegrated the way a high

283

school classroom disintegrates when the teacher leaves the room. The minister smiled sheepishly at Bree.

She forced a smile. "Bet you see a lot of crazy things." Her fingers twined around the curls on her shoulder.

He shrugged. "Groom running away is a first. Did have one guy throw up at the altar. That's why I've got this." He pointed at a plastic bucket hidden behind a flower stand.

Bree surveyed the yellow container. "I'm sure he'll…"

A shout from the front row resounded over the ubiquitous chatter. "This is your fault, Soumil Patel." Mal's mother stood, her arms stretched across her daughters' heads, pointing at her former spouse, gold bracelets jingling, her finger shaking.

Soumil glanced at her. The anger in his gaze would have silenced a lesser woman. It spoke volumes about years of pent-up frustration. But with Faye it was like throwing gasoline on smoldering coals. She raised clasped hands to the ceiling. "Don't you ignore me, you sinful man."

The minister, obviously seeing it as part of his job description to get the situation under control, stepped toward the raving woman. But she anticipated him and marched across the aisle to stand directly above her victim. To Bree's surprise, Soumil neither looked away nor showed any signs of backing down. Her father-in-law to-be, she thought, had certainly changed.

"You taught your son to be weak. Because you are weak." Faye practically spat the words.

Soumil slowly rose to his full height, as though levitated by invisible strings. The audience, seeming to sense a fight, hushed. The minister's "ah-hem" fell on deaf ears as the two sides squared off, measuring each other up.

"Mal simply has indigestion."

At the sound of Soumil's level voice, the guests' faces fell.

"He said whose fault it was." Faye pointed at Bree, whose eyebrows shot up. "And who encouraged him to marry such a woman?"

Stephanie jumped from her bench, with Kacey springing up only a second behind. "Bree's the best thing that ever happened to Mal."

Bree waved at her friend, urging her to sit back down, but unable to repress a smile.

The room waited in silence for Faye's response. The minister seemed about to try his luck again, when everyone's attention was abruptly turned to the other side of the room, where Val, clutching her purse to her chest, swayed on unsure legs. "After all Mom did for you." She shook a finger at her father." Now you're sleeping with another woman. It's disgusting."

Seeming to be bolstered by Val's support, Faye lit into Soumil again. Juli next rose to her son's aid. Then the four Patel daughters traipsed over the marble floor to join their mother. This, the faces on the Patel side of the chapel clearly showed, was a far better wedding than any they had anticipated. Bree cringed as she saw some of the younger members removed cell phones and begin filming. She could just see it: her wedding going viral on

YouTube. She was about to step into the fray when she felt a pull on her elbow.

"Funny." Ryder stood next to her and gestured with his chin at the melee.

Bree glared at him. "My wedding in ruins?"

Ryder shrugged. He pushed his wavy blond hair behind his ears and leaned back. "Funny that they call this family." The corner of his mouth crept up in a grin as some of the Patels marched across the aisle.

Bree noticed Stephanie's relatives had retreated from the front bench to stand against the wall, where Bree's friends had gathered. Stephanie motioned for the minister to join them. She rolled her eyes at Bree and held up the photo of Bree's parents in a helpless gesture.

A giggle grew in Bree's chest. She bit her lips to suppress it, imagining her work colleagues watching the viral video during their free time. But when a bouquet plucked from one of the flower stands sailed out of nowhere through the air and landed in an explosion of pink and orange petals on Faye's head, she lost control. Laughter burst forth through her pursed lips. She leaned on the minister's podium.

"They've ripped the lid off." She spoke between explosions of mirth. "The mess is out in the open."

Ryder chuckled. He slid his hand around her waist, his eyes sparkling. "What do you think, Bree? Time to go?"

She examined his face. Her mind flashed back across the past months and the feeling that had grown within her despite her own protestations. She nodded, unable to speak, surprised at her own acquiescence, but relieved.

Ryder guided her through the aisle, helping her avoid the fracas. When they reached the padded doors, he paused, his look questioning. Bree turned and surveyed the scene. Stephanie was leading a procession of laughing guests toward the place where she and Ryder stood. Mal's family feud had devolved into a screaming free-for-all. Bree felt the last remnant of stress flow from her body down into the glossy floor. She laughed up into Ryder's face. "Did you set this up to help me see the light?"

Ryder bent down and kissed her on the lips, an open-mouthed kiss of deep contentment that drew her in completely, wholly, longingly. The world faded into the background. And in the wedding dress she had thought was for Mal, she embraced the person who had walked her down the aisle.

When their lips finally parted, she entwined her hand in his. He pressed it against his heart. He pushed the doors open and threw one last glance behind them. "It's what I said before. Family isn't what you're given. Family is something you have to create."

They sauntered down the short hallway. Bree felt as though she were gliding an inch above the floor, her dress flowing around her like a cloud, wafting her alongside Ryder. Movement was effortless, her mind free from care or worry. When Ryder tugged her arm, bringing them to a stop, she hung in the air for a moment, like a bird soaring on a thermal.

"It's Mal." Ryder's eyes focused on hers.

Bree's feet returned to the ground. But her heart

beat normally. She disengaged herself.

Mal leaned against the bathroom doorframe with one hand. The other held his stomach. His white tuxedo front was splattered with yellow dots. His face looked green. When Bree approached, he lifted his gaze listlessly and observed Ryder and Bree and the mass of guests behind them with uncaring eyes.

"Are you okay?" Bree reached out her hand to touch his shoulder.

He shrunk away. "Don't touch me. It might be viral." He closed his eyes as a spasm gripped him. "It wasn't the pancakes. I'm sorry I said that."

Bree studied the bedraggled man in front of her, the man she had been about to marry. She hardly recognized him. Who really was Mal Patel, she wondered. And with that thought, she realized she had never seen him for who he really was. She had endowed the man she chose as her life partner with qualities she wanted him to have, fashioned him in her mind as the answer to what she had been looking for. She suddenly understood that it hadn't been fair.

She took his hand. "You were right when you said things didn't fit."

Mal glanced behind her at Ryder. "Doesn't mean they won't fit. They just didn't for us."

Bree kissed him on his bedewed forehead. She slipped her engagement ring from her finger and placed it in his breast pocket. "I hope you find the perfect fit someday, Mal. Forgive me for not being able to see straight until now."

Mal shook his head. "It was both of us." He gave Ryder a wan smile. "Now go. People are waiting."

Ryder approached and took Bree's hand. He threw Mal a salute. "I'll take good care of her."

Mal nodded. "She'll take good care of herself."

CHAPTER 21

At the hotel's main entrance, Bree shielded her eyes from the scorching sun. She stood, blinking, in the bright light. Ryder still held her hand against his chest, and through the fabric of his dark navy suit she could feel his heart thumping. She gazed up at him and he bent down to kiss her again, to the glee of a busload of middle-aged Midwesterners. The group stood in a semicircle around Bree and Ryder, ooh-ing and ahh-ing at their embrace.

One woman tapped Bree on the arm. "Just married, are you?" She winked before disappearing inside with her cohort.

Ryder grinned at Bree. "What you think?"

Bree read the expression on his face. "Are you ready?"

"Ready?" Ryder laughed and scooped her into his arms. "I've been ready since I saw you in line at the car rental."

Bree twined her arms around his neck. "Did you send the roses this morning?"

Ryder cocked his head. "Do you have to ask?"

Bree nuzzled her face into his neck.

Stephanie stepped from among the circle of guests who had followed them. "Stay right there." She lifted the hem of her dress and streaked across the lot. A minute later, a white Hummer limousine pulled in front of the hotel. A tinted window lowered and Stephanie's head popped out. "Had this waiting as a surprise, *amiga.*"

Ryder released Bree's hand and opened the door. She stepped into the air conditioned interior and he carefully folded her dress in after her. He squeezed in and made room for himself by her side. Guests piled in after them. One of those who couldn't fit stuck her head in.

"We'll take cabs. Where to?"

Ryder grinned at Bree. "Bureau of marriage licenses."

***

An hour later, Bree ordered the limousine to stop. "Let's walk." She tugged Ryder's arm. "It's fun to spread the joy."

Ryder nodded. "You're the bride."

She stepped onto the hot concrete sidewalk and he heaved her dress out after her. The sun beat down. In the distance, a white wedding chapel glowed like a shimmering mirage. He removed his jacket and slung it over his shoulder. One hand wrapped tightly around hers and held it against his heart. Behind them, a long line of taxis pulled to the curb like an eddy in a river.

After the assembly gathered, they formed rows

on the sidewalk. Ryder and Bree lead, with Kasey and Stephanie next to them, Stephanie cradling the framed photo of Bree's parents. Passing cars honked. Drivers lowered their windows to wave. Tourists on the Strip stepped aside, pointing and snapping pictures with their phones. A teenage girl glanced up at her mother for permission, then ran to Bree. The procession halted.

The girl gazed at Bree with awe and held up her phone. "You're so beautiful."

Bree grinned.

"Can I take a selfie with you?"

Bree bent over the young girl's thin shoulders. "Don't you want Mr. Handsome in it too?" She gestured at Ryder to join them.

But the girl peered at Ryder and shook her head. "He's nothing special. But you're..." She pulled her eyebrows together. "You're exactly what I want to be when I grow up."

Bree blinked as the girl snapped pictures. Then, watching the young figure skip away with glee, she lay a hand over the necklace on her chest.

Ryder strode toward her. He cupped her face. "See. Other people notice it too." His lips melted against hers as he held her gaze. "*You're* the amazing one."

ACKNOWLEDGMENTS

This book had many friends who helped along the way. Wild at Heart Newsletter readers chose character names and scene locations. I am indebted to the staff at Limitless Publishing for their shepherding of the project from first draft to completion. My editor, Rosa Sophia, was delightful as always. My husband, Ron Strickland's birthday party near Las Vegas provided the impetus for the story setting. And Ron's willingness to critique chapter after chapter helped shape some of my favorite sections and character quirks. I love this book and sincerely hope you do as well.

Onward, to book four!

ABOUT THE AUTHOR

Christine Hartmann grew up in Ohio and Delaware and loves traveling to exotic, romantic settings. After a college semester in Kathmandu, her first three "real" jobs were all in northern Japan, where she lived for almost 10 years. She currently splits her career between her daytime occupation (improving the quality of veterans' nursing home care) and her nights/weekend avocation (writing both fiction and non-fiction books). Her husband, Ron Strickland, is a well-known long-distance hiker, trail guide writer, and the founder of the 1,200-mile Pacific Northwest National Scenic Trail. Christine loves reading, pilates, bicycling, snorkeling, and health foods that taste like they're bad for you. You will often find her at a keyboard, with Ron whispering sweet edits over her shoulder.

Facebook:
https://www.facebook.com/christine.w.hartmann

Twitter:
https://twitter.com/chartmannbooks

Website:
http://chartmannbooks.com/

Goodreads:
https://www.goodreads.com/chartmannbooks